Seduction In Blood

KIM ALLRED

STORM COAST PUBLISHING, LLC

SEDUCTION IN BLOOD
Book 1
KIM ALLRED

Published by Storm Coast Publishing, LLC

Print edition March 2022
ISBN 978-1-953832-12-2

It takes a lot of courage to show your dreams to someone else.

Erma Bombeck

Chapter One

I INCHED ALONG, my toes curled as I pressed all my weight into the balls of my feet. The heavy fog coated the three-inch ledge with slick moisture, making it impossible to see more than a few feet ahead. With little to hold on to, the thirty-foot walk was precarious. At least I'd made a good selection on footwear when I'd splurged on that new pair of light sneakers.

The fog wrapped itself around the building like a thick blanket, almost making me forget I was crawling around the top of a four-story building. It wasn't my first walk around a ledge in the mist, not with the amount of fog we got in Santiga Bay or anywhere else along the California coast. But something hadn't felt right when I'd arrived earlier, and my nerves were on edge. Without a safety harness, it would be a long way down. I pushed the image of that landing away and refocused on the tricky part of the walk, turning the corner into the windy side.

When I poked my head around to test the wind, I could already hear the familiar voice bitching about the weather.

"Can you hurry it along? For Christ's sake, Cressa, I can barely make you out. That is you, isn't it? I'm freezing my balls off with this bloody window open." Harlow couldn't seem to find pleasure in any situation. The one time I'd taken an ill-advised vacation with him to Los Angeles, he'd complained the entire time.

His words fell away with the wind as I focused on my hand-holds. The breeze was minimal with the dense fog, but it was strong enough to push my short locks from my face. I braced against the cold. Not far now.

I was five feet from the window when I planted my foot on a loose piece of cement and slipped. My breath caught as I dug my fingertips into the rough surface of a stone window casing. My heart pounded so loudly it blanketed Harlow's voice, which was more of a benefit than an additional problem. An image of my head split open on the asphalt flashed for an instant, and the muscles in my legs screamed as I pushed down on my right foot. My fingers tingled with numbness as I held on, moving my left foot around for a solid piece of ledge.

Sweat dripped from my forehead, leaking into my eyes, and I blinked away the moisture, trying to make out the dim shadow hanging out of the window. Harlow, his arms flying about, tried to grab my leg. I kicked his hand away when it almost caught me. What was he planning on doing? Dangling me from the ledge by a leg? Why I kept joining his heists, I'd never know. But he was the best mastermind in the business. When my left foot connected with a solid surface, I scurried the last few feet until Harlow's strong arm grabbed my waist and hauled me through the window.

We fell onto the carpeted floor, his body resting on top of mine.

"That is you, luv." His smug grin showed off his perfectly white teeth in the dim light. "I'd know this body anywhere."

"For fuck's sake. Aren't you supposed to be on the bottom if you're saving me?" I pushed against his chest. A wiry man, he was stronger than he looked, and he didn't seem to be in a hurry to move.

"I like my women on their backs. I thought you knew that." His smile, the only charming thing about him, only widened as he took a second to run his hand over me from my upper leg to the edge of my left breast. "But I'm willing to have a go doggie style if you want to roll over."

"Get off me." This time I used both hands to push while I tangled my legs with his, attempting to roll him over.

He tightened his grip as we rolled, so I was locked in his embrace, his hands using my breasts for leverage when he landed on his back.

He laughed. "I see what you mean. I think I could get used to this."

I was ready to punch him in the face, but the third voice that crept through the room was as good as dumping ice water on him.

"I'd suggest removing your hands from her breasts if you want to live past the next minute."

Harlow's smile vanished. "Trudy, Princess, I didn't see you there." His eyes widened as he rolled his head back in a vain attempt to catch a glimpse of his jealous lover.

"Uh-huh." Trudy stomped over, her famous steel-toed boots planted inches from his head. She held out a hand and pulled me up. "Thought I'd save you the trouble of punching him. We need those precious fingers of yours." She gave me a nod before glancing down at Harlow. "Pick yourself up. We still have a sensor blocking us from the room."

Trudy, who wore an automatic rifle strapped around her shoulder, held the weapon in a two-handed grip and whipped it around as she moved back out of the room. She was our muscle, and she stopped just outside the door, monitoring both ways for surprise visitors.

"Where's Stan?" I assumed he would be on the computer trying to get rid of that last sensor, but sometimes there was a hard-wired backup rather than one controlled by a software program.

That was where Harlow came in when he wasn't fucking around. But I imagined that besides him being a prankster, he was simply bored. He was the strategist, as hard as it was to believe, but

3

he had the mind of a genius that was unfortunately wrapped with a foul mouth of sexual innuendos. The trials of a working team.

"He's having a problem breaking the last encryption. We need Harlow." Trudy glanced back in the room. "Today would be good."

Harlow sauntered by Trudy, slapping her on the ass on his way out.

She pointed the rifle at his back and yelled, "Pow." Harlow waved his hand without turning back. "Damn, why do I love that man?"

"Brain damage?" I couldn't help but smile at her scowl.

She shook her head. "God help me." Then, she grinned. "At least the sex is hot."

I waved both my arms before covering my ears. "I don't want to hear it." I cringed. "Too late. Ah, man, now I have that image stuck in my head."

Trudy chuckled as she followed me down the hall where Harlow had disappeared. "I don't know why you didn't just come in the way we did."

"I need the practice, and it makes for a quick escape if I need one. Besides, there's another job I've been casing with the same architectural structure." I shrugged and glanced at the artwork we walked by as we made our way to the opposite side of the historic mansion. "It's a small job. The artifacts will be slow to sell, but I need to stay limber."

Trudy grunted. "They have gyms for that."

"Gyms don't have shiny baubles."

She laughed. "I can't argue with that."

We rounded a bend and took the main staircase down to the second floor. I'd been surprised when Harlow had approved my risky entrance, which had added time to the job, but with the amount of security required to get in the place, I'd go crazy waiting on Stan to bypass the alarms. I'd also been the one who found the job. The mansion was owned by some puffed-up politician who was currently out of state. I'd seen a newspaper article from a year earlier about his purchase of the Alistair diamond. The job required three months of surveillance and influencing one of the staff to confirm the diamond was on site. From there, a hack into the security company told us the type of safes on the premise and their locations.

Luckily, there was only one safe in the second-floor master suite closet. No surprise. Most safes were either in the bedroom or the study. The wealthy just weren't that creative. The actual surprise, however, was that it wasn't digital. Not that it made a difference. I had the tech knowledge to break through any digital safe. But the old-fashioned ones, especially those with sophisticated locking mechanisms, made my nipples tingle. Those were the type of safes that started my illustrious and highly illegal career. The thought almost brought tears to my eyes. I was inwardly laughing by the time we reached the bedroom.

Harlow and Stan were in front of the closet, near a floor lamp they'd turned on. Stan tapped at his computer, working on bypassing the last of the sensors. When he nodded, Harlow entered the impressive walk-in closet and pulled open the false door, revealing the floor safe.

"All right, Pandora, come open the box and let's see what horrors await." Harlow stepped back, bowing low as I ignored his reference to my street name, my focus on the safe.

The security company files were correct. It was a vintage Schwab safe, one of the best in its time, but a newer combination had been installed. Safes weren't easy to crack if you tried to figure out the combination. It was doable if you had the time to manipulate the lock. Time most burglars didn't have, not if they weren't taking the safe with them. Drilling was the next option and the one I used most frequently if I couldn't find the code another way. Fortunately, our inside person—a disgruntled house cleaner—found the last two digits of the combination. Doing my research, I'd discovered it was two numbers in the wife's birth date. I had memorized the birth dates of all the family members, including grandchildren.

If this were my heist and I was alone, I would have enjoyed practicing my skills in graphing the combination. But my expertise lay with the ability to combine my burglary skills with knowing my target. I researched their lifestyle, their habits, and how lazy they were. It was surprising how many people never changed the try-out combinations that came with the safe. After that, the most common combinations were typically birthdays or anniversaries. That's why I kept my jobs to residential thefts rather than jewelry stores or banks.

After dropping my backpack, I rolled my neck, flexed my fingers, and relaxed my muscles before crouching to get a look at the lock. I leaned close and dialed the first combination, immediately knowing it wasn't going to work.

The second and the third combinations didn't work either, so I reset the lock and considered my options. I could pull out my drill, but Harlow was pacing. The soft shuffle of his boots on the thick carpet began to irritate me. I gave Trudy a glance over my shoulder and nodded toward Harlow.

"Come on, Harlow. Let's check on Jamal." Trudy grabbed the back of his shirt and hauled him out.

"Put a foot on it, luv. Time's a tickin'," Harlow mumbled as he was dragged away.

I turned my attention back to the safe, blew out a breath, and tried again. On the sixth combination, I heard the satisfying click and the release of the door. The correct combination had been the daughter's birth month, the son's day of birth, followed by the wife's birth year. It was fortunate they had a small family. I had to give the guy credit—but if I had the Alistair diamond in my safe, I wouldn't have used any number associated with family. Not that I had much of one to begin with.

"Bloody time." Harlow must have been hovering by the door. I'd barely opened the safe.

I stepped back, letting Harlow have his moment to pull out the treasures. I might have been the one to discover the gig, but Harlow had fronted the job and pulled in his team. The money I would see from my share would make a significant dent in what I owed—and the timing couldn't be better. My name had gone on the bounty list two days ago.

Harlow stuck his head in the safe and pulled out three stacks of money that I'd guess to be around a hundred grand, two bearer bonds that would take some time to move but would provide a decent payday, and five jewelry boxes.

Harlow opened each one before tossing them to me. I shook my head at the first three. They were lovely jewels, two necklaces and a bracelet, but they would take time to fence. The fourth held the prize—the Alistair diamond. I took it out of the box and held it up to the light of my headlamp. The team gathered around to take a moment to bask in the glory of our find.

"How much did you say that was worth?" Trudy asked.

"A cool million, Princess. And our little Pandora here already has a buyer. Isn't that right, luv?"

I stuffed the diamond back in the box and tossed it to Harlow. "Just remember that when we split up the take." I ended my obvious threat with a wide smile. "We'll have the money before the week's out."

"Boss, we have a problem," Stan called from the bedroom.

"Is it the patrol?" Harlow asked as he grabbed half the stash while I snagged the rest.

Stan glanced up from his monitor, the glow from the screen making his pale face appear green. "They weren't there a second ago."

Trudy ran to the bedroom window. "I don't see anything."

I crammed the stash in my bag and pulled my backpack on.

"Where are they, Stan?" Trudy's voice, though still calm, held an edge.

He was shaking his head. "They're all around us."

Harlow slammed the monitor shut. "Get your gear. Now."

"There's no need to hurry."

Everyone froze. I did a quick survey of the room, already knowing I wouldn't find an exit, but my gut reaction to run was instinctual.

"And I would drop the weapons." The man's voice came from inside the room near the shadows.

Two more men walked in, pushing Jamal, our exit man, to the floor.

I finally turned, shutting my headlamp off and taking a small step back, hoping the darkness in the room was enough to hide my face.

"Hello, Pandora. I've had a devil of a time finding you."

Chapter Two

MY GUT CLENCHED at the sight of the man standing near a large armoire. I couldn't see his face in the dim light, but I recognized the voice.

I stepped out of the shadows, blinking as one of the goons turned on the bedroom lights. Now that I'd been found, there was no place to run. But how the hell had he found me? No one else would have known about this job. I glanced at Harlow. His face was as white as the proverbial ghost, which told me he wasn't our snitch. A quick scan of the others told me the same thing. If any of them had loose lips, surely one of them would have looked more comfortable under the bounty hunter's menacing stare.

"Sorrento." I kept my tone level and firm, not wanting to appear intimidated while I determined his mood.

Sorrento was an impressive man with powerful shoulders and a barrel chest that suggested a future slide to fat. But now, he was thick with muscle, easily seen beneath the leather vest he wore sans shirt. His biceps bulged to an abnormal size as he crossed his arms. His legs stood apart as if he was bracing himself on a ship, and the muscle in his thighs stretched the seams of his cargo pants. And while all that was enough to scare the shit out of most people who found themselves face-to-face with the man, it was his tattoo that made you pee your pants.

A Cobra tattoo covered the left half of his face, the snake's fangs large and impressive as they arched over the man's eyes. The ink covered a nasty scar. Only rumors surrounded how he received the old wound, each meant to add to his badass reputation. As if being the region's most successful and brutal bounty hunter wasn't enough.

He stepped forward, and the two other equally large men took a position on either side of him. They each carried a pistol in their hand and silver swords on their hips. The blades were meant for magical creatures that could only be stopped by decapitation. The guns would have silver bullets, just in case.

Harlow's crew wasn't supernatural. Neither was I. But a bullet was a bullet.

From the doorway, three more men and one of the tallest women I'd ever seen entered the room and spread out, ensuring each of them was close to one of Harlow's people. We were outnumbered, outclassed, and I was shit out of luck.

Sorrento stopped in front of Harlow and took the duffel from him. He tossed it to the woman, who opened it and looked through the stash. After opening two of the jewelry boxes, she threw one to Sorrento. He removed the diamond and held the gem up to the light. He whistled before turning to me, one eye drawn down as if he was winking at me. "Is this all you have for me, pet?"

"If you had waited a couple more days, you'd be getting a large pile of cash instead of a rock." I crossed my arms, trying to show I wasn't scared. I was actually ready to piss my pants but still hoped to talk my way out of this pickle.

"You must know this little trinket will only pay off a portion of what you owe." He tucked the diamond in his pocket then sat on the edge of a dresser, one leg swinging in a slow arc. "The thing is, I have paper for your immediate capture."

Yeah, I was going to piss myself. Damn. How did this happen? Who else knew about this job?

"We've worked out our differences before." I could come up with something if my brain would slow down and let me think.

He smiled. The predatory grin and long perusal of my body told me exactly where his thoughts were headed.

"Do you have another job for me? Something that would take the sting out of my run of bad luck." My luck had actually been pretty good up to this point, but he didn't need to know he was messing with my record.

"Interestingly enough, I have something like that in mind." He nodded to Harlow. "Take your crew, what's left of your loot, and get out."

Harlow glanced at me, then his crew.

"Don't overthink it, Harlow. Take what success you can from this." Sorrento patted Stan on his shoulder, and I thought the hacker was going to have a heart attack. "And grab Pandora's duffel. She probably has part of your take in it, and she won't be needing it."

Harlow nodded and gave me a pathetic apologetic glance as he removed the duffel from my shoulder. "Sorry, luv."

I nodded. Any assist, and he would end up dead. I couldn't blame him. But if I found out someone from his team snitched, well, that would be a different story.

Harlow glanced at the rest of his team. "Let's go."

Jamal closed up the duffel the tall woman had picked through, swung it over his shoulder, and followed Trudy out. Gone in less than ten seconds. Harlow helped Stan, who shook like an upset chihuahua, get his monitor in his backpack. He gave me one last look before he pushed Stan through the door and was gone.

Once I was alone with Sorrento and his team, I planted hands on my hips, close to my weapons. "So, now what? A ride to your place?"

He grinned again, and that smile, along with his Cobra ink,

made me squirm. "You've always been a smart girl. Except with your finances, that is."

I never caught the signal, but before I knew it, the muscle man, who'd moved behind me, grabbed my upper arms in a grip as tight as a vice. My knees buckled when he kicked my legs out but kept me upright with his own strength.

"We're going for a long drive. I hope you fed the cat." I wasn't sure what he meant. I didn't own a cat. Then, the tall woman bent her head near mine, and I didn't know whether she was going to whisper in my ear or kiss me. It was hard to tell. But all she did was take a deep breath as if she was smelling me.

"Down, Patrice." Sorrento's voice held a harsh edge, which didn't bolster my confidence.

Something stuck me in the neck—sharp and quick. I tried to move my arms, but they were still locked in a fierce grip. I struggled before my legs turned to rubber, the edges of my vision blurred, and I slipped into utter darkness.

Chapter Three

THE FIRST THING I noticed was the familiar feeling of being in a moving vehicle. I tried to remember what had happened, but everything was fuzzy. I hadn't been in a bar, so I wasn't hungover. Then, it all raced back. Sorrento waiting for us, then someone stabbing me in the neck. The asshole had drugged me.

I sat up and hit my head on something hard. It was pitch black, and I checked to see if I'd been blindfolded. My arms moved slowly with the remains of the drug. No blindfold. I stretched out my legs, but they hit a wall before I could fully extend them. Panic set in as I stretched out my arms. The last of the dizziness left me when I realized I was in a box. A vent on each wall my only source of air.

My heart thumped as I reached out to assess how much space I had. I could sit up as long as I bent my back. My arms couldn't fully extend, and I quickly found all four sides of the metal box— steel and most likely lined with silver.

A catch box.

Great.

Don't panic.

That wasn't as easy as it sounded, but Sorrento couldn't keep me in here forever. Not if he wanted his money.

My first task was to slow my breathing and think about what to tell Sorrento to regain my freedom. I'd heard of slave traders. *Stop it.* That kind of thinking wasn't going to calm my nerves. I closed my eyes to help me focus. The vehicle was still moving. I wasn't sure what kind of vehicle, but there wasn't any strong airflow, so I wasn't traveling in the bed of a truck. It must be a van —something that could hold the heavy metal box.

We were on an asphalt road. So, I wasn't being taken down some dirt road to be killed. He could have done that easily enough in the bedroom where they'd caught me. No. Sorrento had different plans. And he was teaching me a lesson by sticking me in a catch box.

I refocused on other sounds to get a sense of where I was, but it was useless. There was nothing but the rumbling from the road. I allowed my muscles to loosen as I swayed with the motion. I cleared my head of every thought, pushing away the fear as it continued to roll in. If I had no place to go and could only await my fate, I would borrow a lesson from an old friend and mentor, who had taught me meditation. I let her calming words penetrate my steel enclosure as I searched for inner peace.

When the vehicle slowed and made a turn, I was ready. I wasn't sure how long we'd traveled since I didn't know how long I'd been out from the drug. But I figured I'd been awake for more than an hour. Wherever we were going, I didn't think we were in Santiga Bay anymore. I stretched my legs as far as they would go, then rubbed them to force the circulation to return. The last thing I wanted when I got out of the box was to collapse like a broken puppet from stiff muscles.

The vehicle stopped, and mumbled voices drew me closer to the air vents. Probably a checkpoint or gate. The distant sound of rusty hinges confirmed one thing. Wherever we were going, we were there. An ugly thought pierced through my peace. What if we were at the harbor, and I was being loaded onto a ship? *Stop it.* I sniffed the air, trying to pick up smells. Fresh-cut grass. Please don't be a cemetery.

Panic returned at the thought of being buried alive before we came to a stop and the engine cut off. I blew out long, slow breaths as the vehicle rocked and two doors slammed shut. I checked my pockets for the umpteenth time. Still empty. All I had was my martial art skills and my wits to get me out of whatever was coming next.

Bright light hit me as the back door of the van rolled up. It took several seconds for my eyes to adjust. I was in some type of cargo carrier, and four of Sorrento's men hovered around the tailgate. I scanned the area behind them, trying to figure out where I might be, but all I saw were large green fields dotted with trees. The air was fresh outside the box—no scent of a harbor. The men just stood there. Waiting for instructions?

I considered asking them questions, but Sorrento's men didn't believe in small talk. I'd hold my tongue until I was in front of someone who mattered. Five minutes later, two of the men drew out long steel poles. They aimed them at the box, and I was grateful they looked too big to fit through the air vents. At least I wasn't going to be skewered. One possibility to scratch off the long list of dire things that could happen next.

The poles scraped along steel, and I realized the bars would be the handles to lift the box out. Two men jumped inside the van, and the box was pushed to the edge, where the other two men waited to grab the poles.

I rolled to the side, my head slamming into hard metal as the box was unceremoniously dropped to the ground.

"Careful with the merchandise." Sorrento's rough voice was oddly comforting until I had time to consider his words.

Merchandise?

My earlier thought about slave traders came back. Would he

really sell me to get his money? They wouldn't get much for me. Certainly not as much as I owed him. Not by far.

The box was picked up again, and when we moved away from the van, I got a glimpse of a massive rock mansion. I couldn't see it all, but the building stretched forever before we disappeared into a tunnel. There hadn't been any fences or guard towers.

The dark tunnel didn't last long before the men moved through large doors and down a bright, richly furnished interior hallway. They continued through another door, one more hallway, and finally, an arched doorway that ended in a vast circular room. A single chair positioned on a dais sat on the far side of the room. A lone man waited as if on a throne waiting for subjects.

Even in my current predicament, I had to hold in a chuckle. This man thought highly of himself.

Two small men in business suits strolled in to stand on either side of the man in the chair, who appeared to be in his forties. A fit man, from what I could see. Sweat trickled down my back as we got closer. I'd seen that face one other time. Right before my old mentor had whispered a warning: "Don't ever find yourself on his bad side."

It seemed I was going to find out what that statement from five long years ago meant.

The men gently settled the box thirty feet from the dais.

"Remus," Sorrento called out. "It's good to see you again, old friend."

Yep. Remus. I was in big trouble if the stories I'd heard were true. Nothing that I wanted to remember now. My bladder was too full for this nonsense.

"That remains to be seen." The man's voice was strong, but he didn't appear to hold any malice toward Sorrento. He sounded bored.

Maybe killing all those people in horrific ways had become a dull sport for him. I was just one more to add to his list. *Stop it, Cressa.* Yep, I was going crazy. At this rate, my first words outside this box were probably going to get me killed, so why wonder what happens next?

"I'd heard you were looking for someone. Someone special." Sorrento paused as he moved to stand next to the box. He was too close for me to see his face, but I recognized the pistol he wore at his side. It was a vintage Colt, and I'd once thought of stealing it until I considered the consequences. I hadn't learned any lessons where Sorrento was concerned.

"What do you have for me?" The man's tone had changed to one of interest. I wondered if he was the type that opened his presents slowly, taking care not to rip the pretty paper. He probably just grabbed an edge and shred the paper in his haste to find his prize. What interesting things people thought about when stuck in a box, waiting to be let out—or killed.

"Something that might clear my debt to you."

I was being traded off. A brand new hell waited for me.

I peered through the vent at Remus. He was no longer leaning back but had perched on the edge of his seat. Did he just lick his lips? Maybe I was dinner. And considering who this man was, that wasn't too much of a stretch.

"Could it be?" Remus stood, rubbing his hands together, but he didn't leave the dais. The two men by his side hadn't moved, but one brought out a notepad and started scribbling in it.

Someone, probably Sorrento, knocked on the box twice. "Open it up."

The poles slid from their brackets and were placed gently on the floor. No one wanted to irritate Remus by showing disrespect. Locks were opened, and more metal slid as the top of the box was removed. Fresh air rushed in. I squinted at the increased light before hands reached in and pulled me up. I wobbled for a few seconds before gaining my footing. Sorrento's men helped me out of the box and positioned me in front of it. They held onto my arms until Sorrento waved them away.

I made a quick assessment of the reception room. Besides

Sorrento, his men, and the three on the dais, six other men were positioned around the room.

I glared at Sorrento before turning my attention to the man in charge.

Out of the corner of my eye, Sorrento straightened while tugging on his pants. "May I present Pandora."

Remus's eyes grew large as he stared at me, giving me a once-over that was at first curious, then lustful, before fortunately settling on shrewd. He stepped down from the dais and walked toward me, never taking his eyes from me as he continued his perusal. Perhaps assessing my value? When he circled me, checking me from all angles, I followed his movements, partially turning when he moved behind me. Based on his slight grin, my reaction seemed to amuse him.

"How can I be assured this is Pandora?" Remus moved in front of me and lifted my chin. I batted away his arm. He smiled, showing his teeth, and I had to force myself not to back up a step. "Feisty. I like that. But I'm not sure if that will work for what I have in mind."

"I can assure you this is Pandora. She's been in my debt for the last three years, and she's the best thief I've seen. Her reputation is valid."

I didn't like where this was going, and I had no idea why Remus would be looking for me. Unless I had unwittingly stolen something from him. Maybe he had a job for me. If it was the latter, all they had to do was ask. Anything to pay off my debt.

"She'll be a handy addition to your pack." Sorrento's salesman-ship could use some work.

Would I be a thief or a toy?

Remus continued to assess me, his gaze shiny with possibilities, but then his expression changed as he let out a breath, his shoulders slumping. "Unfortunately, I also owe favors. But she'll do nicely in crossing one inconvenient debt off my list."

For fuck's sake, Remus was just a broker for a bigger deal. I wasn't property to be traded around like someone's prize mare. Maybe that wasn't the best analogy, considering the circumstances.

"She can be a bit problematic and should probably be kept in chains." Sorrento eyed me with a grin I'd like to knock off his face. "Or the box."

Asshole.

Remus turned on Sorrento with a speed that surprised me. "I gave you a pass for presenting her in the box. You know my feelings where catch boxes are concerned. You'll take that atrocity out of my sight when you leave." He glanced at his men. "It's making the wolves chafe."

Sorrento paled and motioned to his men, who replaced the lid, slid the poles into place, and moved the box outside the door. He bowed his head. "I'm sorry. It was the only thing I felt was safe enough to transport her."

Remus laughed, deep and hearty. "So, your four beefy men can't handle this slip of a girl." His men laughed with him, but they watched me with menace, or perhaps hunger, in their eyes. Remus turned back to the men on the dais. "Mark Sorrento's debt paid."

He turned to Sorrento. "But if she proves not to be Pandora."

Sorrento didn't back down. "Then my debt is doubled." He smiled. "I'm not worried."

Remus nodded. "Good. Because Trelane won't be as accommodating, and my owed favor will pass to you."

Sorrento paled again, but his defiance didn't deflate. "Still not worried."

I ignored Sorrento as I tried to recall where I'd heard the name Trelane before.

"Glenda," Remus yelled. "Come get this girl. She'll need to be cleaned before we leave."

Sorrento bowed to Remus and backed away. Before he turned to exit, he gave one final warning, nodding toward me. "This one is slippery. I suggest keeping her in chains."

"There's nowhere for her to run. If she tries, any one of her six new bodyguards," he nodded toward the men in the room, "will rip her apart before she makes ten yards." He turned to me. "Remember that girl." When a robust woman entered the room, Remus pointed toward me. "I want her bathed and dressed to meet Trelane." He glanced out the windows. "You have two hours before dark. He should be available then."

Sorrento gave me a last, almost regretful glance before disappearing out the door.

I gave the six men a quick assessment. They weren't as large as Sorrento's men, but they were wiry like Harlow and no doubt quick. I shrugged. In two hours, they wouldn't be my problem. It wasn't until Glenda had grabbed my upper arm in a tight squeeze and pushed me to another door that I remembered where I'd heard the name Trelane. I wheezed, and my knees almost buckled.

Trelane was the notorious city outcast. And an ancient vampire.

Chapter Four

I stared out the window, grateful for a more luxurious ride than a catch box. At the sound of ice cubes dropping into a glass, I turned toward my host. Remus, also known as The Wolf, traveled in style. The limo was well-appointed with a white interior, and I stared down at my clothing, wondering how much filth I was rubbing into the matching leather seats. The carpet was so thick I wanted to run my toes through it. A light musky scent mixed with the rich smell of leather and something a little more sinister floated between us.

A dark partition had been raised between the driver's section and the back, which had plenty of legroom. I huddled on the long cushioned bench, and The Wolf sprawled on one of two console chairs. He poured what looked to be vodka into the glass.

He glanced at me and lifted the crystal decanter that he'd pulled from the chilled section of his liquor cabinet. What the hell.

I nodded. When he reached for the tongs to select an ice cube, I murmured, "Neat."

He raised a brow and poured two fingers into the glass before leaning over to hand it to me.

I forced myself to sip rather than gulp the liquor, but my

nerves wanted me to down it and beg for more. After two long sips, my courage returned. "I didn't know the packs were into slave trading."

I waited. Was he going to censure me? Hit me? Eat me?

Instead, he laughed. "Ah, my dear, I'm afraid Sorrento has given you the wrong impression." His expression darkened, and he swallowed a large portion of his vodka. "He knows how the shifters feel about catch boxes. And while he may have paid his debt in a more than acceptable manner, his actions won't go unpunished, if that gives you any peace for the way you were treated."

I tried to hold my surprise in check. A shifter being more polite than a human. But I had to admit, Sorrento wasn't your model human by any stretch.

"Yet, you have no problem with him trading me off to pay his debt." I swallowed the rest of the vodka. The liquor replaced my fear with irritation.

"Is that what you think? That you've been traded off to be a slave?"

I managed a half-shrug.

He laughed before finishing his drink. He lifted the crystal decanter. When I raised my brow, he followed with a shrug of his own. "We have another forty-five minutes before we arrive at the Trelane estate. We might as well enjoy the ride."

I offered my glass, and this time, he poured a larger serving for both of us before setting the crystal bottle back in the refrigerated cabinet. It had been a while since I'd had anything as fine as this vodka. Not only was it worth sipping, if I drank much more, all my inhibitions would be gone. That wouldn't be wise until I knew more about my situation.

"So, how would you classify my abduction and..." I waved my hand around the limo, which I had to admit didn't suggest horrible captivity. But a hostage was still a hostage.

"As a human, you probably don't know much about magical

creatures. But, from my research into Pandora, you know the underworld." When I didn't respond, he asked, "Am I wrong?"

I shook my head. The more I learned about my situation, the easier it would be to find a way out. One in which I was still in one piece.

"This world revolves around those who have and those who don't. Even in the mundane world of humans, people borrow money or other material items, typically in exchange for money or credit. In the world of immortals, money is king, but the only credit we use are personal favors, which are as valid as any written contract. But unlike debt collectors or lawsuits, anyone not following through on a favor owed is punished more...directly."

I took a large gulp of my drink and turned to the window. No sane person would ever go back on a favor owed to an immortal of any species. Not without a death wish or forever looking over your shoulder.

When I didn't say anything, Remus sipped his vodka as he stared out his window. "Sorrento said you owed him a sizable debt you've been unable to pay."

"He didn't give me enough time to repay it. I was in the middle of a lucrative operation when he caught me. If he'd given me two more days, I would have handed over a tidy sum."

The Wolf considered my words. "Still leaving a rather large balance."

I couldn't argue.

"Sorrento has his own debts and favors to pay. As do I. It's how the world works. The only question is the degree."

That spurred my curiosity. What type of favor would my debt require? I straightened from my growing slouch. The leather seats were scrumptious.

"Let me assure you. No one is trading you off as a slave, per se."

When I narrowed my eyes, he only smiled and sipped his drink.

"It's not you personally that is of interest. It's your talents."

My eyes grew wide. Did this shifter think a sex slave was any better?

He chuckled. "Your skill as a thief."

I blinked. Sorrento kidnapped me in the middle of a heist so I could perform more heists?

"Unless Pandora's reputation as a thief is only matched by her skill in the bedroom." He grinned, and for the first time, he let the lust, along with his teeth, show through his heated gaze.

This time I sneered, but I couldn't help the blush creeping to my cheeks. I wouldn't categorize sex as one of my specialties. A growl might have slipped out to cover my embarrassment, which only seemed to please him. Wolves.

"Sorrento said you were feisty. I would suggest you keep that in check. Trelane doesn't respond well to disobedience."

"If someone wanted me for a job, all they had to do was ask."

He shook his head. "That's not how it's done. And besides, I'm not completely sure if your skills will be enough to clear my own favor. Hence, the refund declaration Sorrento made."

Great. Not only did I not know my fate as payment for debts owed, but it also seemed I could be returned like some broken doll. I was beginning to feel like that unwanted Christmas gift that kept getting passed around.

"Then why go through all this trouble?"

"Because, my dear, with great risk comes great reward. And when the hunt becomes personal and the stakes are high, one can't afford to work with contractors."

Before I could ask what he meant, a bell chimed, and Remus set down his glass to retrieve his phone. He read the text then glanced my way. "There are magazines in the side panel if you wish. I'm afraid I need to take care of some business for the remainder of our drive."

I turned toward the window, pulling my legs up and curling into myself, my glass of vodka tight in my grip. I nursed the rest of it as I watched the passing landscape. Remus had lived on a large estate with wide-open fields that edged a forest. Now that I understood he was the area's alpha with a large pack, it made sense. Plenty of space to run with no one watching.

We had driven through the city and were now headed along the coast. When we broke out of the forested landscape to find glimpses of the ocean, I noticed the sun dipping toward the horizon. It would be dusk when we reached our destination. The witching hour. Or, in this case, vamp hour. And for the first time, I wondered what Ginger had thought when I didn't come home. She'd warned me about this last heist. I snorted. I don't think this outcome was what she'd worried about.

The limo made its last turn into a private drive and stopped at a twelve-foot gate. I glanced around, my first inclination to review the security. The stone walls were as tall as the gate, and though I couldn't see much from this side, I was certain the wall surrounded the entire estate.

When the gates opened and the limo moved forward, I straightened, marveling at the vast expanse of lawn and giant sycamore trees as we wound our way up the drive. The trees opened to reveal the mansion, and I cringed. The hairs on the back of my neck rose in protest.

The gothic three-story monstrosity appeared to be in shadows with the sun setting behind it, casting an unearthly orange glow around its stone structure. It was out of every horror movie I'd ever seen, and a cold shiver settled deep in my bones. I set my glass in the console and wrapped my arms around my middle. Ominous lights glowed from several windows—sentinels watching our approach. It wasn't until we pulled up to the front door that I noticed unnatural shadows in the recesses of the mansion. Two moved closer to the door. The others remained as motionless as statues. Maybe my eyes were playing tricks, but I didn't think so. As a thief, I was used to working with limited light and saw well in the dark. The vamp had personal guards.

When the driver and another man got out, the first thing I

heard and smelled was the ocean. The crashing waves had been muffled by the soundproof limo. The combination of salty air and rotting fish was a familiar smell one would expect at a fishing dock, not at the mansion of the city's most notorious bloodsucker.

Both passenger doors opened simultaneously as Remus and I were assisted out of the vehicle. The Wolf led the way. The driver and the other man, who I assumed was a bodyguard, escorted us to the door. If I'd been in the same situation, I would have brought more men, especially as I noted the number of shadows increase. But I assumed men like Remus and Trelane had to play nice if they lived in the same city, at least while guests at each other's homes. And I assumed Remus must be a guest since he was using me to pay off a favor.

The door opened as if by magic because no one met us. But after we walked through, I saw a diminutive man standing behind the massive ten-foot wood door. He must have some magical strength to have opened that door, or maybe it was just hollow. I took note of the handle and locking mechanism, which didn't appear to be anything more than one would expect to find in an old mansion. The only question was whether there was an alarm if the door opened, what triggered it, and who was notified.

The inside was what I'd expected. Paneled walls, deep-green wallpaper, and paintings with diverse subjects and time periods— angels, battlefields, royal courts, and dance halls. But they all had one grisly thing in common—blood. Every painting had death portrayed in some brutal way, even in the most colorful and airy scenes. What a dismal place to live. And what did that say about the owner? Even the furniture was dark wood. Then, I felt the color drain from my face. Did they keep everything dark so no one could see the dried blood spatters of a meal gone bad?

I shivered as we were led through another set of tall doors that brought us to a formal living room. The black leather sofas and chairs seemed out of place, as did the squared, smoked-glass coffee table positioned between them. A crackling fire filled the hearth that was large enough to walk in and cast the same orange glow as the sunset.

In front of the fireplace, a man stood with his back to us, his hands clasped behind him. He seemed to be staring into the flames, and if he'd heard us enter, he gave no indication. His finely tailored suit molded to a lean build, but I guessed there was some hard muscle under the dark cloth. His hair, the color indistinguishable in the firelight, was pulled back into a ponytail. *One of those guys.* Hadn't he heard that fashion style was long dead? I mentally shrugged. Oh yeah. He was also long dead.

The four of us and the six vamp minions that formed a semicircle around us waited for our host to notice. I glanced at Remus, but he didn't seem bothered by the lack of felicitous greeting. A minute later, our host turned. The low lighting and the glow of the fireplace kept him in the shadows, so I wasn't able to get a good look at his face. But his gaze seemed to track over each of us before resting on me. And though I couldn't see him well, the pressure of his perusal felt like heavy hands on my shoulders, his eyes raking my soul. An instant later, it vanished.

That was weird.

He stepped into the light of the room, and when he glanced at me, he quirked a brow, probably still trying to figure out who or what I was. But I couldn't focus on that. His gaze bored into mine, and while I'd heard of vampires being able to entrance people, I didn't think that was happening. I wouldn't have been able to tear my gaze away, even if he wasn't a vampire. The man to which I was being traded into indentured service was stunning enough to make my panties wet.

Chapter Five

"WELCOME, REMUS." The vamp swept his arm to the side to encompass his home. "Would you like a drink?"

"That would be most welcome," The Wolf replied.

"Sergi, would you please pour a vodka over ice for our guest?" He took a seat in one of the leather chairs and waved a hand for us to sit.

After the drinks were served, Trelane leaned back, casually holding the glass on his thigh. He studied Remus. "What brings you to this side of town?"

I unclenched my jaw. Trelane hadn't asked who I was, didn't offer me a drink, and hadn't looked my way once after his initial inspection. Most people were polite enough to ask my name or offer me a glass of water. The only thing stopping me from storming out was the six vampires, three wolves, and this rude ancient bloodsucker.

Two could play that game. I ignored the men and began a slow scan of the room. I kept my ears open while I checked out the valuables, but the men weren't saying anything of interest. What I did find fascinating was the antiques. I'd been looking for less than five minutes and found three things worth stealing. There was so much crap in the room, stuffed in bookcases, curio cabinets, and table-tops. Would anyone notice a few missing items? Just souvenirs from my time here.

"Pandora!" Remus shouted.

I turned to him. "Sorry, what?"

I glanced at our host. Although his arm hung lazily over the side of the chair with his whiskey glass gripped by his fingertips, he stared at me with a fierce scowl. Inside, my flight instincts blared until all I heard was buzzing. Outside, after years of being a cat burglar and scaling some incredibly difficult buildings, I'd learned to stay focused. So, I glared back before turning to Remus.

The Wolf had finally lost that casual look, a splotch of red forming on both cheeks. Maybe I would end up someone's dinner after all.

"Mr. Trelane asked about your specialties. He already has two thieves on retainer."

If he had two thieves, he was right in questioning his need for a third. If he didn't need me, maybe The Wolf could use me. But he might trade me off to someone else. What's behind door number two? I didn't want to take the risk.

"After all," the vamp added, "a thief is a thief."

That pissed me off. "Oh, really?" I scooched until I perched on the edge of the couch. "Can your thieves climb any building in this town, get by any sensor, or crack any safe? Can they do all three?" I made sure my scowl was better than his since we seemed to be in a contest for the crown.

When Remus cleared his throat, I broke eye contact with the bloodsucker and sat back, arms crossed. What the hell was I doing? My pride was going to get me killed.

"Have you not heard of Pandora?" The Wolf asked.

"I'm not normally in need of a thief." The vamp drained his glass and set it on the tabletop, which forced him closer to me. Only a few inches, but enough to whiff a wickedly tantalizing and heady aroma—cinnamon and cloves. Was the scent coming from someone adding spices to the fire, or was it from him? Good God.

He pulled out a phone and typed a message. The vamp stared at the phone, and though it appeared he was just waiting for an answer, there was something else going on. Thin lines formed between his eyes, which looked unfocused as if he was thinking—or planning. And I wasn't sure what that meant for me.

I was dying to squirm in my seat—the silence deafening. From somewhere, a grandfather clock ticked with each swing of the pendulum. A floorboard creaked above us. I glanced at The Wolf, but he stared at his own phone. I felt like I should have whipped mine out if I had one. I rarely took my phone on operations, leaving it in my beat-up, multi-colored Jeep or at home if I had a crew. Someone always had one if we needed it. At least mine was currently safe at home. Harlow always carried his, and I'd walked to the local bar to meet his crew. Was that last night? I never asked how long Sorrento had me drugged but assumed no more than a day.

What seemed like hours but couldn't have been more than five agonizing minutes, the vamp's phone chirped, bringing him out of his trance. After reading what must have been a pretty short message, he nodded to Remus.

"A week trial. If, at the end of that time, I have no use for her, she'll be returned, and your debt will be reinstated."

The Wolf considered the proposal while I continued to fume about two supernatural beings trading a human. Like I didn't have rights. Then, I remembered who was in the room—three shifters and seven vampires. Who was I kidding? Being human wasn't exactly an advantage here.

"I accept your proposal." Remus set his glass on the table. "But you must promise she'll be returned unharmed." At least the shifter was in my corner. Then, he shrugged. "Or she would be of no use to me."

Of course, I was only as valuable as the skills I had to offer.

How did I get myself into this mess? But I knew the answer. Had known the risks. And now I was on the backside of that decision. I sat straighter. Whatever my actions cost, they'd been worth the price. Nevertheless, I gulped when The Wolf and the vamp stood to shake hands. It was done. I wasn't leaving this horribly depressing mansion, and a deep sense of claustrophobia overtook me. I might never leave it.

Remus stopped long enough to whisper, "If you need anything, or find yourself in trouble, just contact me." He slipped me a silver-colored business card with a number on it. Cheeky for a shifter to carry silver business cards.

He strode out with his two bodyguards behind him. Once the front door shut, the silence intensified, the sound from the grandfather clock pounding like war drums as I awaited my fate.

The vamp nodded, and the other six figures disappeared from the room as silently as they'd arrived. He stared at me briefly before calling out, "Anna, please make up a room for our guest. The west-side corner suite on the second floor should do. And Anna?" A woman, who I hadn't seen, stepped forward out of the shadows. She was younger than me. Was she a vampire or just a human servant? "Pandora will require a wardrobe. I'll provide a full list, but a change of clothes for this evening and tomorrow will be required immediately."

Anna nodded and disappeared into the shadows, her tiny footsteps receding down the hall.

"I apologize for my poor manners. Had I known you weren't one of his pack, I would have been more hospitable. But Remus only mentioned the meeting was of some urgency."

I was tongue-tied. He was sorry for ignoring me? Didn't see that coming. I guess I was one step higher on the ladder than I thought.

He glanced at his watch. "And this meeting has put me behind schedule." He sauntered to a side table where he retrieved a tablet, the device seeming futuristic in this gothic setting. His lips moved as he typed, and I wondered if he was talking to someone that only a vamp could hear or to himself. I almost smiled. The behavior seemed so human.

"Have you eaten?"

Another surprise. "Not recently."

He nodded, still perusing the tablet. "Lucas will take you to the kitchen. Cook usually has something available. By then, your room should be ready." He laid the tablet down and turned to me. His expression had softened to a friendlier visage, which only made him more attractive. Good grief. "I'm sure you understand I can't give you any freedom until we've gone over the rules. We can discuss those tomorrow. Lucas will be your guard for this evening. All I ask is that you remain in your room. If there's anything you need, Lucas will show you how to contact Anna."

Then, he walked out the door.

I turned around, wondering who Lucas was. No doubt a vampire.

When no one arrived, I took the time to investigate the room more thoroughly, not knowing if I'd ever get another chance. I wasn't sure how far my chain would go.

I picked up what appeared to be a Fabergé egg. Real ones were so rare. I'd only seen one in a museum and another in a magazine. Based on the other treasures in the room, I didn't question its authenticity. Why wasn't it in a locked case? Oh yeah. Vampires. I wasn't an expert on antiques, but as a thief, I had to know the value of objects when negotiating with a fence. When I began pilfering, what seemed a lifetime ago, it had been a game. Then it was a way to stay alive.

I discovered how quickly I picked up the right skills, and my notorious career was launched. I'd begun with stealing simple stuff that was easy to unload—ordinary jewelry, small electronics. The money was decent, but the jobs had been limiting, so I began picking up other trinkets. That opened new avenues for learning when I started working with various crews around Santiga Bay and all points south to San Francisco.

"If you'll follow me." The voice made me spin around. Another good-looking vampire. This one was the California surfer type. Blond hair cut short on the sides but longer on top, letting a little fall over one of his crystal-blue eyes. But rather than a bronze tan, his skin was pale. His expression was stony, yet there might have been a slight twitch to his lips when he glanced down at my hands. "Were you planning on stealing while you're here?"

I turned to put the egg back where I'd found it. Then waited for the heat to leave my cheeks. Could vampires read my thoughts?

"You'll need to learn to be less obvious. But a thief handling precious antiquities will always raise a brow." He clapped his hands. "Come now. Cook doesn't like to be kept waiting."

I took a cooling breath and turned to him. He hadn't moved, his arms held behind his back, but his expression had changed to one of impatience if I read those brows correctly. I strode toward him, pushing my fear down as I got closer, but before I was ten feet away, he turned and marched down the hallway. He didn't speak, and that was fine by me. I turned on surveillance mode, checking out each room as we passed, sketching out a floorplan in my head, and making note of exits.

The kitchen was massive, with two sets of ovens on the far wall and a long counter with two double sinks and cabinets to the right. In the middle was a huge island, almost as long as the counter. A table that fit twenty was on the other side of the room. Probably an eating area for the servants or lower-ranking vamps.

Next to a window, a table for two sat in a corner nook with a single place setting, a glass of water, and an empty wine glass. Outside the window was nothing but blackness.

"Sorry, we're late." Lucas motioned me to the table before dropping onto a stool at the island.

Cook was not the stocky old woman I was expecting. This guy was a bruiser. If he was a vamp, he was the first ugly one I'd seen.

His features were marred with two ragged scars. The first ran from his hairline, down the middle of his forehead, and across the edge of his left eye, while the second traveled from his right cheek to his upper lip. His dark shaggy hair was tucked into a hairnet of all things. I had to stifle a laugh. The net seemed so out of place on this man who was well over six feet tall and, with those shoulders, must move through doors sideways.

His dark eyes pinned me like a bug to the floor. Once again, I wondered if I might be on the menu.

"Sit," he barked and pointed toward the nook.

I almost ran to sit down. This was not someone I was going to mess with. One slap of his hand could knock me out for days.

For his size, Cook moved around the kitchen like a ballerina. His movements were mesmerizing as he put a plate together and set it in front of me. My stomach growled at the scent, and I almost drooled at the sight. Aromatic lasagna, green salad, and garlic bread. He returned with two small dressing servers.

"This one is Italian, and this one is my special dressing, refined after many years." He waited. I had a feeling he wasn't going to leave until I made a selection. I glanced at Lucas, who was grinning now. He nodded toward the big man, which could only mean one thing.

I stared at the dressings, not wanting to know what made Cook's dressing special, but I pointed toward it, and his smile deepened the creases of his scars.

"Excellent choice." He poured a small amount on the salad before setting the serving dish down. Then he brought a bottle of wine and held it up. When I nodded, he poured a glass of red. "This is a pinot from the valley. Very good." He left the bottle then returned to his side of the kitchen to continue cutting vegetables.

I ignored the two men as they begun chatting about some problems with the groceries. The lasagna was out of this world, and I polished off most of the food in short order, deciding to take my time with the salad and bread while drinking as much wine as possible. The pinot was starting to work its magic as my shoulders relaxed, and the tension I'd been holding since waking up in the catch box began to diminish.

With nothing else to look at, I turned toward the dark window. Based on my calculations, the window should face the ocean, but it was difficult to tell with the light fog that had rolled in.

I was savoring the last of my wine when I noticed a light moving slowly through the mist. The bright glow cast a single figure dancing in and out of the darkness. Before kneeling, the figure stopped and set a lantern on what looked like a tall grave marker. All I could discern was the hooded shape.

Blinds snapped shut, and I fell back, surprised to find Lucas frowning down at me.

His demeanor changed back to his original bland expression, though tiny frown lines that hadn't been there earlier creased his forehead. "I'll take you to your room now."

"Who was out there?"

He bent closer as if he didn't want Cook to hear. But I think it was more his way of ensuring I paid attention. "That is none of your business."

Chapter Six

DEVON TRELANE SURVEYED the neighborhood as Sergi, his driver for this evening, eased the limo down the street. He would have driven himself, but it had been a long time since he'd walked these streets, and in this neighborhood, the owner of the block changed frequently. And though shifters and vampires shared the streets equally, it didn't mean they got along. There were rules, but here, where few watched, they were more suggested behaviors. Like one should floss every day, but truly, how many people actually did that? Well, maybe the shifters after each meal. He chuckled at the thought.

Shifters and vampires weren't supposed to kill each other. But accidents happened. As long as it didn't turn into civil war among the magical, no one questioned what went down in the Hollows. As a Council Elder, Devon should be protected, but he was under censure. And no one, other than his vampire family, would be concerned if a censured Council member met a grisly fate in this part of town. This time his laugh turned menacing. That would please some of the Council while making other's lives so much easier. So, for this meeting, he'd asked Sergi to drive him.

Sergi would have followed him anyway. He sighed. On the one

hand, he appreciated his stalwart friend's concern for his welfare. On the other, there wasn't any place Devon could go on his own without one of his trusted friends following, even at a discreet distance.

"Go around once more." Devon thought he recognized the building, but he wanted to be sure. It seemed seedier than the last time he'd been here, but that was a long time ago. And he'd been a very different person in those days.

Sergi repeated their drive down the main street of the Hollows, then turned down a side street. After another block, Devon tapped his side window and pointed to a building on the left. Sergi nodded and drove another block before pulling over. The limo would be noticeable, but it wouldn't be the only one. Devon had counted three while they circled. There would be more parked in the back allies. While most of the action in this area involved drug deals and off-book, small-stakes gambling, more dangerous games occurred in club basements and abandoned warehouses on the edges of the district. That was where the big money was, along with the instinctual nature of being a magical creature.

In all-human neighborhoods, where drug kings ruled, expensive cars would be jacked and stripped if they weren't well guarded. In this district, anyone who fucked with a shifter or vampire would be hunted down. Maybe not right away, but the perpetrator would be forever looking over their shoulder until one day they would no longer have their head.

So, Devon let his guard down when he sensed Sergi following him. His bodyguard would be barely visible to anyone other than an older vampire. When Devon reached the house, he gave it a close scan as he walked by, then turned down the next alley, deciding to approach from the rear.

To most, little could be heard from the building, but Devon's oversensitive hearing detected voices from the basement, even though music blared from the nearby clubs. Vampires had exceptional hearing, sometimes too good, and newly created vampires required many months of training to separate superfluous noise. It took decades to distinguish a single voice in a room of hundreds.

Two men leaned against the building, monitoring the back door. Devon barely glanced at them as he approached. Sergi would station himself someplace in the shadows, only following Devon inside if he sensed trouble.

The Den had been his home for a long time. Not an overly original name for a shifter club, but its clientele weren't the discriminating type. When he'd first stumbled through the doors, half-mad on Magic Poppy, the outlawed juice of the Blood Poppy, this club was the only place willing to take him in. A decade passed before one of his still-trusting friends found him. It took two more decades before he walked away and never returned. That was thirty years ago.

The stairs creaked with a long squeal that sounded of age and broken dreams. When he reached the top step, one of the men shifted to the right to block the door. Devon decided not to give the security team a hard time. The doors had been his first assignment working at the club, not because of beefy arms or a thick neck—he didn't have either—but for his fangs. Everyone had their specialty. Devon simply stared at the man until he bowed his head and returned to his leaning spot. The men were older shifters, rough around the edges but ready to intimidate the uninitiated or the foolhardy. They recognized vampires and never questioned the elders. At least, that was one house rule he remembered, and it seemed that hadn't changed.

He pushed through the door and strode through the first-floor rooms. Small-time poker games, hook-up rooms for dalliances with magical creatures, and two bars that served cheap liquor. The upper-floor rooms, used for personal playtime, were the same, and he had to smile at the owner's deference toward predictability. Stepping down from the staircase, he surveyed the main room one last time before heading toward the kitchen, where stairs led down to the basement—the real action took place there.

Decker, the shifter who'd owned the club when Devon had lived there, had dug the basement deeper to support the high-walled cages made of thick, silver-lined wire required for magical fights. Additional rooms extended beyond the fight area, where darker fantasies played out. Turning away from that part of the basement, Devon pushed his way through the crowd to the bar. He hadn't come for the fights. He'd turned his back on that part of his life when he'd left the Den and had no desire to return to it.

The crowd thinned in the lounge as they moved toward the cage fights that would soon start. He found a spot at the end of the bar and sank onto the stool, surveying the room but not seeing anyone he recognized. Although that was best, it left him melancholy to know everyone he'd known had moved on—one way or another.

"Well, if it isn't Devon Trelane. I thought you'd be dead by now."

Devon smiled before glancing up to find the tall, shapely blonde saunter toward him. As usual, her thick mane of hair was piled high on her head, and her dark, penetrating eyes returned his perusal.

"I didn't see you come in." Sabrina's brows scrunched together as she studied him, and he tried not to squirm. She had a knack for looking straight through someone and instantly gauging their weakness. "You've changed."

"Maybe." He smiled, honestly pleased to see her. They'd had good times long ago, and along with Decker, she'd saved him from himself.

"I still see the shadows, though." She frowned, and Devon sensed her distress, as he had the last time she'd confronted him. The last time they'd spoken.

Devon had no reply, and she shrugged. "But you're still with us. That's something."

He gave her a slight nod to put her at ease. "Does Decker still come by?"

She laughed a deep, throaty chuckle that caught the attention of a randy group of shifters at a nearby table. Devon gave them the stare, and they straightened, heads down, before returning to their conversation.

Sabrina pinched his arm. "Stop that. I've had my eyes on those boys all evening. Don't go scaring them away." Her smile could light up the darkest of rooms, and Devon couldn't help but laugh.

"I'm glad to know some things truly don't change."

"Decker should be in soon. He still owns the place."

"I should have known better."

"I'd say. Can I get you a drink while you wait? Your usual? If it's still your usual." She pushed back a lock of his hair, her fingers lingering on his cheek. "I liked you better with your buzz cut. It showed off those marvelous cheekbones."

He ignored the comment but grabbed her hand, rubbing her palm before letting go. "The usual will be fine." He didn't drink tequila anymore, but she didn't need to know that. And he admitted he was in the mood for something...different.

"It really is good to see you." She poured his drink, turning quiet. When she placed the drink in front of him, she leaned in. "Listen. Decker isn't the same as you remember him. Oh, he can still be his grumpy old self, but..." Sabrina glanced around and put a hand over his, "he can't let go of the past."

It shouldn't have shocked him. Something that horrific was hard to shake. "Some things never go away. You know that."

Her gaze darkened for a split second, and she wiped the bar down before continuing, her voice low. "It's been getting worse. He holes himself up in that office for hours at a time. And it's not because he's doing books. He has someone who does that for him now."

When Devon didn't respond, too busy staring into his drink, Sabrina gave up. "Anyway, I thought you should know."

She turned to attend to another customer before Devon responded. "It's why I'm here."

She stopped for a second before nodding and hurrying off.

Devon sat back and surveyed the crowd. He didn't sense any humans, only young shifters and vampires. Too young to have been customers while Devon had worked here. There were two older creatures, but when his gaze brushed over them, he didn't recognize them.

He nursed his second drink and, not for the first time, considered the package that had been delivered that evening. He'd been shocked and a bit outraged when Remus brought a woman to pay off a debt. He'd honestly assumed she was a new pack member or The Wolf's lover. Sometimes, Devon couldn't get an accurate read on the newly created shifters. Not until after they'd shifted a few times. And it wasn't unusual for shifters to keep humans as their sex partners.

She hadn't appeared happy in Remus's presence, which was why he'd assumed her a new shifter. Some weren't brought over willingly. And while Remus had his dark fantasies, he usually didn't go for such young ones. The woman's milky skin gave her the appearance of a vampire, but that's where the comparison ended. He'd sensed the anger and fear before he smelled it seeping from her pores. Yet, her face hadn't shown anything other than boredom. It fascinated him until he'd shoved it away, assuming Remus owned her.

It wasn't the first time Devon had taken a human as payment for a debt, though it had been decades. While it was a permissible trade in their world, Devon found it distasteful. He chuckled to himself. Sabrina had been right—he had changed. His first instinct had been to turn down the offered payment until he discovered she was a thief. Devon hadn't lied to Remus. He did have two thieves on retainer, but they lacked the right skills. His interest piqued, and never having heard of Pandora, he'd sent a message to his first-tier guards to see what they knew about her. Devon had received more replies than he anticipated, but everyone agreed on two elements: highly skilled and a mystery. Meaning no one knew who Pandora was.

After all this time, Devon had found a way to not only pay back Decker but solve his own problems. But could one human redirect the course of his life?

When Devon pushed his drink away, he noticed the original crowd, who'd moved to the cage fights, had been replaced with a new group of customers. He was turning back to his ruminations when he spotted him.

Decker had his head down and didn't spot Devon at the bar. Sabrina was right. Decker looked horrible. His physical appearance hadn't changed in all this time, but Devon sensed the pain and defeat in the tired eyes and sagging shoulders. If the man had walked into any other shifter club, he'd be an easy target. But in his own club, the man had enough bodyguards to drop his defenses. Still foolish.

Devon laid money on the bar and followed Decker toward the office. It wasn't until Decker started to open his door that he spun around. His eyes widened, a smile almost touching his lips when his bushy brows formed a line over his hardened gaze. "Do I need a bodyguard for this unexpected visit?" He glanced past Devon's shoulder. "I don't see any of your people."

Devon gave Decker a thoughtful look, curious why the man would think he'd come to hurt him. Perhaps he should have stayed in touch before now, but he pushed the guilty thought aside. This was important, and he'd waited far too long for this moment. He gave Decker an eerie smile.

"I think we may have a way in."

And without another word, Decker straightened, his eyes brightening, and he gave Devon a large, wolfie grin. He ushered Devon in before slamming the door shut behind them, neither of them spotting the lone vampire lurking in the shadows.

Chapter Seven

THE WINDOW of my room stretched across two walls meeting at a corner, providing an enhanced view of the property. The scenery was breathtaking—a grassy, treed landscape overlooking the ocean. Yet, I couldn't take my gaze away from where I'd spotted the mystery person with the lantern the night before—two gravestones near a large sycamore tree.

Nothing mysterious after all. It wasn't unusual for older estates to have a family plot. I'd seen a similar one on a job last year. Had it been Trelane paying respects? With vampiric night vision, he wouldn't need a lantern. Why would any vampire? That was the interesting part.

I tore my gaze from the window and leaned against the wall, jonesing for coffee, and hearing the grumbling of my stomach, needing breakfast as well. I'd woken before daybreak and watched dawn chase away the shadows as the house woke, creaking in an oddly comforting way. As large as it was, the house I grew up in never made noise, probably because it wasn't nearly as old as this place and didn't have enough stories to tell.

There had been soft murmurs in the hall at one point, just past seven, but they'd drifted away. I thought to check my door to see if it was locked but wasn't ready to greet the day. Or meet the vampire. Anna had laid out a nightgown, which I'd left at the bottom of the bed, preferring to sleep in my tank top and undies, but I figured it didn't hurt to have something close in case of a midnight visitor. I had no idea if vampires slept and had to admit, most of my knowledge about them was half-truths and scarier fabrications.

Anna also supplied a pair of black pants, a tailored shirt, and a sweater. It took me fifteen minutes to decide whether to wear what was left for me or put my old clothes back on. But my clothes stank, and I was still feeling petulant about being kidnapped. I didn't want the reminder that I was to blame for striking that deal six months ago, knowing damn well I wouldn't be able to pay the debt back in time. And who makes deals with loan sharks with connections to magical creatures? An idiot—that's me.

The house was warmer than I expected, so I dressed in the slacks and shirt but left the sweater on a chair, curious if the garment meant I might be allowed outside. Trelane did say I could walk freely around the house, but he might have meant just the interior.

Seven days to prove to him I was worthy of whatever deed he had planned. One job, and I would be clear of my debt. That seemed too easy.

The knock surprised me, though I'd been expecting it. I glanced at the old clock that ticked away on the mantel above the barren fireplace. I stood and cleared my throat, but my "come in" still sounded raspy.

Lucas entered and, after giving me a quick once over, nodded his acceptance. Glad I made someone happy.

"Devon wasn't sure if you were awake yet. Since you hadn't come down, he asked if you would join him for breakfast." Lucas glanced around the room, maybe checking to make sure I hadn't tied the bed linen together to make an escape. Not that it hadn't crossed my mind, but where would I go that a vampire couldn't find me? Or worse, a hungry pack of wolves if this didn't work out.

"I would have gone down earlier, but I wasn't sure of the house rules." I stood and ran my hands down my slacks. I hadn't worn anything this nice for...well, that didn't matter. I preferred my jeans and black cargo pants.

Lucas laughed. "House rules?" He shrugged. "I suppose there will be one or two for you, considering your position here, but this house isn't nearly as formal as most."

"You mean as most vampire homes?" His statement seemed to have left that part dangling.

He bowed his head then waved an arm toward the door. It was clear he wasn't going to say more, so I strode past him, almost walking out of the short-heeled pumps I'd been given. One size too big. I wasn't going to run away in these. I remembered the way to the kitchen and was almost there when Lucas grabbed my arm and steered me toward another room. Of course, a dining room. I should have known that. When I lived with my mother and Christopher, meals were always taken in the dining room, never the kitchen. If I remembered my previous life, sticking only to the protocols for meals and such, this week would go easier. I could focus on the job, not how to survive breakfast.

When I entered the dining room, Trelane was the only one there. After a quick scan of the wood panels, dark-red carpet, and long banquet table with only two place settings, I walked the length of the table, standing just to the left of him.

He read a newspaper, a phone lying to his right. There was a coffee service but no food.

Trelane glanced up. "There you are. I wasn't sure if you'd already eaten this morning. Do you usually sleep in this late, or are you catching up after the last two days? I can't imagine it was comfortable sleeping in one of those dreadful catch boxes. They're not even fit for shifters."

Two days? What had Sorrento given me? Ginger would be freaked.

He waved a hand for Lucas to leave, then stared at me. "Have a seat." He rose to pour me a cup of coffee. "I wasn't sure how you took your coffee, so I asked Letty to bring cream and sugar."

"Black is fine." After sitting, I took the napkin lying on the plate and draped it over my lap. I scratched at my pants before pulling at the collar of the shirt.

Trelane grimaced. "Those clothes aren't right for you, but it was all we had available on short notice. It also seems the shoes are too large."

How the hell had he noticed that?

He shrugged. "You seem to be shuffling your feet." When one of my brows rose, he shook his head. "I can't read your mind, but it's obvious you're uncomfortable with the clothes. And you didn't have any problems stomping around yesterday in those sneakers of yours." He pointed to his head. "Sensitive hearing." Then, he smiled.

And my stomach did a little flip that irritated the hell out of me. But hell's bells, the man was gorgeous. And those full lips? I glanced around the room, anything to take my eyes off of them. "You have a lot of antiques."

He laughed. "Already scoping the place out. A true thief at heart."

My cheeks heated. "Sorry. I didn't mean..."

He waved a dismissive hand. "Stop. One of the first things you'll need to learn is how to respond to off-handed comments. And how to deflect them. I've arranged time with Anna to go over the more domestic aspects of your training. I'll instruct you on the rest. Between Anna and me, we should have your mannerisms and repertoire, if not perfect, enough to pass muster."

I was too deep into figuring out what he meant about training to realize I'd been insulted. By the time it hit me, Trelane was staring at me.

"Another perfect example. I know you weren't expecting my comment about training. And even as I told you what the training was about, you sat there with your mouth open instead of coming up with a witty remark."

I wondered how he might handle a kick to his midsection. Instead of glowering, as I'd prefer, I kept my expression blank. I might not be a linguist—I knew big words—but I'd learned how to school my emotions many moons ago. Back in the dark days. And in this business, I'd only honed it.

Expecting to see Trelane's renowned temper, he threw back his head and laughed. It was so surprising, and such a sensuous sound, all I could do was marvel at the sparkle in his eyes. They were probably tears of mirth at my expense. Somehow, I didn't mind, which only stoked my irritation.

"Fascinating. I didn't think silence could be better than a smart reply, but you've outdone yourself." He stared at me as if determining whether his little thief might have more value as a mime. He drummed his fingers on the table. "Anything Anna or I can teach you will be icing. There's so much more to do in seven days, and it's not nearly enough time."

I began to squirm under the intensity of his gaze, which changed into something more. I wasn't sure what but felt rattlers in my stomach and smothered them with a nervous laugh. The phrase was something Harlow said whenever he thought a job was going bad.

"I'm not sure I understand what you're expecting me to do." His gaze never left me, and if I didn't know better, he was staring at my lips. Heat rushed through me, and I tried to think of anything that would get my mind off his own lips before my cheeks turned as red as the carpet.

Then, those luscious lips turned into a grimace. "For some time, I've been searching for an artifact. Something stolen from me. I've recently discovered its location but haven't found anyone with the appropriate set of...skills, if you will, for the task. To be honest, I'm not sure you have what it takes either, but you're the closest I've found with the most potential. The timing, however, is..." he shrugged, "unfortunate. That is why I was willing to absorb The Wolf's debt, and yours, if the next seven days prove successful."

Before I could ask more, Letty returned with a large tray that she set on one of the cherrywood side tables. The aroma made my stomach growl, and I lowered my head, not wanting to see Trelane's knowing look. All thoughts of him disappeared when Letty set down a plate teeming with scrambled eggs sticky with cheddar, diced-fried potatoes that smelled of onion and garlic, several slices of crisp bacon, and a gigantic biscuit. I sipped several swallows of coffee before trying the eggs. I closed my eyes in bliss.

I was halfway through devouring my meal when I took a break to slurp more coffee. Trelane watched me as he stirred his eggs with a fork, something glinting in his gaze like he had a surprise he was waiting to spring. Then, I noticed his plate of food was different from mine.

I'd always wondered if vampires ate. The few I'd run across hadn't been eating in a restaurant or having a pleasant conversation at someone's dining table. Trelane stabbed at an egg-white omelet speckled with green, which I assumed was spinach. A single-serving fruit bowl was filled with a variety of melons and berries. He was either a light eater or this was the typical diet for a vamp. I decided to hold my questions for Anna.

Besides, I wasn't typically a large breakfast eater, preferring a bagel with cream cheese. These large meals were reserved for celebrating a successful job when I had a few more bucks in the bank. So, I took another swig of coffee, decided to ignore the vamp, and went back to shoveling in the food. Though I did try to use the appropriate utensils.

When I couldn't stuff one more bite, I sat back, hands on my stomach, feeling like a well-fed feline who just wanted a place to sleep it off.

Trelane had finished his bowl of fruit and was sitting back, thumbing through his phone. He raised a brow when he glanced over to see Letty removing my plate and set the phone down. "I apologize for ignoring you while you ate." He pointed to the phone. "I don't usually allow phones in the dining room, but I've been waiting for a message. Not that you left much room for conversation."

My first instinct was to respond with one of my witty retorts, but I gathered this was another of his tests. The man would drive me mad, making me question every word I spoke. "The dining options were less than convenient in the catch box."

He nodded with satisfaction, and I could have slapped myself for the tiny bit of pleasure I derived from his approval. Good grief. I didn't need his blessing. Except, playing by his rules and showing I was a team player could seal the deal on my leaving this place in one piece.

He ran a finger back and forth along his jaw. His direct gaze made me want to squirm, and when I turned mine away, I noticed his silver ring. A square black stone with a pyramid set in the middle. "I'm afraid this breakfast was the last large meal for a while."

I blanched. He wasn't going to feed me?

"Don't pout. You'll be well fed here, but probably not what you're used to."

I grabbed my cup, holding it close as if he meant to deprive me of my bliss—my morning coffee. I was scared to ask what I'd be eating.

"This particular job will put you in the heart of vampire society. High society. You'll be mingling with the city's most respected and most dangerous vampires. To fit in, you'll need to have a particular look with discerning tastes. And you'll need to eat what vampires eat."

I sat back, the grease of my breakfast threatening to revolt.

He laughed. "I'm not asking you to drink blood wine. But I do expect you to eat nutritious, organic meals. Besides excellent hearing, we have a unique sense of smell." He tapped his nose. "We can smell someone's blood when they get close. We can tell its purity and the contents of their last meal. For example, if I were to meet with you in two hours, I'd know you had garlic and onion in your meal. It wouldn't stop me from drinking your blood if I had a mind, but that very scent would tell another vampire that you probably don't belong to anyone. I'm far too old to worry about having to drink very often, so I don't keep humans in the house. But younger vampires require a drink more frequently. Even those a century old still keep humans close for feeding." He shrugged. "They don't need to; they just prefer the old ways." He shook his head as if he found that disgusting. Perhaps just uncouth. Either way, it made me feel a little better. I shouldn't have to worry about him sneaking into my room in the middle of the night looking for a sip. I reflexively rubbed my neck.

He glanced down when his phone vibrated. His jaw clenched, and he held his cup so tightly, I thought it would shatter. Not good news. After a couple long minutes, he took a deep breath and turned to me, returning to our conversation as if never reading his message.

"My point is, where we'll be going, you'll need to not only act the part but smell the part as well. Otherwise, no one will believe why you're with me."

He stood. "I'm afraid I have something to attend to. Anna will start your training this morning. I should be back this evening for our session. A couple of rules for your stay here. You have the freedom of the yard, garden, and anywhere in the house on the first and second floors. The third floor is completely off-limits. Any questions before I leave?"

I had a dozen, but it was obvious I wouldn't have his full attention. And I preferred trying to get answers from Anna. "Just one."

He tucked the phone in his pocket then gave me his undivided attention.

"What am I being trained for?"

He gave me a slow perusal, and this time, it was more heated. The desire to squirm returned. Then, he gave me that million-dollar smile. "To be my human lover, of course."

Chapter Eight

Devon stared at the formidable structure with mixed feelings. It had been years since he'd been called to speak with the Council, and he'd always known or suspected why he'd been summoned. This time was different. For the last several years, he'd been on his best behavior, staying out of the limelight. His business ventures held no connections to Council business, so he was a little nervous about the reason for this visit.

It didn't escape his attention that he'd been summoned to the highest court the minute he began a mission to recover what had been taken from him two centuries ago. But worrying before he had reliable information wasn't his style. He pushed his concerns aside as Sergi pulled the limo into a visitor's parking spot.

"Do you want me to come in with you?" Sergi calmly checked his pistol, chambering a round of silver bullets before tucking it back in his pocket. He also carried two silver daggers hidden inside his jacket. The silver wasn't enough to kill a vampire, but struck in the right place, it would slow one down.

Devon scanned the parking lot, searching for the conspicuous red Rolls Royce belonging to the one vampire he didn't want to see today. The car wasn't visible, but that didn't mean the man wouldn't show up before Devon left. And he was the one person who worried him enough to bring a bodyguard. It wasn't unusual for anyone called before the Council to arrive with one. Anything could happen. Devon was a Council member, albeit not active, which guaranteed his right to an entire security squad. But at this point in Devon's relationship with the court, a full team would make him appear threatening and would be an unfortunate political maneuver.

If he'd given it more thought, he would have brought Lucas, since his third guard, Bella, was away on assignment. But he needed Lucas at home with eyes on Pandora. Someone might have already learned of his new guest. The Wolf wouldn't have said anything, but Devon didn't know who'd brought Pandora to The Wolf. He would need to remedy that.

"Stay at my side until someone says otherwise. I'll decide then whether to make a stink over it."

They exited the car together, and Devon felt for his own weapons. They wouldn't be checked at the door. Everyone carried when at the Council building. Unlike human legislative branches and courts, Council meetings and judgments had become bloody in the past; the defendants always had the right to a last battle. He didn't think that would be the case here. Official papers would have been drawn if Devon was accused of a high crime, but leaving weapons behind would be foolish. Council members had been assassinated before, and no one with any sense would walk in vulnerable.

Security was expecting him, and they passed the two men through without comment. One member of the security detail nodded, a sign that confirmed Devon still had friends in the building. More than one would expect for such a notorious Council member, but the truth was, he had many more, yet few would make any outward sign of acknowledgment.

His first surprise was finding the Council's chamber doors closed. A Council page waited for them, and Devon raised a brow when he slid a glance to Sergi, who responded with the barest of nods. Be prepared.

"Master Trelane, the chamber is silent today. Mistress Stanton will see you in the solarium. If you'll follow me." The page turned without waiting for a response. No one said no to a Council summons, wherever the meeting might be held. Although, this was highly unusual.

Devon was tempted to recheck his text. He was positive the summons had stated a meeting with the Council, not a single member. He shook off the nerves creeping over him. Sergi remained silent but kept pace as the three walked through long, quiet halls, turning right and left as they ventured deeper into the building. The solarium was on the opposite side of the building from where they'd entered. Devon knew every possible exit, even those in the catacombs. The tunnels beneath ran to various outbuildings on the property, and one exited half a mile away in an old cemetery crypt. That one had always been Devon's favorite, a tribute to the false stories of vampires sleeping in mausoleum sarcophagi to hide from the sun.

A woman dressed in soft shades of lavender sat in a high-backed chair centered in the middle of the room. Giant ferns, assorted potted plants, and exotic orchids filled the solarium, all healthy from the bright sunshine that filtered through the glass walls and ceilings. Light-colored shades perched on the woman's nose as she thumbed through an immense tome. Probably one of the Council law books based on the size and age of the book.

"Thank you, Barnes. That will be all. Please shut the door on the way out." Her voice carried a rich timbre, and she never lifted her gaze from the book.

The page bowed then left without another word.

Devon waited, knowing the game, but it didn't stop his short temper from rising. Sergi planted his long legs next to the door with his arms crossed in front of him. The only thing missing from the scene was the loud ticking of a clock. But vampires didn't need clocks—they always knew the time. Clocks of any type were mere affectations, and Devon rubbed a finger over his Rolex, not ashamed by his love of timepieces.

After a long silence, the woman shut the book and tossed it on the table next to her as if it were no heavier than a napkin rather than the several pounds it weighed.

"Devon. It's been too long." She smiled, and even through the sunglasses she wore, Devon saw the smile reach her eyes.

Breathing a long sigh, Devon returned the gesture with a slight bow. "Far too long, Isabella."

Isabella Stanton was one of the oldest vampires on the Council and had always been his friend. But they'd kept their distance over the last two hundred years, in keeping with the decorum of tradition and rules. There wasn't any single magical creature that presided over the Council. Each member was equal, but if there would ever be a high ruler, his money would be on Isabella. No one played the game better than her.

"I wish our meeting didn't have to be under these circumstances." She leaned back, her body melting into the chair and her wickedly long fingernails tapping against the wood.

"And what circumstances would that be. I didn't receive any paperwork." What in all the holy hells was this about? Devon felt Sergi tense behind him.

She considered her response as if she hadn't already played this scene over a dozen times before his arrival. "I admit this is awkward, as the Council doesn't typically get involved in other Council members' business, whether they're active or not." She took a moment to flick an imaginary speck of lint off her gown. "There's been a rumor that you might be planning something... unsavory. Something that could affect the terms of your censure."

A muscle ticked in Devon's jaw, and he dared not glance at Sergi. And he hoped Sergi would give nothing away, although the man could hold a mask better than anyone he knew. "The Council now dabbles in rumors rather than facts?"

Isabella grimaced, and her words came out in a growl. "It's distasteful, I agree." She stood and stepped down from the chair, the long folds of fabric falling around her and scraping the ground as she wandered to a side table where several pots of orchids encircled a bronze head of Vlad, one of the original Fathers of their race. She ran a finger over one of the orchids—a Holy Ghost, or Dove Orchid as they're also called—that Devon knew to be her favorite.

"The Council wouldn't have even considered the information except for the reason of your censure. In fact, even with that, the Council deemed it unworthy of further discussion unless proof could be provided."

Devon relaxed, but only partially. Isabella was warning him, giving him time to circle the wagons, if necessary.

"May I ask what the rumor entailed?"

"No." She leaned down to sniff the orchid and frowned. "I do wish the fragrance was more like a rose. But I love them just the same."

Isabella turned and squinted at him. She'd never been one to embrace the light, preferring to stay in the shadows like most vampires, venturing out only at night. Devon had been like that when he'd been active on the Council, but his time with Decker regularly forced him into the daylight. Over time, he'd acclimated to the brighter light, only wearing shades when the sun was at its zenith. With the Council living up to some of their oldest traditions, Devon always questioned the reason for a solarium. Just one of the many oddities of the place.

"Did you receive the White Egret Orchid I sent at Christmas?" Devon asked.

Isabella floated over to him. He didn't have any other way to express it. She'd always given the impression she was walking on air, and he'd always wondered how she managed that. Vampires couldn't fly or hover as far as he knew.

"I did. It was a lovely gesture." She reached out and placed a palm on his cheek. "It's always good to see you, Devon." She hesitated as she ran a thumb over his skin. "Please take care." Then, she floated out the door.

Devon stood quietly, thinking over the quick meeting. Someone had shared a rumor, something that might be connected to the Council's censure of him two centuries earlier. He glanced at Sergi, who wanted to say something, but Devon shook his head. Every room in the building was wired with the ability to record sound. There was no question the sound recording was turned on after she left. His gaze fell on the book Isabella had been reading.

He strode over and studied the front cover. The *Ordo Autem ad Originem*. The Origin of Order. He'd been right. This particular book documented the laws governing the Council's composition, how business was conducted, and how a council member could be censured, along with the remedies for such. The size of the book only demonstrated how complex vampire society was. It hadn't been a coincidence that Isabella had chosen this volume. One more reminder of what was at stake.

"We'll get nothing more here. Let's go." Devon strode past Sergi, who turned to follow him out.

They'd reached the halfway point to the main entrance when a man stepped out from behind a column in the long hallway. He was dressed in black, his finely tailored suit emphasizing his raw magnetism, lean muscles, and chiseled features. His equally dark hair was pushed back with hair gel. All he needed was a cape and widow's peak to complete the image of a storybook vampire.

"Devon Trelane. What brings you to our hallowed halls?"

"Ever the drama king, Lorenzo. I have every right to be here, as long as I avoid chambers unless commanded." Devon clenched his jaw, wishing he could stake this ass and take his head, but he would end up forfeiting his own life in exchange. He had other plans for Venizi.

Lorenzo Venizi had been Devon's enemy since he'd first heard the man's name. With the longevity of immortality, the raw emotions of vengeance and revenge should fade over time, but Lorenzo proved it could grow and fester if nurtured correctly.

The man's lips thinned, and Devon sighed. He didn't have time to play games. Not today. There were too many other things on his mind. He didn't have to pay homage to Council members, certainly not ones he preferred to throttle. He only had to be respectful in the chamber. The rules didn't apply in the halls, so he strode past Lorenzo, ignoring the man's glare. Sergi remained at his back until they exited the building.

When they reached the car and had driven a block, far out of Lorenzo's hearing range, Sergi finally spoke. "How did they know you're up to something?"

Devon stared out the window. "I think we have a tail." But how much did they know? "Take me to Oasis. And call in the team. Call in everyone. Level two alert."

Chapter Nine

ANNA PULLED out the third evening dress, this one a deep jade, and held it up in my horrified direction, looking at the dress and then me, then back to the dress. She seemed satisfied with her assessment and slipped it onto a hanger before carefully hanging it in the closet. I hugged the jeans and a pullover sweater, terrified she might see them and tell me they were a mistake. All the previous boxes of clothing contained dress slacks with matching blouses, sweaters, blazers, casual knee-length dresses, and formal evening gowns.

There were a handful of tank tops and three pairs of workout pants, along with the prerequisite undergarments and nightwear. The stack of shoeboxes was almost as tall as Anna. I stared down at the bed next to me, my eyes glazing over at the little silk bags of jewelry. There was a brooch, and I wondered if the stick pin was long enough to poke my eyes out. Did Trelane really think these were the type of clothes I wore?

"Devon has a good eye, but you still need to try these on. If you don't want to do it with me, you'll need to do it on your own tonight. If we need to exchange anything, we must do so quickly.

Your first engagement is tomorrow evening, and you'll be expected to wear one of the evening gowns.

"What?" Other words floated around, but Anna seemed too sensitive a person to hear them.

Anna closed the closet, and relief washed over me that there weren't more boxes to open. "I'm sure Devon will explain when he returns. Maybe we can start with those?" Her gaze wandered to one of the stuffed chairs by the barren fireplace.

Dark slacks, a pink blouse, and a blazer lay across the chair like evil sentinels from my past. A pair of pumps sat on the floor. I hugged my jeans tighter and could only imagine the wild look in my eyes, like someone pulled out of a jungle, abandoned as a child and left to scrape out a meager existence. I snorted. Not too far from the truth, if you could call Santiga Bay a jungle.

Anna sat on the corner of the bed and gave me a conciliatory smile. "I wasn't used to the flurry of gifts when I first arrived, but Devon is quite generous. Is your hesitation because you're not sure of his intentions?" She glanced at the jeans clutched in my hands. "Or maybe you're not used to the style of clothing?"

I must have given some indication of the latter, although I felt frozen to my seat. I'd decided to take Trelane's comment about being his human lover as weird vampire humor.

She nodded. "The slacks and blouse aren't as restrictive as they appear. And we can try a dress a little later, just long enough for me to ensure the size. Then we can put it away until tomorrow. Is that a deal?"

I slid my gaze to the clothes on the chair and then to the closed closet. I knew how foolish this was. They were just clothes. But honestly, I couldn't understand what clothes had to do with stealing something. Or why I was being so stubborn. Was it the clothes, Trelanes's overbearing persistence that I only required one pair of jeans, or the memories the clothes raised from a past I didn't want to remember?

I heaved a sigh, knowing the answer, and let the jeans fall to my lap.

Anna nodded and stood. "I need to check on a couple of things. Why don't you change then meet me in the front foyer? We'll take a stroll around the yard."

"We can go outside?"

Her laugh was a tinkling sound like the chatter of songbirds. I could see why Trelane would like Anna. And that thought put a different spin on the duties of a personal assistant. I instantly gave myself a mental head slap. What did that matter? I pushed any niggling arguments on the topic aside.

Seven days. I could do this.

"Of course, we can go outside. Devon wants you familiar with the grounds. It's been decades since they've had trouble, but anyone who spends more than a day or two here must know the property and all the exits."

He didn't care if I knew the exits? I didn't have to ask about the trouble. The magical world was known for its own brutal rules around territory, perceived slights, and in-house battles. The fact he seemed more concerned for my safety than any attempts I made to escape surprised me. When I thought about it, it made sense. If I escaped, he'd be out nothing. The Wolf would still owe a debt, and I'd be running not just from Sorrento but The Wolf as well.

Before leaving, Anna took the bags of jewelry and placed them on the dresser then reached for a small ornamental box. "I'll find a more suitable box to store your jewelry." She pushed one of the bags to the side. "I suggest wearing these so you can get used to the earrings. Devon noticed you had pierced ears."

She left me to stare at my room with a different eye. There were no bars on the windows, and they all opened. And while I was on the second floor, it wasn't as if that could hold a cat burglar adept at scaling buildings. Maybe Anna was right. Lucas was no longer at the door, though I sensed he was probably close. I let out another long sigh. I wasn't a twelve-year-old anymore, and I needed to stop acting like it. After finding a drawer for the jeans, I ran a hand over them before shutting them away.

Trelane had bought them and the sweatshirt. I glanced at the comfortable workout clothes. He knew I needed something of my own, and instead of bringing me comfort, it grated that he was trying to make me feel welcome. How idiotic was that?

After changing into the new threads, I had to admit they fit well and were more comfortable than I thought. The pants had some stretch to them, and even though I hated pumps, I could run in them if I had to. I bent and twisted, attempting a couple of my more sedate martial arts moves, and found the clothes unrestrictive. I didn't think I could do a full side kick without ripping something, but if I was put in that position, I didn't think a split in my pants, however embarrassing, would be my biggest concern.

Anna waited for me in the foyer with a basket in one hand. She beamed at me. "You look marvelous. The clothes fit well. I told you Devon had a good eye."

I lifted my arm, showing her a bracelet I'd found in one of the bags of jewelry. "What's this?" The bracelet was silver with a black, opal-shaped stone. I pointed at the pyramid symbol, which didn't accurately describe the design. The overall shape was a pyramid, but it was made of three interconnecting triangles—two at the base and one centered on top.

She glanced at it. "It's the House Trelane symbol. You only need to wear it to the functions Devon takes you."

"Does everyone have one?"

"Of course, but Devon isn't a stickler for enforcing rules." She swung the basket.

"What's the basket for?" I asked, steering the conversation away from the clothes, Devon's eagle eye, and house rings.

"The lilacs are blooming. I thought it would be nice to have some for the dinner table this evening." She waltzed out the door, and I followed, shutting it behind us.

"Where's Lucas?" I hadn't seen my bodyguard or whatever he was since breakfast.

"Oh, he's around." She waved a hand in the air, which I assumed meant he could be anywhere on the grounds or in the house. "He said something about new business to attend to."

We meandered through lush gardens framed by sycamores, maples, and a larger California Buckeye. The morning dew had already dried under the filtered sunlight.

"Have you lived here long?" I had to admit, now that I'd had a good night's sleep, a hearty breakfast, and clean clothes, even if not my preferred fashion, I was curious about my surroundings.

"About six years now. My father requested I come here after his death."

"I'm sorry."

She gave me a sad smile. "Oh, it was a long time ago now. And I'm quite happy here. Devon and his family have made me very comfortable."

"Family? He's married?"

Her burst of laughter surprised me and completely changed her. She looked even younger than before. "I doubt he'd ever do that. No. I'm speaking of his vampire family. He's an alpha."

I shook my head. "I thought that was what the shifters called their leader."

She nodded. "As do the vampires. Devon is also a Council member, so it's only natural he would head his own family."

I glanced around. There had been six vampires in the audience chamber when I'd first arrived. Since then, I'd only seen Trelane and Lucas. "Where is everyone?"

She didn't respond, and I thought she was determining how much to tell me, but when I glanced over, she was gone. I turned around to find her kneeling next to a flower bed, carefully snipping buds with tiny clippers. She jumped up when she was done and handed me one.

I smelled it. I'd never seen this variety of flower before and found the scent a little too musky for my taste. "It's beautiful." Which was true enough if one didn't get too close to it. I cringed at the thought of it being on a dining room table.

"Devon only keeps a handful of his people here. He doesn't want anyone thinking this house is anything special." She shrugged. "Everyone must have duties elsewhere today." She turned us down a wide dirt path littered with dead leaves and bits of shredded bark.

I'd been keeping my eye on the ground but stopped and glanced up. In front of us was the longest archway of vines I'd ever seen. The leaves, fresh with a spring green color, had filled in the gaps, giving the path the appearance of a long tunnel.

"Great, isn't it? In a month, it will be covered with purple and red flowers that will last all summer." Anna skipped through the living tunnel, turning in a circle halfway through before moving on.

By the time I met up with her on the other side, she was snipping lavender lilacs from a large bush. When she'd filled the basket, she led me down a path that ran toward the grave markers I'd seen the previous night.

She stopped at a bench just shy of the markers and sat down, patting the spot next to her.

"Can I ask a personal question?" I wasn't sure about the proper etiquette, but I needed to know. When she nodded and glanced up with an expectant expression, I leaped. "Are you a vampire?"

That tinkling laugh again. "Oh no, but I'd like to be."

"What?"

"That's why I'm here."

I must have appeared perplexed because she set down the basket and turned toward me. "My father worked for another vampire, one closely aligned to this house. I grew up with vampires."

"Did they drink your blood?"

Her eyes grew wide, and then she shook her head, giving me one of those where-do-you-get-all-this-from looks.

"I'm sorry for asking. I really don't know anything about this world."

Her shoulders relaxed, and she sighed. "I had no idea. Now everything makes sense." I could tell I was going to get an earful. I wasn't wrong.

"Long ago, I mean hundreds of centuries ago, vampires lusted for blood to survive. Or so that was the thinking. But once their presence was discovered by a growing human population slowly becoming more educated and more superstitious, vampires couldn't feed as often. They soon discovered they didn't have to drink blood as frequently to survive. Next, they learned that the older a vampire got, the less he needed to feed. They also learned to tolerate food, as long as it was grown naturally, or what today we'd call organically. And boy could they put away the liquor without any lasting effects."

That was information I didn't know. "But why would you want to be a vampire?"

She looked at me like I was a dimwit. "Because of their immortality and superior intelligence."

"Superior?"

"Oh, yes. Devon speaks eight languages, is deeply knowledgeable in the sciences, math, and economics. He's also a master strategist. None of this came from schooling. It developed over time by reading."

I stared at her, not believing the superior bit. Some people could just remember facts better than others. But she answered a few other questions, and now I knew she was human.

"My father was never interested in becoming a vampire, and at first, I admit he wasn't happy with my request to become one. But as he got older and closer to his own mortality, he gave in to my desire and asked his mistress if it were possible. She didn't want the responsibility but knew I could be useful in this house, so an exchange was made.

"An exchange? They own you?"

Another laugh that was starting to grate on my nerves. "I can leave at any time. By exchange, I meant that Devon had a personal assistant, and he didn't need two. The one he had would have to leave before I could join his household. By the time my father died, Fatina was ready for a new assignment and expressed interest in joining my old house." She tilted her head. "You have a dark history, don't you?"

I sat back. "Why would you say that?"

Anna shrugged a shoulder. "You seem to see something sinister in the simplest things." She stood, grabbed her basket, and walked toward the ocean.

I sat for a moment, digesting everything she'd said. I'd have to do more research before I believed anything she said about vampires. She was obviously biased by living with them her whole life. Yet, I was irritated that she might be right about me seeing everything through a dark lens. Maybe we were both biased by our upbringing. But wasn't that true for everyone?

When we walked back to the house and reached the grave markers again, I needed to resolve another curiosity. "Who's buried here?"

She didn't even glance over. "It's the family plot from long ago."

"Who's the person who visits it in the middle of the night?"

Anna stumbled but caught herself. "I should tell Devon this walkway needs repairing."

I looked down but didn't see anything that would have made her stumble unless she'd caught a heel. Or hadn't been prepared for my question. I stopped and turned toward the house. I quickly found my corner room on the second floor, then raised my gaze to check out the third floor.

A curtain was drawn back, but it was impossible to see if

anyone was there. Until the curtain dropped back in place. A cold breeze from the shore washed over me, sending shivers down my neck. Trelane had warned me to stay away from the third floor. And why did I always want to do the exact opposite of what I'd been told?

Chapter Ten

FOR SOME REASON, I thought the training room would be in the basement, but it was a startlingly empty first-floor room tucked away in a far corner of the house. It was the size of a ballroom, and I idly wondered if it had once been used for fancy society parties. My new sneakers squeaked on the polished wood surface as I surveyed the training equipment. A twenty-foot-by-twenty-foot mat had been placed in the middle of the room. Several feet away, three ropes hung from the ceiling. On the other side of the mat, an equal distance away, stood a ten-foot wooden post. Another rope ran in a taut incline from the top of the post to a climbing wall. Five feet farther down, one last rope hung from the ceiling. I found the placement of the objects odd but ignored them, assuming Trelane would tell me what they were for.

In a corner, toward the back of the room, a door led into what I assumed would be a storage closet, but it held a treadmill, an expensive stationary bike, and a rack of dumbbells. No one was in there, and I wasn't sure why a separate room was needed. I shrugged. One more mystery in a house full of them.

A single bench had been placed in front of a floor-to-ceiling mirror that stretched a good length of the wall opposite the climbing wall. I sat down to remove my shoes and socks before stepping to the middle of the mat to take a position.

Trelane was running late. He'd missed dinner, so I ate alone in the dining room—a green salad filled with raw vegetables, a slim slice of salmon, and focaccia bread. No alcohol since I would be training. That had been an hour ago, and I was ready to rumble.

Not knowing if the vamp would show, I began with some exercises to warm up my muscles. I was soon running through a series of martial arts moves that increased my heart rate and brought a sheen to my skin. I had been trained in three martial arts styles— karate, Jiu-Jitsu, and Shaolin kung fu. Any of the three could be used for therapeutic mental conditioning, defense, or killing. I practiced for self-defense and to stay limber. Enhanced technical advancements in security had forced me to scale buildings and bend around laser sensors when I didn't have someone who could hack them. But I knew one or two moves that could kill—if necessary. I'd never had to put those particular skills to use.

I was thirty minutes into a martial arts exercise and coming up out of a roll when I stumbled. Trelane stood no more than ten paces from the mat, watching me.

Devon Trelane—vampire and absolutely hot specimen— standing in a tank top that showed off his lean muscular arms and sweatpants that hugged his trim waist. He was barefoot with his dirty-blond hair tied in a ponytail and a rakish stubble that made him look twice as dangerous as he already was. His blank expression revealed nothing except the hard line of luscious lips.

"Your form is sloppy." He strolled around the mat, inspecting me from head to toe as if I was a soldier in his army.

And all I could think about were the last words he'd spoken to me earlier that day. That he was training me to be his human lover. Right now, I was thinking maybe that would be the better option. I glanced around the room, rethinking how the few training elements might be used and hoping he wouldn't break anything, like my arm or leg—or both.

His brows lowered as I turned to follow his path around the mat.

"Defend yourself."

And before I knew it, he came at me. For a while, he was in the defensive position. But after my previous workout, my energy quickly waned. And before he powered up to land me on the floor, he stepped off the mat. A sign the match was over, but not the training.

"In a one-on-one fight, you'll never escape a shifter, let alone a vampire."

"I wasn't trained for that." I wiped the sweat from my brow and worked to get my breath back to a normal rhythm.

"Obviously."

Not a drop of sweat showed on his chiseled features. Not a strand of hair had come out of his ponytail. Maybe vamps didn't sweat.

"I was going easy on you." It was a lame response, but all my brain could handle. This wasn't how I'd pictured the training sessions.

He didn't laugh, and I wondered who the real Trelane was. The charming and thoughtful man from this morning, or the unsmiling killer who couldn't wait to put me down like a dog? I wasn't liking his idea of training, but maybe he'd had a change of heart. I'd be happy to go back to The Wolf if I only knew whether that was a better option. Unfortunately, I didn't know, and either way, I wasn't getting out of today's session.

"If you can't fight your way past one vampire, you're useless to me."

I really hated being called useless.

With hands on hips, I narrowed my eyes. "I'm a thief. If you want me to steal something, then I would expect you to protect me. Or have one of your goons do it."

He moved so fast I didn't see the first hit—a kick to the back of my knees that dropped me to all fours. Before I could push myself up, I buckled from his next attack. I managed to deliver a kick of my own as I recovered, and when it landed, it felt like I'd hit a cement wall.

I stumbled back, wincing as the pain raced up my leg, but I was still standing. He circled me before coming to a stop.

"I'm not a babysitter, nor are my goons." This was said with a sneer.

He really wasn't happy with me, and I didn't know what I'd done to create his wrath. This was the vamp I'd heard about. The dangerous outcast of Santiga Bay.

I dropped my arms and stood straight. If he wanted to come at me, so be it. But I wasn't going to play his games. "Then you're not as smart as I thought to risk your thief. If anyone else could do what I can do, you wouldn't be going through this trouble. So, stop being an asshole."

He stared at me, and I thought he might be considering my words. Then he stepped onto the mat, coming within a foot of me. I refused to back away.

"Step into the red circle."

"What?" I had no idea what he was talking about until I glanced down. Why hadn't I noticed the colorful circles and squares before? Or maybe I had and assumed they were random designs.

"If I have to repeat myself, your training sessions will have to be increased."

The red circle was barely four feet in diameter. Once I stepped inside, there would only be inches between us. I swallowed hard, then stepped in. There was no way I'd survive longer training sessions.

"And what is this supposed to teach me?" I only glanced up as far as his lips, not wanting to look into his eyes. I was tall, but he still had a good four inches on me. I wasn't sure his lips were the best choice and lowered my gaze to his chest.

Without warning, he leaped to the closest rope, his

momentum swinging him as he undulated his body to increase the height. When his rhythm reached its peak, he released and flew toward the climbing wall, catching on with one hand before grabbing the taut line that ran across the room. He crawled along the rope, hand over hand, feet pushing him along until he reached the wooden post. In a blink of an eye, he swung from another rope, heading straight for me. Not sure what to do, I planted my feet, braced myself, and squinted until I heard the soft thud of his landing mere inches from me. I glanced down to confirm he stood within the red circle as his warm breath washed over me.

I replayed the entire scene in my head. The image was unbelievable, yet there he was, so close I could almost hear his heart racing. Did vampires have heartbeats? There was still much I didn't know.

When he didn't say anything and only glared, I should have returned the gesture. But I wasn't always the smartest one in the room.

"You're nuts if you think I'm going to learn how to do that."

I felt the hit to my shoulder almost before I saw him take the two quick steps back before kicking out. The force of the kick spun me, and he slammed a hand into my chest that sent me flying. I hit the floor, the momentum sliding me across the smooth wood, too stunned to stop my trajectory. Before I crashed into the oncoming wall headfirst, I was picked up and slammed against the hard paneling. Trelane's hand grasped my neck, holding me up on my tiptoes.

I scratched and pawed at his arms, barely able to breathe. My heart pounded so fast it blocked out everything but the rapid beats reverberating in my head. My blood froze.

The vampire's brows furrowed over glowing eyes. The piercing blue of his natural eye color had turned an iridescent silver. They would be beautiful if he wasn't frowning, his lips twisted in a sneer. Then his frown receded as the color of his eyes darkened with bits of blue sprinkled within the silver.

He bent his head and ran his lips along my jaw. The scent of cloves and cinnamon circled around us, filling my senses, invading deeper parts of me as I warmed from the inside out. My nether regions tingled as he breathed deep, taking in my own scent. A hand caressed my hip, lingering as his lips moved toward my mouth. When the tips of his fangs slid across my lips, I heard a moan.

His hand released my neck as if he'd been burned. I dropped to my feet and braced the wall to stop from falling.

He pushed back several paces, his gaze locked on my lips. I couldn't help it. I intuitively licked them, and he took a step closer. I wasn't sure what changed, and though his eyes still glowed, they had settled into the deep silver-blue of a winter moon.

I blinked, and whatever was going on, the motion seemed to wake him, and he stepped back. His expression changed, and his shoulders drooped as he hung his head.

"We're done for the evening." His voice sounded raw, and he didn't look at me again as he strode out of the room.

My breathing slowed, and damn it all, I couldn't help but notice the person hidden beneath the twisted emotions as he stormed away. Hell's bells, he was a fine-looking man.

Get a grip, Cressa. He almost killed you.

But had he?

I glanced around the room and shivered. My legs shook as I picked up my shoes and socks, but I found enough residual energy to race from the room, not stopping until I reached my bedroom. I didn't slam the door, but I made sure it was locked.

Once in the shower, I replayed the entire training session. Trelane had been irritated when he'd entered the room. Had he been mad at me or someone else? Maybe he was just reminding me of who he was—who vampires were. I had to admit, if they were all like him, their physical abilities were exceptional and not something to take lightly.

He'd told me I would be introduced into vampire high society.

Surrounded by them with little to no defenses. Whether he meant his actions to drill that point home or not—he'd succeeded.

But it was the last part that shook me. Was he going to kiss me? I snorted. Right. Kiss me with his fangs out. But after I toweled myself off, I stared at my reflection in the foggy mirror, running a finger across my lips. I still felt the sensation of his fangs as he traced the same path. The tingle in my nether regions returned.

"Stop it." And with that last scold, I threw on the lightweight dressing gown and slipped into bed. But try as I might, I couldn't shake the sensation of his fangs across my lips, and I reached down to cup myself as those silver-blue eyes followed me to sleep.

Chapter Eleven

THE NIGHT WAS warm with the scent of honeysuckle and roses. That seemed odd this time of year. It was only spring, but maybe I was in an enormous greenhouse. When I pushed away a vine that had grown over the stone path, a thorn pricked my finger. A deep-red drop glittered in the moonlight. I sucked my fingertip, the taste of copper sharp on my tongue.

I turned, thinking I'd heard someone, but no one was there. Where was I?

I didn't remember getting out of bed. I glanced down, surprised to see my satin nightgown reached mid-thigh. That wasn't right. The one I'd gone to bed in had been cotton and touched my knees. Hadn't it?

I kept walking. Someone waited for me, and I didn't want to be late.

The narrow path led me through lush vegetation bursting with blooms whose heady scent competed with the honeysuckle. Some of the flowers I recognized, others were as foreign as the garden. Yet, I knew where I was going. Had some sense of what was waiting for me. And that knowledge spurred me on with an excitement and yearning almost as unfamiliar as my surroundings.

He'll be here soon.

I hurried, pushing past leaves as long as my arm until the path opened up to a stone grotto. Two dusky-red Japanese maples edged the sides of the alcove. A stone bench stretched across the grotto, leaving a secret place to read or meditate. Surrounding it, a patch of lush grass grew so dense I could already feel the blades tickling my toes.

Our place.

I ran my hands through the maple leaves, then lifted my head to suck in the sweet scent of roses, its vine growing over the top of the alcove. I picked a flower, crimson red in the moonlight, before sitting on the bench. It was so peaceful. The sound of trickling water calmed me, and I knew it was the fountain in a small pond on the other side of the garden.

How did I know this?

The anticipation grew, and I closed my eyes to lessen the aching need to see him. To touch him. I opened my eyes.

Devon.

His shirt was open halfway, revealing a smooth, powerful chest, and I remembered the feel of his pecs, his ridged stomach. Thick, wavy hair hung to his shoulders, giving the impression he'd just woken or had been caught in a summer breeze on his way here. His eyes didn't glow the pure silver of his nature but the silver-blue of his heightened passion, and they caught me in their snare. I ran a tongue over my lips, pleased to see his fierce smile widen to reveal the tips of fangs. His hands balled into fists. He was never as patient as he claimed to be. Not when he knew what he wanted.

I waited. Let him come to me. I was surprised by his careful control as his steady march clearly shouted his intentions. The goosebumps raced across my flesh, and I felt myself grow wet. He knew how to tease. But still, I remained seated.

When he stood in front of me, I lifted my head and lost myself in his gaze. How many times had we played this game? And I never tired of them. Almost wept with the sweet promise of pleasure, the easing of the ache between my legs, and the strength of his arms as he held on tight.

Devon held out a hand, and I took it. He brought it to his lips, his fangs brushing against the warm skin. Then, he pulled me up, wrapping an arm around my waist as he slid his fingers down my neck, making me shiver. He bent down, burying his nose in my hair while his lips nibbled my ear.

"Cressa."

The way he said my name never failed to heat my blood, full of desire and hunger with that touch of impatience. I smiled and wrapped my arms around his shoulders, feeling his muscles bunch as he lifted me so I could wrap my legs around his waist with my dressing gown hiked to my hips.

His body molded to mine, wrapping me in his spicy scent and making my skin glow with equal need. I ran a hand over his hair, grasping a handful to pull his head back so I could see the need in his gaze as I kissed him. His lips were molten hot, and he found no impediment as his tongue pushed through to meet mine, branding me.

I pulled him closer, wishing we were skin on skin and wondering why not. I tugged at his shirt as his lips moved to my neck. The scrape of his fangs re-energized the goosebumps, and I shivered.

He pulled back, and his eyes bored into mine, hot and greedy. "Are you sure, Cressa?"

My eyes popped open, and I jumped out of bed, tripping over the sheets and falling to the floor.

What the hell just happened?

Was that a dream? I sat on my ass and recalled the entire scene. It was so real. I touched my lips. They were damp, and I still smelled the roses and his spicy scent.

I dragged myself up and stumbled to a chair, not ready to return to bed. The whole dream, and yes, it had to have been a dream, was the most realistic and erotic I'd ever experienced. And with a vampire? Where had that come from? I remembered his glowing eyes, and I sighed in relief.

Devon's glowing eyes at the training session. My fear had combined with some weird attraction to him. I half shrugged. It wasn't my fault he was knock-out gorgeous. My subconscious had played tricks on me. I snorted. I'd even called him Devon and was now thinking of him that way. I ignored how nice it sounded when he called me by my given name, not the code name of Pandora that had started as nothing more than a taunt.

Thankful I'd determined what had happened, I crawled into bed, but the pressure of my hands on the mattress made my finger twinge. I felt the spot. It was tender, and I reflexively stuck it in my mouth. I tasted the coppery scent. Something had pricked me. Then I remembered the vine.

DEVON TURNED, gaining his bearings. He knew this place. But the scent of honeysuckle and roses made this the wrong time of year. And then he felt the pull, and he turned to follow the path. He wanted to run, but he forced a steady pace, knowing where he was going.

Would she be there?

He wasn't sure who she was. Or did he know? And the thought made his blood flow stronger, hotter. He batted away the leaves that blocked his path and increased his pace. But when the vegetation receded and he found himself facing the alcove, he froze.

She's so beautiful.

His heart pounded painfully in his ears. This was their place. Her eyes were closed, and she held a crimson rose to her nose, breathing in its strong scent. He took a step, and then another. He had to control himself, and he tried to pull in his fangs, tried to roll back his lust. It was so difficult.

Her eyes opened, and she saw him. And smiled.

He'd known she'd be here, waiting for him, and he'd counted the hours, the minutes before this moment.

God's blood he wanted to sweep her off that bench and lay her in the cool grass. He felt his hands close into fists as he held himself in check. He moved toward her—slow and steady. His little thief waited for him. That was all right. There was no place for her to go. She desired him as much as he craved her.

When he reached the bench and looked down on her, he caught the scent of blood. He brought her hand up and kissed it, immediately finding the finger that had recently been pierced.

"It was just a thorn." Her hurried whisper made him shiver with anticipation.

The roses. They grew wild in the garden and always reminded him of her heady scent, prickly nature, and untamed passion.

He pulled her up. The need to hold her in his arms chased all other thoughts away. Then she was holding on, and her lips tasted of raspberries on a warm, sunny day. Her legs squeezed his waist, her hands in his hair, her tongue eager for his. He was ensnared by her very essence.

He tore his mouth away from hers to run his lips down her neck. Her tangy scent, combined with her squirming body, crazed him. His fangs released, and he ran them over her heated flesh, quickly finding the strong pulse under her delicate skin. He licked the length of the vein, heard her moan.

"Cressa."

He wanted all of her, not just her sweet kisses that consumed him like no other. Her breasts pressed against his chest, and he wanted to suckle them, to become lost in her. Her fingers plucked at the buttons of his shirt while he pulled her nightgown down, just a quick nibble along her breast.

"Are you sure, Cressa?"

And when he could wait no longer—he stumbled.

Cressa had vanished.

Devon's eyes snapped open. He didn't move. He couldn't have even if the house were on fire. His body ached with need, his arms so empty.

What in holy hells had just happened?

He knew he'd been dreaming. That was clear from his surroundings. He was no longer in the garden but in his bedroom at his coastal estate. And Cressa was on the other side of the house.

Cressa.

Was that her name?

He focused, trying to push the fog from his mind. The only time he'd heard of living dreams was through strong blood bonds, but he hadn't fed from her. And why such an erotic dream?

He couldn't deny the attraction he'd felt since first seeing her. But his focus was on his mission. His revenge.

Then he recalled the training session. So foolish. He should have sent Lucas in his place. Hours after meeting with Isabella, he'd still been so angry. His long wait over the centuries was close at hand, but only days into the mission, the Council had been warned. Now he played a dangerous game. It was all within his grasp, but it came down to a single human female—one that seemed to arouse more than mere curiosity.

After a punishing training session that only spurred his temper, he'd almost bitten her. When her intoxicating scent wrapped around him, all he wanted was her in his arms. He'd almost kissed her. A human. That made the dream all the more impossible if they'd never shared blood. He wasn't even sure that type of blood link was possible with a human.

What could have made the dream so real that he could smell the roses and honeysuckle, catch the scent of her blood, and taste the sweetness of her lips? From what he understood, not even blood bonds were that realistic.

He ran a hand over his chest and felt the imprint of her hands as they slid to his shoulders, her fingers tugging at his hair in her own desperate need.

Another possibility crept in, but it was too outlandish. Nothing but folklore. The idea had been something he'd considered for years, but he'd never been able to find anyone who could tell him more.

He pushed it all aside. The dream had been nothing more than a wayward attraction heightened by the tempestuous training session. But when he closed his eyes to attempt sleep, he fell under the influence of the way Cressa's legs had wrapped around him and the erotic hunger in her eyes when she claimed his passion.

Chapter Twelve

BREAKFAST WAS GOING to be awkward. Which was why I hadn't moved from my room. I'd slipped into my jeans and sweater, the only items that could separate me from Devon and this house, even if he'd been the one to purchase the clothes. They were the closest to being me, not what he wanted to make me into. Even if it was only for a job.

And though my dream had been nothing more than an illusion, thorn prick aside, how could I even look at him without turning fifty shades of red? If I stayed in my room for another hour, he should be done with breakfast and be too busy to wait for me. My stomach growled its frustration, and I glanced around the room, wondering if it would be a problem to add a small coffee pot. But if I was only going to be here a week, what was the point? I could hold out for an hour.

Ten minutes later, a knock jarred me. They were constantly checking on me. This was only day two, and I was already tired of the routine.

Another knock.

"Pandora, you need to come down for breakfast." Lucas's tone was eerily reminiscent of my mother's when I was being petulant.

"I'm not hungry." Well, that sounded grown-up.

"Trust me. What Anna has planned for your morning session may not be as taxing as the training room, but I can guarantee it will bore you to tears." When my only response was silence, he sighed loudly enough for me to catch without vampire hearing. "Instead of paying attention as you should—because believe me, Anna will report everything you master, and what you don't, to Devon—you'll be thinking about how hungry you are and how silly it was to skip breakfast."

My stomach gurgled in agreement, and I covered it with my hands as if it would block the sound. It wasn't that loud.

"I can hear your stomach from here. You're going to need as many calories as you can absorb for your afternoon training sessions. Devon won't be available in the mornings."

That lifted my spirits.

"You can at least come down and grab something to bring back to your room, but honestly, while you're down there, why not stay?"

He stopped. I didn't hear him leave, but I wasn't sure I'd be able to. They could be sneaky when they wanted.

I opened the door and, with my head down, shuffled past Lucas. I was grateful he didn't say a word.

Anna waited for us in the dining room, breakfast already on the table.

"I'm sorry if you waited for me. The food is probably cold." I sat with a chagrined expression, truly sorry for ruining their meal.

"Cook heard Lucas go up, so the plates just arrived." Anna dished out scrambled egg whites while Lucas passed the bowl of diced fruit around.

The room quieted as we ate. I hated the silence. It was fine when I was alone, but not when I was with others.

"I thought you weren't allowed to eat in here." I was never great at the art of conversation. And this was one of those awkward moments when I proved it. When Anna and Lucas glanced at each other, I realized how rude I'd sounded.

Lucas nodded as he pushed his plate away. "I understand. Yesterday morning, Devon wanted time to speak to you alone without everyone stopping by to see the new house guest."

"We're all so busy with our duties, we sometimes forget to stop for a meal, or we take them at odd hours," Anna added. "But Devon likes his rituals, meals being one, so when you're available, he expects you to attend all meals unless told otherwise."

I should be thankful he wasn't at breakfast this morning. Maybe by dinner I wouldn't turn into an idiot when I saw him. Before I finished the last of my fruit, footsteps brushed along the carpet behind me. When Devon walked in, my body vacillated between run-like-a-bunny panic and the desire to quench the burning ache between my legs. I cringed at the heat that flooded my cheeks and dropped my head to focus on my plate, wishing there were more than two bites left.

"Devon." Anna sounded surprised. "I thought you'd already left."

"It's all right, Anna. One of my appointments was canceled, so I have extra time this morning."

I raised my head long enough to see something pass between Devon and Lucas. Great, now I was thinking of him by his first name. After that sultry dream, it was impossible to think of him any other way. And how would that change our relationship? It's only a name, Cressa. "Could you pass me the toast?"

I needed something to keep my hands busy and had asked the question of Anna, who was closest to the basket. But I hadn't realized Devon hadn't sat yet and was surprised when he offered the toast. I lifted my gaze to his, hoping my face wasn't as red as it felt, unsure what to expect.

The sparkle in his eyes and the charming smile wasn't what I'd expected, and all I could do was squeak out, "Thank you."

"You're quite welcome." He sat at the head of the table as Letty hurried in with a bowl of oatmeal and fruit. He nodded to her, and she glanced over the table, retrieving dirty plates before hustling out.

"If you're finished with your breakfast, I need some time with our guest. Lucas, if you could check in with Sergi, he has some updates to our timeline. And Anna, our evening plans have changed. I received an invitation to a tea party, and I'd like to take Pandora."

Anna picked at the edge of her napkin, her gaze darting around the table. Her milk-white skin paled, which told me this tea party wasn't what it sounded like. Even Lucas appeared perplexed. My skin itched, wondering what this was about.

"Is Pandora what we should be calling you?" Devon asked.

At first, I didn't realize he'd asked a question, too focused on the intent of this party. Then the question slammed into me. We'd never discussed my name, and I hadn't seen a reason to give it up freely. I wasn't sure what difference it would make, but I had little left of my dignity or freedom and clutched at the tiniest bit of control.

When I met his glance, there was something there I couldn't read. His expression carried only a smile with no hint of what he might be thinking. Why was he being nice to me again? I couldn't help but remember the dream and the warm glow that coursed through me when he'd said my name. My true name. And for a brief, terrifying moment, I wondered again if he could read my mind—or my dreams.

"I had the impression Pandora was more of a code name."

I shrugged. "Not of my choosing. I'm not even sure who started it. Maybe Harlow. He likes nicknames."

"So, what should we call you?"

Screwed six ways till Sunday, I thought and held back a snort. At the end of the day, what was a name?

"Cressa."

A quick flash from those icy blue eyes before he dropped his head to take a bite of oatmeal.

"She doesn't have an appropriate dress for this type of party." Anna pulled at her fingers, still seeming out of sorts.

Devon sipped his coffee and laid a hand on hers. "I've already arranged for something. Everything will arrive this afternoon." He glanced at me before directing the conversation back to Anna. "Today, I'd like you to focus on etiquette at formal dinners, banquets, and balls. The differences are archaic and a nuisance, but something we have to live with."

When Lucas and Anna rose, Devon raised a hand. "One more thing. Just a light lunch today. I'd like to start our training session at two sharp. And Lucas, I'll need you for that."

They both nodded before leaving. Lucas slid me a smile that relaxed my shoulders and eased the tension in my neck. I wondered if he knew how grateful I was to know he'd be my instructor this afternoon.

I played with the toast, eating the bits without butter or jam and leaving most of it in crumbs.

Devon finished his oatmeal, poured himself another cup of coffee, and held the carafe up in offering. I nodded. He ate two bites of fruit before sitting back. "I wanted to apologize for my behavior last night."

My gut wrenched at the thought of the dream.

"I received upsetting news that dredged up old memories and put me in a foul mood. I had no business being in the training room with my temper. I should have sent Lucas."

I felt stupid when my first thought had been my erotic dream and not the terror I'd felt in the training room. But it was all drowned out by his apology, which I hadn't expected. He didn't seem the type to do that often.

"I admit I was a little confused." More than a little, but after his concession, I decided to let him off easy. I convinced myself it had nothing to do with the way his hands had caressed me in the imaginary garden.

He sat back, clasping his hands over his stomach as he watched me. Seeming to have made some decision, he rested his head on the back of the chair as he stared at the ceiling. "The news I received yesterday will impact our mission. And while I can't divulge more on that topic, I can share that we'll have more eyes on us than I'd planned."

"I don't understand why I need to attend parties if you only need me to steal something."

He remained relaxed but lowered his head to meet my gaze. "You haven't spent time in the vampire world, have you?"

I shook my head.

He sighed. "We're an ancient race who've spent many centuries hiding, running, or pillaging. When we moved from the dark ages to a more enlightened existence, a governing body was created. The older vampires believed a Council was our only chance of survival if we were to live among humans and not be hunted by them. Later, two shifters were added to the Council to maintain a fragile peace amongst the magical creatures. Our rules are old and archaic, and while we don't religiously adhere to most of them, the older the vampire or the higher in society one rises, the more the rules are followed."

He reached for his coffee and a couple more bites of fruit as I digested the information.

"You're worried I'm going to stick out?"

His smile sent tingles through me. "You will definitely stick out, but that has nothing to do with understanding our rules."

What did that mean?

"Overall, we're a bored species. Many of us pursue enough business interests to keep us occupied, and we're constantly fighting over territory. But when you live a long time, it's difficult to find anything that amuses you. The instincts of a vampire can be hard to fight. And while we may seem disinterested or sedate, I can assure you, there's not a single vampire that wouldn't see a human as easy prey."

I swallowed hard. "Does that include you?"

He held my gaze. "Yes."

I fidgeted in my seat. I was living on a roller-coaster.

"I don't want to lie. But that doesn't mean I don't possess enough control to deny my genetics. Humans simply don't have the strength or the intelligence to outmaneuver a vampire. That doesn't mean we act on our baser instincts. At least, most don't."

I supposed that was meant to make me feel better.

"What I'm trying to say, rather poorly, is that you need to understand how dangerous even the most sophisticated vampire can be. And I would argue that the most polished, the most aristo-cratic of us, are usually the most deadly."

I nodded, suddenly understanding his point. "Probably because that is how they gained their position or, if born to it, how they perceive keeping it."

He nodded with an expression that seemed pleased with my assessment. "And now that you know that, you need to become comfortable in a room full of unscrupulous vampires. I need to know you won't panic during the true mission."

It made sense. He'd told me earlier that I would be going into vampire high society, but I had no idea what that meant. I had mingled with society's elite, but they'd been human. And though it was more than I wanted to know, it had come in handy as a thief.

I wasn't sure how to approach my next question, especially after last night's dream, but I had to ask. Had to know. But I couldn't look him in the eye, so I reached for the carafe and topped off our coffee as I asked, "What did you say my cover story was?" I knew damn well what he'd said but hoped he'd meant it figu-ratively.

His gaze darkened, and I focused on my coffee cup, ignoring that stirring in my loins. "You're a Blood Ward. This is a human who wishes to become a vampire."

"Like Anna?"

His brows rose. "She told you?"

"I thought she was already a vampire, so she told me her story."

He nodded. "I see. In practical terms, yes, Anna is a Blood Ward, but her story, as you call it, is different in that she's been raised in a vampire household. Most Blood Wards are humans who become aware of us, and for a variety of reasons, want to become one of us. But like you, they have no real understanding of our history, our values, our customs, or our rules. They must go through a training period where they learn to let go of their human instincts and learn what it is to be vampire."

"Students."

"The Wolf didn't tell me how intelligent you were."

"Maybe I'm part vampire." It was meant as a joke, but Devon didn't laugh, and his intense gaze made me uncomfortable again.

Ignoring my remark, he continued his lecture. "As my Blood Ward, the others will assume you're also my lover, being trained in the art of seduction and manipulation. You'll need to reflect that in how you present yourself at any gathering I take you."

There wasn't any way to stop my cheeks from flushing with that remark.

"Only in appearance, of course."

I still couldn't look at him and nodded as I stared into my coffee cup. Would this conversation be easier if he were only half as attractive?

He stood. "Anna will be upset if I take too much of your time. She has quite a lot to teach you today."

I didn't move but also didn't want to be the little mouse. "Thank you for the background. It's helpful."

"I'll see you this afternoon."

I waited until I heard his footsteps retreat down the hall before I let out a breath. Why the hell did I have that dream? This evening was not going to go well.

~

WHEN DEVON RETURNED to his office, Sergi was waiting in the antechamber, studying his tablet. He followed Devon and plopped into a chair in front of the desk, scowling at the sun's glare.

"Sorry." Devon touched a pad, and blinds dropped from the ceiling, darkening the room. Devon preferred light in his office, but as an elder vampire, he tolerated it more than most. And though Sergi was almost as old as him, his friend preferred the old ways.

Sergi barely nodded, used to Devon's peculiarities. "I have a surveillance and security plan, but there are gaps. We might need to bring in consultants."

Not what Devon wanted to hear, but nothing he hadn't expected. He had a large family, but it had never been as extensive as Lorenzo's. "Leave it with me, and I'll consider it. I have something else I want you to do."

Sergi tapped his tablet, probably forwarding the plans, before focusing on Devon.

"I want a background check on Cressa." Devon picked up a white crystal he kept on his desk and rubbed its edges.

"Cressa?"

"Pandora is just a code name for our guest."

Sergi typed in his tablet. For someone who preferred the old ways, Sergi had become both adept and passionate about technology. "Last name?"

"She didn't say." When Sergi raised a brow, Devon waved a hand at him.

"I know it might be difficult, but I need as much as you can find, as quickly as you can. And include her family, two generations back if possible."

Devon ignored Sergi's expression when it changed from boredom to curiosity. He had no doubt Sergi wanted to know what scent he'd caught. Time would tell if fate laid a hand upon his shoulder or proved he'd lost all his senses.

"I would prefer you didn't ask The Wolf about her if you can avoid it. She mentioned someone who'd given her the nickname Pandora. Someone by the name of Harlow. If this person knows she's a thief, then he would run in the same circles."

Sergi nodded, pleased with the information. There was no doubt his security expert would build a decent portfolio, but would it be enough for what Devon needed?

His dream had been too realistic. Any other time, he might have considered it nothing more than his own flight of fancy with such an attractive woman in the house. But Cressa's reaction to him at breakfast wasn't what he'd expected. The last he'd seen of her in the training room, she'd been terrified of him. And she should have been. He'd barely been able to control himself, and he could have unintentionally hurt her. But instead of fear this morning, her cheeks had flushed. He needed to know—no—had to know if she was truly human.

Chapter Thirteen

THE HUGE SYCAMORE tree I'd noticed from the window the day before was a scant ten yards from the family grave markers. I strolled that way, glad for the sunny skies and warmer temperatures, even if it might only last a day. Spring was like that on the coast.

Anna's session had bored me to numbness, just as Lucas had predicted. Why would any culture have three different etiquette techniques depending on the type of event? Especially a culture raised on drinking blood rather than eating. Perhaps that was the reason in itself—to prove they could be civilized. But it was to the point of overkill.

When Anna confided that the main trick was to watch what everyone else did, I stopped paying attention to her rambling. Based on her short temper before breaking for lunch, I'm positive I failed every point of her lesson.

She was so irritated with me, she claimed to have another task that prevented her from dining with me. With Lucas out on some errand, this was my opportunity to snoop. That was what thieves did, and since everyone in the house knew I was one, shame on them for leaving me alone.

I found Cook washing fresh blueberries. "Ooh, I love blueber-ries. We had a cook when I was little that made the best blueberry scones." I leaned over to get a better look, and he shooed me away.

"No one gets close to the food until it's prepared," he chided. "So, what brings you to my den?"

"I'm on my own for lunch and thought I'd grab something to take outside."

Cook was quite pleased to pack me a small picnic. No one had asked him to do that in decades, which had been my only clue so far that he was a vampire. A vampire cook. Who would have thought it?

"Why would a vampire want to be a cook?" I hadn't meant it as a slight, and fortunately, he didn't take it as one.

He sliced thin sections of roast beef and turkey to place on thick slices of homemade sourdough bread. "I came from a poor house. Even with centuries to build wealth, wrong partnerships can have long-term consequences. To lighten the load on our Father, many of us in his house helped where we could." He stopped cutting the tomatoes as he stared into the distance. "I remember the first time I was up to my elbows in flour, making my first loaf of bread. I can still feel that joy I had from making some-thing. When I joined Devon's family, I was encouraged to go to school."

"You're a trained chef?" With my background, growing up in a wealthy neighborhood, I knew a little something about the subject from the dozens of chefs that had come and gone before I left.

He nodded and pointed his knife to a small plaque on the other side of the kitchen. I wandered over to read the inscription: "Institute of Culinary Education." One of the most prestigious schools in the world.

"Why aren't we calling you chef something?" I'd also learned from my family's kitchen that chefs were typically cranky, stuffy, and without a drop of humor.

"Those people are crazy—too temperamental. All I want to do

is cook, so the name stuck. I like it." He wrapped the sandwich in plastic and placed it in a small basket next to a cup of fruit. Then he added a bottle of mineral water and shooed me away with a quirky grin.

I glanced around to find the best place to sit since the grass was still damp from the overnight mist. I dropped to a bare spot that had caught enough sun and leaned against the tree to stare at the two grave markers.

Even at this distance, I could see the names were barely legible. I couldn't make out the last name from here, but it didn't look to be Trelane. It appeared the year of death was some time in the early 1900s. Devon's off-handed comments made me think he was much older, which only piqued my interest at whose markers these belonged to if they didn't bear his last name. Maybe they were on his mother's side of the family. Or they could be human.

I was halfway through my lunch when I glanced up at the house and almost dropped my fruit cup. Had the blinds moved in that third-floor room? My uncontrollable urge to sneak about shouted at me to take advantage of being on my own. I swallowed the rest of the fruit, shoving everything else back in the basket.

Before heading back to the house, I took a moment to stop at the grave markers. The first names were entirely worn away by the salt and rain. I could make out a few letters of the surname, but they were only vowels, an "a" and an "e". Not nearly enough. There was only one date, equally difficult to read, and I assumed it was the date of their death. I could confirm the first two digits on one marker were definitely a one and a nine. The last two numbers were readable on the second marker—a two and a five. It was impossible to tell if they had died at the same time, though the headstones were similar in style.

I turned to head for the house. This time, I distinctly saw movement on the third floor.

Almost racing back, I left the basket on a side table in the foyer, promising to return it to the kitchen later. I didn't want Cook to know I was back in the house, so I paused to listen. Vampires could be noisier than one would think, but they were typically deathly quiet. All I could hear was the ticking of a clock. I strolled to the staircase, just a girl going to her room, but when I reached the second floor, I stopped again.

Silence.

I didn't know where Devon's room was. I wasn't even sure which floor. That could be his room on the third floor, but that didn't make sense unless he kept someone locked in there. That was a creepy thought. He didn't seem the type, but how would I know after just two days? I had to stop thinking about that dream. Dreams were manifestations of our subconscious, not reality.

Taking the silence as my cue, I tiptoed up the last flight of stairs, grimacing when I hit a soft board and the screech reverberated in my head. I froze, waiting to see if anyone heard me and would come running. I had no excuse for being up here when Devon had explicitly told me to avoid the third floor. Had he known at the time what an open invitation that had been?

I smiled. If he discovered me, it would be a teachable moment on what not to tell a thief. Continuing on, I treaded carefully until I reached the third floor. A tall bookcase sat against the wall, slightly to the left of the stairs, and I scurried to stand beside it as if it offered some unique hiding place. With the shadows created from dim hall lighting, it was better than some places I'd hidden on my jobs. I peeked around the case and glanced down the opposite hall of where I wanted to go.

There was nothing but shadows as far as I could see, but I slinked that way, just to get a feel for the floor plan. The hall stretched for what appeared to be half the length of the mansion and was filled with decorative tables, two chairs, and a full-sized armored statue. I sighed. Every old mansion came with one of those. I counted ten doors in all, five on each side. When I reached the end, I was somewhat disappointed, positive I would have found Devon's master suite. There was a door, but it was smaller, less grand than the other doors, and I assumed it must be a storage closet.

I had little time before someone came along, and as much as I wanted to see what was inside, my goal was on the other end of the hall. I retraced my steps and was almost back to the staircase when I heard the click of a door opening. It was from behind me. I'd never make it down the stairs without being seen, so I dashed to the bookcase and slid into my hiding spot.

I pressed as far back as I could go, wishing someone had stuck a fern or some other tall houseplant next to the bookcase. Anything to stay covered. I held my breath as the heavy footsteps grew closer, muffled as they were on the carpet. It must be a man. One of the vampires? Would he be able to sense me?

I glanced to my right, hoping there was something else I could hide behind, but there wasn't enough time. Besides, there wasn't anything more than a small bench next to a tall floor lamp, which was thankfully dark. The only thing I had going for me was that the bookcase didn't sit flush with the staircase. Whoever was coming wouldn't see me if they were focused on the stairs, as most people would be.

If they stopped partway down and turned to look back—that would be a problem.

The footsteps slowed as they reached the staircase. I forced my eyes to stay open but lowered my gaze and waited for shoes to appear. It might be superstition, but I was a true believer in knowing when someone was watching me. It was a sixth sense someone in my field implicitly trusted.

Would a vampire believe the same thing? I smirked. I had no doubt of it.

The shoes stopped at the top of the stairs. Crap.

When I raised my gaze, I glimpsed a male figure. No one I recognized from this angle. He was checking his pockets. Seeming satisfied, he continued down. I refused to take a breath until I heard him jogging down the next flight of stairs.

I gave it another minute, knowing I should race back down before someone found me, but what kind of cat burglar would I be if I did that? Maybe I could say I was practicing for the job. I almost snorted before peeling myself away from the bookcase and turning to the right. After a few steps, I saw past the shadows to a much shorter hallway with double doors at the end. I could barely make out the carved scrollwork in the poor light.

This was more like it. The only question was whether this was Devon's room or someone else's. Like maybe the cloaked figure that had stood next to the graves that first night. I racked my brain, trying to remember the person's size, but even with the lantern, I couldn't guess whether they had been male or female.

The only other door in the hallway was another closet door on the left, not far from the double doors. I inched closer, my senses on full alert for anything behind or in front of me. I should be scanning everything, but I couldn't seem to pull my gaze away from the door handle.

When I stopped a foot from the door, I leaned my ear next to it. Nothing. I placed my hand on the wood, and though I wouldn't know unless I tapped against it, it seemed solid. If someone was moving about on the other side, I should still be able to hear something.

I closed my eyes, focusing on any sound from inside the room. Even a ticking clock would give me an indication of how thick the door was. But the only noise that greeted me was silence. I stepped back, considering my options.

I'd be crazy to try the handle.

What if Devon found me snooping? Would that cancel the trial period? I wasn't sure what to think when my first reaction to that thought was one of disappointment. Of course, I wanted to leave, but I wasn't being mistreated nor constantly monitored. Standing in front of a door on the third floor where I'd expressly been told not to venture was proof of that.

The dream I'd tried so hard to forget tumbled through my

head again. The smell of honeysuckle, the prick of the thorn, the erotic feelings that had swept through me when Devon found me and pulled me into his arms. The memory was so vivid, I took another step back. The intensity of the ache between my legs surprised me and made my cheeks heat.

I shook my head to dispel the images. Of all times to remember the dream. It had been easy to shake the vision off before. Why was it so difficult to do that now?

Whatever I'd hoped to find up here, I only confirmed one thing. Whatever lay beyond these doors took up ample living space. As I took another step back, the barest sound made me glance down.

The doorknob turned.

My heart thumped wildly as I backed up two more steps. My instinct to run beat against my head, screaming for me to move, but my feet were stuck in place. The knob stopped. Then it turned back the other way.

Was it locked?

I didn't see a deadbolt. The only lock appeared to be a keyhole. Would the knob still turn if the door was locked?

When it turned the other way again, I found the drive to force my feet to work and backed up several paces. Then, not caring if anyone caught me, I flew down the stairs, hitting the second floor hard before turning left toward my room. I was halfway to the door when I heard my name.

"Cressa?"

I stopped, my heart pounding so loudly I barely heard him.

I turned to face the music. Devon stood farther down the hallway, and I had the presence of mind to note that he'd been coming from the other end of the hall. So, his room must be on this floor.

"Why are you running?" He strode toward me. If he was suspicious, it didn't show. He looked concerned.

Think, woman. You've gotten out of worst scrapes than this.

I gulped air and pushed my hair back, taking as much time as I could to come up with a plausible excuse. I took in his workout clothes, which didn't disguise his toned body, and decided sticking close to the truth would be best.

"Cook made me a picnic lunch. It was such a nice day and...I fell asleep. I thought I might have lost track of time." Don't ramble. "I didn't want to be late for training."

He stepped closer. "Your cheeks are red. I hope it's from running. It wouldn't be good if you got too much sun."

I must have looked confused, and he smiled.

"Vampires might be able to travel in daylight, but I doubt you'd find any willing to sunbathe. And while everyone will know you're still human, they would expect you to give up certain behaviors."

He didn't suspect anything, and I was so relieved I couldn't help but get a bit snarky.

"So, no golden tan for me?"

He quirked his lips. "Only if it was your natural skin tone."

"Ah. So, no tan lines."

His gaze warmed. "Would I find any?"

I gulped. That sounded more intimate than it should. I pulled myself together, avoiding his gaze by staring at his lips, which honestly wasn't any better. Damn that frickin' dream. "Some mysteries aren't meant to be revealed."

He smiled, and my knees went weak. His voice was nothing more than a whisper. "And some enjoy a challenge." When I didn't respond, couldn't respond, he nodded, knowing he'd won that round. "You have five minutes. Don't be late."

His steps echoed down the hall of the first floor before I moved. I was stripped down, pulling on my workout clothes, when I realized something. If he had come from his room on the other end of the second floor, who had turned the doorknob?

Chapter Fourteen

Lucas held out his hand, and I grabbed it, fairly certain I wouldn't make it off the mat without his assistance. My legs were as rubbery as my soggy fettuccine. I never could cook.

"Sorry about that last move." Lucas did look apologetic, which only irritated Devon if the sneer on his lips and light glow in his fierce gaze was any indication. He'd been warning Lucas all afternoon to stop apologizing every time I hit the floor—which was a lot.

We'd been working for two hours, which had felt more like eight. I was winded and sore, discovering muscles I didn't know and hoped to never know about again. For the first twenty minutes, Devon and Lucas sparred while I watched. I could tell by their tentative moves they were holding back. They used a combination of various styles of martial arts. I was familiar with most of them, but they mixed them up in ways I'd never considered. Deadlier ways. Methods that could elude a vampire.

The problem was, when I attempted the maneuvers, my body wouldn't obey my commands, which was too familiar with my singular, rote routine. Lesson learned. And when I became more fluid in my movements, the two vampires responded by moving faster. Completely unfair. The more tired I became—my movements slower, my time on the mat longer—the more Lucas wanted to pull back until Devon snapped at him. After the third bark to stop taking it easy on me, Devon stopped asking.

I thought he'd relented until I saw the glow in his eyes. Then I wished he'd start yelling instead of finding myself pinned to the wall again. But he controlled his temper better than our first training session because he hadn't moved past his current agitated state for a solid half-hour.

"Leave us," Devon snarled, never taking his heated glare from me. Well, his tolerance lasted longer than I'd expected.

"Sir." Lucas's response was barely audible.

Devon waved a hand, and Lucas backed up but glanced my way. Not wanting to get him in any more trouble, I nodded. Devon couldn't kill me—I had a job to do.

"I'm not going to ask again. You have other work to do." Devon's growl got Lucas's attention, and he turned for the door. Before he opened it, Devon whispered something I couldn't hear.

Lucas must have heard because his shoulders relaxed, and he gave Devon a slight nod before leaving.

Not sure what might happen next, and not wanting to find myself on the mat again, I limped my way to the single bench in the room, dropping with a silent cry for my tortured body. I leaned against the wall, waiting for my breathing to return to normal and the sweat to dry.

"You're not focusing." His tone lessened from seriously angry to irritated, and I glanced up.

Devon hadn't moved from his spot across the room. He leaned against the wall with his arms crossed. His hair was damp, confirming that vampires did sweat, and I followed the light sheen that emphasized the lean contours of his muscles.

"I'm trying," I bit out my response, knowing it sounded weak. But, good grief, I'd been fighting two vampires for hours.

"You're not."

That pissed me off. I glared at him. Then I had to go and open my mouth. "You're using moves I'm not used to, and if you haven't noticed, the odds are two vampires against one human. It's pretty obvious you've never trained anyone before."

His eyes flashed with a dangerous glow, yet his lips quirked for a heartbeat. Was there hope he wouldn't wipe the floor with me? He uncrossed his arms and strolled toward me. I didn't squirm, but it took every muscle in my body to remain perfectly still. Was I supposed to wave my arms when a predator approached? I was pretty sure running would be a wrong move, but freezing like a proverbial sitting duck grated on my nerves.

"You knew every move we made. I've seen you perform them." He paced ten feet from me. Far enough away to not seem threatening, but I knew he could pounce that distance in a single move.

"Not like that."

"It shouldn't matter."

"It wouldn't if I had varied my routines in my training." I hung my head but kept my eyes on his feet so I knew where he was.

When silence was his response, I braved a glimpse. The glow of his eyes had receded, but his expression was still stony.

"At least you learned one thing today."

"I'm not sure what you're hoping to accomplish. How can one human hope to fend off more than one vampire?"

"You can't. You'd be lucky to handle one, even after months of training. Not unless you had a sword that could take a head. You might be lucky enough to pierce or shoot them with silver, which wouldn't kill but would at least slow them down."

I memorized those options, wondering where I could get silver bullets. Or better, a silver dagger.

As I suspected, he was in front of me before I knew it. I held my ground. He knelt, forcing direct eye contact, and for a moment, I saw something close to approval in his stern gaze.

"Have you considered the value of the skills you're learning?

How they can be used in your favor when you've worked off your debt here?"

I snorted. "Right. But I'm confused. Am I supposed to seduce my next mark with a kick to his groin or to his head?"

He braced the bench on both sides of me until I heard the subtle crack of wood splintering. He immediately pushed himself up and backed away. "You need to be smarter to live as you do." His temper changed to frustration. "You'll be able to infiltrate any high society party to run surveillance on your next mark and have the additional skills to outmaneuver any security personnel."

That made me pause. Damn, if he wasn't right. I'd been so caught up in this mission—in him—to consider what would happen once I left here. I needed to keep my head in the game.

He picked up his towel and a box no bigger than his hand before strolling back to me. His gaze was the usual icy blue with a bit of apology in them—if only for a moment. He held the box out to me.

I laughed. When his brows knitted in confusion, I quipped, "This is a little big for a ring, isn't it?"

His smile was genuine. "It hadn't occurred to me that you might have family or friends who might be worried about you. And you have no way to communicate with me, if needed."

I was stunned and stared at the box. Afraid to hope, I picked at the wrapping. Sure enough, it was a brand-new phone. The protective plastic still covered its surface, and a charger rested beside it.

"I took the liberty of adding my number in addition to one for Lucas and Sergi. I trust them both with my life, and by extension, yours. You can add anyone else you need."

That was a heady feeling—bodyguards I could contact. "And I can call anyone?"

He paused for a moment, then shrugged. "I'm not your keeper, Cressa. At least not permanently. I've been so focused on preparing for the mission and used to everyone knowing their roles, I forgot you're not used to living in a vampire household. My apologies."

I wasn't sure how to respond, reeling as usual by his swift mood changes. Who knew vampires could be so conflicted?

"I'll have Anna call the masseuse. You have time for a long bath and a nap before Cook sends up a light dinner. And I imagine Anna will want more time than necessary to prepare you for the party."

I groaned. I was too tired for a party.

He was already across the room, far enough not to have heard my vocal complaint. Although, I was sure he did and just didn't care. The mission and all.

Before he left, he stopped long enough to glance over his shoulder. "And Cressa, I've been training men for battle for more than five hundred years. I think I can manage training a martial arts expert, even a human one, to fend off a vampire or two."

OVER FIVE HUNDRED YEARS OLD? I knew he was ancient, but I'd never really considered what that meant. I had to stop thinking about it. It was all I'd been doing since returning to my room. The upside was that my ruminations drowned out Anna's constant instructions. I'd barely gotten any peace in the bath.

After a two-hour nap, I was grumpier than before as Anna tugged at my hair. It couldn't possibly be as tangled as she made it seem, and I was sure to be half-bald by the time she finished. But after a wash, air dry, and brutal brushing, my hair glistened.

Satisfied with herself, Anna nodded. "I'll be back in an hour to finish. Try not to damage the hair."

She'd seemed like such a nice person when we'd first met. I didn't know if her attitude had grown more distant because she took her duties too seriously or if she was bossy by nature. More likely, her irritation grew because of my disregard for her expertise on vampire society. I felt a bit guilty, but I wasn't sure I could be the perfect student she wanted me to be.

Once Anna left, I picked up my new phone, now fully charged, and dialed my roommate and best friend. Okay, only friend. But we really were besties. When Ginger answered, I smiled with relief.

"Who is this?"

"It's me."

"Cressa? Where are you?" Her voice carried a slight screech when she was worried.

"I'm safe. Somewhere on the other side of town." I sat up straighter, pulling my knees to my chest. It was rare to find Ginger speechless. I'd expected panicked, but not quiet. "I know I should have called sooner, but I didn't have my phone."

After a pause and what sounded like a quick hiccup of breath, she whispered, "I know. Howler brought it by a couple days ago. Said you were picked up by Sorrento."

"Yeah."

"This is my fault."

"No," I bit out, angry with myself that Howler had been the one to tell her. I calmed down, knowing she was listening now. "We've talked about this. We knew this could happen, and to be honest, it's a bit of a relief I've found a way to clear the debt."

Another long pause. "And how exactly are you doing that?"

I grinned at her tone. "Not on my back or my knees."

"That's good, because with your skills it could take years."

"Funny." But I couldn't help grinning at hearing her sass return.

"I suppose someone wants you to steal something?"

"Something like that. Listen. I'm not sure how much I can tell you, and I really don't want you to get mixed up in this. I should be done in a few days and home next week at the latest."

When silence greeted me again, I knew something was off. She should be scolding me for not checking in. This silent treatment was something else, and the hairs on the back of my neck went up. "Is Sorrento bothering you?"

I heard a door close before she responded. "I thought you split because of your stepfather."

A chill went through me. "What?"

"He came looking for you."

Now I didn't know what to say. "Did he hurt you?"

Her laugh was shaky. "I told him to fuck off and slammed the door in his face. But there's a black SUV that drives by a couple times a day and sometimes parks down the street. What did you do, Cressa?"

I ran a hand through my hair then cringed, hoping I hadn't messed up Anna's work or I'd have to sit through another painful brushing.

"I haven't seen him for at least six months. The last time I checked in with April, he was out of the country."

"Well, he must think you did something because he wants you in the worst way. Someone calls your phone about three times a day. It's not a number I recognize, but I'd bet it's him."

"Are his goons threatening you?"

"Nah. They're just annoying. I was thinking of setting Bulldog on them."

Bulldog was what we liked to call our neighborhood watch. He got the name for his nose, which had been broken so many times it was a wonder he could breathe through it. He was six-seven and well over two hundred pounds of rock-hard muscle and bad attitude. He ran a small gang that kept our street safe and never bothered us.

"He must know about the SUV."

"Oh, yeah. He's doubled the crew on the corners. They've tried talking to the driver, but the SUV drives off whenever one of Bulldog's crew steps up."

"Shit. I'm sorry, Ginger."

"Not your fault." Her tone was just as pointed as mine had

been earlier. "Wherever you are, and whatever you're doing, I think it's good timing. I'd stay away until this blows over."

"You should delete this number. I wouldn't put it past them to steal your phone."

"I've already added you to my contacts under the name of Stuart with a rating of maybe."

I laughed. If a guy caught her attention, and they got far enough for her to save their number, she'd add their first name with a rating on her "would I fuck them" scale. I winced when I realized the name she'd selected. "That's not fair. Stuart was a nice guy if a bit of a stalker."

"Which would have been impressive if he wasn't always falling over his big feet."

"You know what they say about big feet," I quipped.

We both laughed, and it was the first time I'd felt like myself in days.

"I gotta go." Ginger sounded hurried. "I'm late again. But seriously, girl, you need to stay away. Are you really okay?"

I glanced around the room at the scattered clothes and the silver tray with the remains of a gourmet meal. "Yeah. I am." Suddenly, I realized how good I was being treated, considering why I was here.

"Then stay put. And don't call for another day unless you're in trouble."

Then, she was gone.

I dropped my head to my knees. Why the hell was my stepfather looking for me? And what the hell was April up to?

Chapter Fifteen

DEVON SHOVED HIS TABLET ASIDE, pushing thoughts of Cressa away with it, resigned to stare out his office window. There hadn't been a window before he moved in, but if he was going to have to live and work in this stodgy old place, he'd damn well have a window. It was odd for a vampire, but that was what blinds were for. The sun had set two hours earlier, and nothing but his own reflection glared back at him. Was he doing the right thing? Now that he'd set the wheels in motion, he asked the question often, but the answer was still elusive. He'd thought himself a better man than the one he was two hundred years ago, yet the anger burned deep. If he hadn't been handed the key to his revenge, he might forget one day.

But circumstances as they were, he would never be allowed to forget. So, until he came to a final decision whether to move forward, there was no harm in preparing. They were far from the point of no return, and he could right a few wrongs in the process.

When a light tap came from behind him, he glanced at the spot behind his reflection to watch Sergi enter.

He studied his friend, looking for a sign, but the man had learned to hide his emotions centuries ago. Though Devon found it interesting when Sergi strode to the bar and poured himself a vodka. He must have uncovered something. Devon moved to the couch in front of the fireplace, and Sergi handed him a glass of scotch before taking a seat.

They were lost in their own thoughts as they contemplated the fire and sipped their drinks. After years of service, Devon knew better than to rush Sergi when he had something to report. The man had his own way of easing into a topic. And they had time before Cressa would be ready.

"Everyone but Bella and Jacques have arrived at Oasis. They should be in place by tomorrow."

Devon raised his brows. He hadn't expected everyone to be so close. "Excellent. Arrange a dinner sometime after my next training session with Cressa."

Sergi nodded. "I found some general background, but not nearly enough."

Devon frowned. It wasn't really a surprise with only a first name and her street persona to go on. He finished his drink and stood, intending to refill his glass. Instead, he grabbed the scotch and vodka bottles and returned to the couch, topping off Sergi's drink. They could drink all night and never get drunk. That's not what messed up vampires. But that was another chapter he'd buried for good.

"What do you have?" Devon asked after he'd kicked off his shoes and settled his feet on the coffee table. His left foot ached where Cressa had slammed her heel on his instep. For being barefoot, she didn't hold back, and his lips twitched at the memory.

"Her birth name is Cressa Langtry, but she was adopted by her stepfather fifteen years ago. There's no father listed on her birth certificate."

A chill ran through him, but he didn't respond, positive Sergi had more.

"Her mother, Willa Langtry, married Christopher Underwood

twenty years ago. They have one daughter—April." Sergi stopped and sipped his drink.

When he didn't continue, Devon understood he'd missed something significant. He sat up, pulling his feet from the table. "Christopher Underwood. The same man who owns Plexor Industries? The one who kept outbidding me for that stretch of land along Crescent City?"

Sergi nodded.

That didn't make sense. Cressa had grown up in a very wealthy environment. Why was she stealing? "Did you find where she's living?"

"On Baker Street with a young woman by the name of Ginger Morrison."

"That area is close to the Hollows. A rough neighborhood."

"They live in a rundown apartment building. A gang protects the area."

"Why would she be living there, stealing from the rich?" It could be signs of a troubled youth. Kids with affluent parents didn't always get the attention they deserved. It was a problem in vampire society as well. Maybe it was her way of payback for something. Did her family know how she was making her living? Did they care? He snorted before taking a drink. Cressa could be a handful.

He suddenly had the urge to rip the stepfather's head off without any reasonable explanation, other than disgust that while he lived in a mansion, Cressa survived in squalor among the city's most dangerous criminals. Another thought made him inwardly scowl. Maybe her strange dreams had created a problem. Or did her dreams only confuse her and make her rebel? Devon understood that possibility all too well.

He was left with too many unanswered questions. "Anything else?"

Sergi shook his head. "I'll have more in another day or so."

"I'd like daily reports on her phone calls and texts. And GPS if she leaves the property for any reason."

"Is she allowed to?"

Devon considered it and shrugged. "I don't want her to be a prisoner. She's smart and knows there isn't anywhere she can run. Don't suggest it, but if she asks or leaves on her own, don't stop her." He wanted to know whether she'd return on her own. "Focus on the fathers. Reopen the files on the Crescent City business venture. Let's dig deeper on Underwood. I want to know everything he's into—legal or otherwise." He paused. "Especially otherwise. Regarding her biological father, I have to know who he was. I don't care how you do it, except for harming Cressa or her roommate."

Sergi polished off his drink, stood, and returned his glass to the bar.

Devon set down his unfinished drink and laid his head back, closing his eyes. He had so many balls in the air; did he have time to sort out the mystery of Cressa? But if he was going to use her for the mission, he had to know what complications she brought. More importantly, he had to understand more about her dreams. He sighed as he remembered the party. As if on cue, a tap sounded at the door.

He straightened his suit before leaving his study. He'd asked Anna to bring Cressa to the library, which would be more relaxing than his office. He wanted to go over a few items before they left since their drive would be short. But when he walked through the door and found Cressa standing in front of the fireplace, her fingers tracing the delicate outline of a figurine as the low fire surrounded her in an unearthly glow, he forgot what he had to say. And that was before she turned to face him.

I CRINGED. I didn't have to turn around to know Devon had walked into the room. He had a presence beyond the soft sound of his footsteps. And, of course, I was holding a priceless figurine, and having him watch me made me feel every inch the thief that I was. It was irrational. I was self-aware enough to know I projected those feelings, but his timing was eerie just the same.

My first instinct was to tug at my hemline. I'd been fussing with it since donning the high-end dress made of a deep emerald green that was almost black. The front had a high neckline, and the fabric hugged my body as it flowed to a few inches below my ass. But the material swept low in the back, leaving nothing but bare skin to the base of my spine.

Even with the fire, the room had a chill, and with my legs and back bare, I should have had goosebumps. But I was so nervous about what to expect at the party that I seemed to have developed an internal radiator. When I screwed up the courage to greet Devon, the heat level jumped up. He'd stopped a few inches inside the door, and his eyes glowed that silvery blue I remembered from the dream. The one I'd understood to reflect his desire. It should have terrified me. Not in the "he might want me for a blood snack" kind of way, but in the way a man might devour a woman. And after the dream, I couldn't help but wonder what the real thing might be like.

I wasn't a virgin, and he was the most exotic man I'd ever met. Would it be so bad to be his human lover for what was left of my seven days? When someone cleared their throat—maybe him— the moment was broken, and I returned to my senses. I was here for a job. The fact he could make a girl's panties wet with his tailored suit and dirty-blond hair styled with a bedroom-messy look wasn't my fault. I dragged my gaze away to the figurine I was still holding.

"Sorry," I whispered as I lifted the object, happy to talk about my thieving ways rather than deal with the volcanic fervor threatening to suffocate me. His intense gaze never wavered, but his lips twitched. "Seems I can't help myself, but I assure you, I was only looking."

The twitch turned into a smile that did nothing to settle the twinge between my legs. "I suppose it comes with the job. Once someone knows you're an infamous cat burglar, it's hard to pick up the cheapest of trinkets without someone thinking you might steal it. Vampires have a similar problem."

I grinned. "Once a bloodsucker?" Had I gone too far with that one?

His smile never faltered. "Something like that." He studied me, but this time it carried no sexual heat. Not like before. "I was going to discuss a couple of things before we left. This party was unexpected but couldn't have come at a better time. I want to ensure we make the right impression, but we can discuss it on the drive."

When he stepped aside, waiting for me to exit first, I stumbled over the carpet. Faster than lightning, he was by my side, his hand on my elbow to steady me.

"Are the shoes okay? Do you need a different pair? Something with less heel?"

"They're actually comfortable. It's just been a while since I've worn heels."

"Good. Because they show off your best attributes."

"My ass?"

He chuckled, and the deep sound sent a warm shiver up my spine. "I was going to say legs, but ass will do."

We'd been driving for five minutes, and he hadn't said another word to me. He'd given instructions to Sergi, who I suspected was both driver and bodyguard, as we drove down the long driveway. I perused the limo, finding no fault. The man was a class act, and while he stared at me, I focused on the stocked bar, sorry I hadn't downed a shot or two while waiting for him. When I couldn't take the silence anymore, I finally glanced at him.

It was disconcerting when he didn't seem to care that I found him staring. Was it one of those vampire things? He didn't seem aware of how uncomfortable it made people. He probably did, but that wasn't what made me want to squirm in my seat. I had expected him to drill me on social etiquette for a tea party. From what Anna described, this type of party was a vampire's Saturday night meat market.

"Could my stunning beauty hold a vamp at bay before I stake him, or do I have something in my teeth?" I meant it as a joke, something to break the silence because I had to do something. His stare was creating all those little triggers that reminded me of the dream garden. Maybe it would be better to get down to the nasty and be done with it. Then we could get back to the mission.

If I expected Devon to be embarrassed by his staring, I should have known better.

"You'll want to stay close to me at the party. The house will have a nightclub atmosphere, at least in the main ballroom, but the other rooms will seem more like a social gathering. Don't let the sedate nature of those other rooms fool you. The vampires will be looking for their next fix, so there will be a mix of humans as well as lower vampires."

"Lower vampires?"

"Vampires not of noble birth or high rank. They could also be a fledgling, a newly made vampire whose creator released them into the world prematurely, and now they search for a new master. Everyone of worth in this club is focused on one thing—finding a new sex slave. And for those with lesser scruples, finding a human to use for sex and blood." He shook his head with a sneer. "These are some of the lowest of our species."

"And you thought it would be fun to show me off as your human sex and blood slave?" I wasn't sure how that sounded, but I was certain some of my shock and anger showed through.

"Not in the way you think. The second reason for the party is that it provides cover for deal-making."

"Because you can't do that without a searching-for-a-new-sex-slave party?"

"Not for illegal deals with people you would never normally socialize."

I snorted. "Backroom dealings you don't want your socialite buddies to know about."

He smiled. "There are vampires of all social levels at the parties. And because of their primary nature, no one can guess what happens behind closed doors. And since vampires have no social bias to one's sexual nature or preferences, not like in the human world, there's no judgment on what happens behind closed or open doors."

He almost wiggled his eyebrows on the last statement, and I wondered if there would be wild orgies for all to watch. I stared out the window, his words not helping to squelch my earlier nerves.

Sergi pulled into a long, circular driveway filled with other vehicles dropping off guests—limos, luxury cars, high-end sports models, and an equal amount of what looked like mom cars. But everyone walking up the steps to the mansion sporting several Greek columns was dressed in their finest. After Sergi parked, then opened my door, I glanced at Devon.

His gaze had turned molten as he perused me from head to toe, lingering on my legs and the juncture where they met my short dress. He raised his eyes to skim over my breasts, well hidden behind the silky material, ending at what had to be my stressed expression.

"And what exactly are we hoping to accomplish here?" I tried for a disinterested tone, but I think it was more of a squeak. I was supposed to be his Blood Ward and his lover, but wasn't sure how far he would take the game.

He smiled. "I do have a contact I need to catch up with, and I originally had a plan." He winked. "But now, I think we'll play it by ear."

Chapter Sixteen

DEVON WRAPPED an arm around my waist as I exited the limo. Sergi, playing the consummate chauffeur, nodded at both of us before returning to park the limo as if our outings were a typical event.

"Try to relax." Devon's warm breath tickled my ear. To those watching, which were more than I expected, the gesture would appear intimate. Perhaps the whispering words of wicked things he'd do to me later. I shook my head, pushing away the rogue thoughts.

"I'm not used to all the attention," I whispered back.

Devon pushed back strands of my hair and brushed a finger across my cheek. His smile could shatter hearts all over the city.

I smiled in return, hoping it didn't look more like a grimace as we walked up the steps. The evening air was cool, and I tried to shake off the goosebumps. Anxiety replaced the heat that had over-whelmed me earlier. The weather didn't seem to bother the vamps. Dozens of them loitered on the wraparound porch, and though they watched our approach, Devon barely registered them.

Before we entered the main doors, Devon's hand slipped from my waist to around my hip. I clutched my handbag and tried a timid smile. Was that what they expected? No. These were bold people with expansive desires, so once inside, I went for the haughty look my mother always wore at society events.

Devon stopped in the middle of the foyer. Now I understood why so many were on the porch. The place was packed, making the room extremely warm. While Devon scanned the room, I did the same, though I'm sure for different reasons.

"Let's take a walk through the first floor before going upstairs." Devon turned us to the left, heading for double doors that should lead to a large sitting room if the floor plan matched most mansions.

"Upstairs?" I lifted my gaze past the grand staircase bordered by decorative balustrades that seemed more fitting in a hotel.

He lowered his head to whisper in my ear. "It's not exactly what you think, but knowing this particular host, Gruber will have private rooms available on the third floor if you're interested."

I glanced around, refusing to blush. Several couples with straying hands fondled each other while in conversation with others. I turned on my broadest smile, and feeling bold, I squeezed Devon's firm ass. My response must have been unexpected because he seemed caught between shock and interest as his round eyes warmed with a soft blue glow. I thought he might kiss me, his gaze growing with intensity, until someone called his name.

"Devon. I can't believe my eyes."

Devon didn't respond as heat built between us in the jostling crowd. But the presence that stopped next to us drew his attention, and he pulled me closer as I slid my hand to his waist.

"Margo." Devon's tone was reserved, and though the woman's engaging smile didn't falter, something in her eyes flashed. If I'd been alone in a room with her, I'd want that dagger Devon kept insisting I carry.

"It's been years." She didn't seem to notice me as she planted a kiss on his lips and lingered longer than what most would consider polite, even in this sordid gathering.

I reflexively squeezed his waist tighter before realizing what I'd done, and Devon immediately pulled back. Interesting. Had his pulling away been a reaction to my response or just part of the charade? It bothered me that I wasn't sure which it was. And it was silly, of course. But I didn't have more time to ponder as Margo's hawk-like stare gave me the onceover as if I was something cloying that had stuck to Devon on his way in rather than his companion. His Blood Ward.

I stood taller, outwardly undaunted by her cold perusal. When she blinked, I was pleased by my petty win.

Devon pinched my hip lightly, just enough to consider the movement a caution. He didn't have to tell me this woman was dangerous.

"Let me introduce you to Cressa. My Blood Ward."

Margo didn't hold back her surprise. "Really." Her gaze took on a thoughtful expression, sizing me up like a meal rather than competition. Had these two been a thing?

She leaned in, and Devon's brick-like hold refused to let me back away. Was she sniffing me? Wondering if I was the right vintage, like some expensive port?

Her smile turned wicked and seductive. This woman couldn't be what Devon wanted me to emulate. I needed to have a long chat with him, because I was missing part of the playbook.

"It's been a long time since I've taken in a Blood Ward." She ran a hand down my arm, and I wasn't sure what aura I was giving off, but it seemed to entice her. "You are teaching her...everything?" When her hand grazed my breast, I realized what she'd meant, and it was all I could do not to lean toward her.

"Of course." He pulled me away. "But it's too early to be handling the merchandise."

Her laugh was intoxicating, and Devon's words of me being nothing more than a shiny bauble to be auctioned off irritated me. Her scent drew me in, and I must have leaned toward her again because Devon took a step back, pulling me with him.

"Stop it, Margo. I won't ask again." Devon's tone turned hard as ice, and after a moment, Margo shrugged.

"Can't blame a girl for trying." Before she turned away, she gave Devon another wicked grin. "Do keep me apprised when you're ready to turn her out. I'll pay extra if I can be her maker." She slid a hand down his cheek, rubbing her thumb over his lips. She winked at me before melting into the crowd.

I wasn't sure what had happened, but I was sorry to see her go. Devon pushed me through the crowd and down a busy hall, opening doors as he went. When he found what he was searching for, he shoved me inside. It was a closet. Spacious, but still a closet.

He found a light switch, and I glanced around, feeling a bit shell-shocked.

"Look at me," he barked.

I lifted my head, not sure why he seemed so angry. "Did I do something wrong?"

"No. I did." He lifted my chin higher, peering into my eyes. "Give it a minute, and your head will clear."

I wasn't sure why we were in a closet. Or what he was talking about. I felt fine.

After a moment, he pushed me to the wall before taking several paces back. "I should have expected it, but most wouldn't be so bold."

"What are you talking about?" My head did feel a bit fuzzy.

"I'd meant to teach you how to block during our first training session." He sighed. "I'd been too distracted." He leaned against the door, arms folded across his chest. "Vampires can mesmerize humans. You've heard that, right?"

Is that what had happened? "I've heard all kinds of things about vamps, but most of it has turned out to be wrong."

"Not this."

"When did she do it?"

"Staring into your eyes while she touched your arm."

"She was so irritating when she first came over, but then I

didn't want her to leave." I wrapped my arms around my waist. "I don't think I can do this."

"You can. One of the rules for a Blood Ward is no touching unless I give approval. Margo knows better. But I should have anticipated that with this type of party, someone might take advantage. We need to stick together all evening. Okay?"

"Staring into my eyes while touching. Got it." My dream of the two of us in the garden came rushing back. Is that what Devon had been doing in my dream? His stare had been just as intoxicating when he'd kissed me.

"Cressa."

"What?" I glanced up. "Sorry. Trying to get my game face back."

He smiled. "You can do this. Just stay close." When I nodded, he opened the door, checked the hallway, and grabbed my hand to lead us through more rooms.

We didn't talk much, but that didn't stop him from talking it up with everybody else. And they all commented on how long it had been since seeing him. Did everyone know everyone in the vampire world, or was there something special about Devon? People seemed to go out of their way to greet him. And he nodded politely, speaking more with some than with others, which I assumed meant he knew them better, or they were more worthy of his attention.

He shared introductions, and most had the same expression as Margo when they learned I was his Blood Ward. Either Devon hung in different crowds, or this guy didn't get out much. After the first few hellos, I noticed Devon's charm with some and his cool indifference to others, finally understanding that he knew the game and played it well. That little itch I got when I sniffed something interesting flared. It was obvious he wasn't just a notorious vamp with a raging temper who made deals with shifters. I hadn't asked Anna the right questions and suddenly couldn't wait for my next session with her.

After an hour, I must have been waning because Devon shifted his attention to me, signaling to the others he was done with the intros. I was grateful when he steered us to a table and lifted a hand to a waiter who dropped two glasses of champagne and a plate of appetizers on the table. Devon studied me, probably judging how long before I keeled over. I blamed the heels.

DEVON TOOK the opportunity to slide his hand to Cressa's ass as he directed her to a chair. He'd noticed her shoes bothering her but hadn't said anything. She'd refuse to sit if he mentioned anything that made her appear weak in this crowd. And while he'd kept a hand somewhere on her delectable body all evening, he knew it annoyed her. Yet, she played her role, changing from demure lover to ice princess, taking her cues from his own behavior as they made the rounds. Her ability to adapt fascinated him.

He slid her a side glance as she popped an appetizer in her mouth, her eyes closing with delight. She'd surprised him several times when she made possessive gestures—her hand closing around his arm, his waist. She'd even given his ass a squeeze every time Margo came into view. The garden dream was never far from his thoughts each time she touched him, and it reinforced his decision to discover what she was.

"You seem to be doing well." He turned his body toward hers and lowered his head, making the discussion appear intimate.

She nodded as she nibbled a cheese ball. "I remember most of the players you said were important, but I think I'm going to get Raul and Gruber mixed up. Gruber owns this house, right?"

"Yes. If you think this house is outlandish, you should see Raul's. He's the more flamboyant of the two. They're cousins, which explains most of the similarities. I got the impression Raul was irritated that Gruber matched his hair color. They must be feuding again."

"Ah, so those blue spikes of hair on Gruber was a ploy and not a sign of a bad hairstylist?"

He smiled. "I'm not sure."

She snorted and sipped water. "What's with this Margo?"

"Be careful of her. Our history is complicated, and if you must know, I can give you the highlights when we're home. There are too many ears here."

She scanned the room, her gaze darting to the ceiling before returning to the crowd. "And eyes." She resumed eating as if she'd merely been looking for someone.

"I've seen a camera in each room, but I don't know if they can pick up sound." Devon assumed they did but was curious what his new cat burglar saw.

"Based on the security panel at the front door, I'd say they're using a Gibson 5000 system. Top of the line. The cameras can zoom and are most definitely wired for sound, but with this crowd..." she waved a fork at the room, "even the Gibson wouldn't be able to narrow in on any particular conversation more than ten feet away. In a room with only one or two people speaking, it could probably pick up a growling stomach from across the ballroom."

Devon leaned back. "You noticed the security panel and could determine the system based on that?"

She shrugged before stuffing a crab-filled mushroom in her mouth. Her tongue slid out to lick her lips, and the dream flashed again. Devon felt a stirring in his lower regions that he'd been fighting all night. Did she have any idea the effect she had on him? He hoped not.

"I can't help but notice the security system when I walk into any house, even yours. It comes with the job. The high-end systems add their own modifications to the panel that makes them distinct. And, in reality, there are only a handful of vendors on the market worth their salt." She drank half her glass of water and nodded to

SEDUCTION IN BLOOD

one of the far corners of the ballroom where the banquet tables had been set up. "This room and two of the larger sitting rooms have two cameras." She gave him a dazzling smile. "Did I pass your test?"

"I admit I'm impressed." She had surpassed his expectations and appeared to be taking the job seriously.

She gave a half shrug but couldn't hide the soft rose that stained her cheeks. "Can I ask why everyone seems surprised to see you? And they were shocked when you introduced me as your Blood Ward."

Devon dropped his gaze and picked at his food.

"Something else to discuss in a different setting?" She snorted. "Always a mystery."

Before he could respond, someone called his name from several tables away. "Devon Trelane. How good to see you after such a long time. Are you still hiding in that dreadfully dour house?"

Devon's muscles tensed when he recognized the voice—Lorenzo. They'd just seen each other a day ago. But this was a public venue where Lorenzo could show how outgoing he was while hiding the animosity. Cressa must have sensed his tension because she laid a hand on his arm and gave it a light squeeze. Was she concerned for him or worried he'd vamp out? He gave her a tight smile, surprised to see a worry line on her forehead.

"And who have you been hiding from us?" Lorenzo strode up to the table, his eyes laser focused on Cressa. "Are the rumors true that you have a Blood Ward? And after the last one failed so miserably." His gaze devoured Cressa, who gave him a pleasant smile before dropping her gaze to review her plate, moving her fork around as if unable to decide which appetizer to select.

"I didn't know you enjoyed these types of parties." Devon attempted an even tone, but it was hard not to wipe the smirk off the man's face. *Ignore him. This was all part of the plan.*

"They've been rather dull of late, but now I'm glad I came. I could always use another female in my house."

Devon felt Cressa tense through the leg she'd leaned against his, but somehow she managed to pick up her champagne glass and appear nothing more than a timid companion as she sipped. He half expected her to toss the drink in Lorenzo's face.

"You're not looking for business partners here, are you?" Lorenzo asked. A sneer that could be mistaken for a bland smile crossed his face. "I'm sure I don't have to remind you of the censure laws."

Devon winced, wishing Cressa hadn't heard that. But what did he expect bringing her to these events? Someone was constantly rubbing his face in it. "I'm quite aware of the laws, as I'm sure you know."

Lorenzo smiled and refocused on Cressa. "I'm surprised anyone would want to be a Blood Ward to an outcast, but maybe she knows her beauty will be enough to place her in a more noble house."

If Cressa was paying attention, which Devon had no doubt she was, it would be impossible for others to tell. She nibbled the last of a sauteed shrimp, her tongue licking her lip before she swallowed. Then she ran a hand over his arm before sliding it below the table, resting it on his leg. Devon couldn't help but smile at Lorenzo.

"Was there something in particular you wanted?" Devon wanted the man to go away before Lorenzo said anything else he'd have to explain. But he enjoyed Lorenzo's annoyance at Cressa's attentiveness.

"Isabella noticed you were here and has called an informal meeting in the library. For some reason, she wants you there. Perhaps she's finally caught you at something. But never fear, if she has you hauled away, I'll be happy to ensure your Blood Ward finds her way home." His gaze sparkled with insincerity.

Devon wasn't concerned about Isabella. If she'd had an issue with him, he would never have left the council chambers the day before. It was more likely she wanted to remind everyone of the rules that Lorenzo tended to ignore. One thing was certain, Cressa would learn to use a dagger and carry it with her whether she liked it or not.

He glanced at her, momentarily lost in her adoring eyes. He gave her hand a squeeze, pleased with how well she played the game. Was that Anna's doing, or was Cressa a natural? He leaned in to whisper in her ear. "You're doing well. But I can't avoid this meeting."

She ran a hand down his cheek and drew closer. "I'll stay out of trouble. No staring if someone touches." Then she kissed his cheek before kissing his lips with the gentlest of touches, and he felt his cock stir. The minx.

Chapter Seventeen

I GAVE Lorenzo a slight smile before squeezing Devon's arm as the two men strolled off, but when the vamp glanced back at me, I changed it into a sultry smile. In reality, it might have come across as gas. Lorenzo was a handsome man, with bits of gray at the temples, and his suits were as tailored as Devon's. But the man was a leech. *He could use another female at his house.* What an ass.

Now that my feet had a chance to rest and I was fully sated with food and water, I decided to roam. My first stop was a restroom, and I found myself waiting in line between two vamps who hadn't seen each other for what sounded like years. I suppose in the vamp world, a decade or two was similar to a few months in my feeble human world. I leaned against the wall, eyes closed, soaking in as much information as I could, surprised when Devon's name came up. Good to know I wasn't the only one who couldn't get naughty thoughts out of my head whenever he smiled.

After taking care of business, I wandered the halls and rooms, slinking into dark corners or sticking to the edges. Most of the vamps either didn't notice me or didn't care. It's amazing how well you can blend in with poor posture. When I passed a hall where the library must have been, there were no less than eight vampires stationed a few feet apart, including Sergi. Everyone Devon was meeting with seemed to have their bodyguards. What I'd give to be a fly on that wall.

The second floor had an expansive open landing with couches and overstuffed chairs made for lounging. Four hallways led to gaming rooms, entertainment rooms, and a few bedrooms if the partially dressed vamps sneaking in and out of them were any indication. The private rooms were on the third floor, and I'd seen a set of elevators in the back of the house I assumed Gruber must use to get to his master suite. The second floor wasn't nearly as crowded as the first floor, but I still managed to appear inconspicuous. Devon's name cropped up in scattered conversations, and I realized the stares I'd received all night weren't because I was anything special. There were dozens of beautiful women for the guests to ogle. I was unique because I was on the arm of Devon Trelane, who apparently didn't get out much.

Then I remembered Lorenzo making a comment around censure. Devon was on the vampire naughty list. What did one have to do to piss off other vampires? From the tidbits of conversation I'd overheard, the guests were excited to see him, not fearful.

The gaming room had conjured all forms of kinky ideas in my head, and I was freakishly disappointed to discover it was a room with a billiards table, a dartboard, and several tables with multiple chess and backgammon games in process. I grabbed a glass of champagne and found a quiet place next to a large fern to watch a woman kick ass at billiards.

I didn't know how long I'd been watching when two men stopped on the other side of the fern. I kept my head down but managed to get a glimpse of blue-spiked hair through the large green fronds. It was Gruber, but the other man had his back turned toward me. His tall frame and broad shoulders blocked most of Gruber.

A groan and soft clapping turned my attention to the billiards table, where the woman had won her match. They were racking the balls for a new player when I heard Devon's name again. Had anyone noticed me as other than just eye candy? Reminding myself that was a good thing, I focused my attention on the two men while appearing to watch the games.

"I didn't know he'd be here. He hasn't been to one of these gatherings for years. And never with a woman, let alone a human." Gruber's high-pitched voice was easily recognizable.

"Perhaps the rumors of him going mad are true. Either way, it doesn't impact us, not with the Council keeping tabs on him." The big man had a deeply accented voice from somewhere in eastern Europe. While I couldn't precisely place it, it felt familiar. Maybe something I'd heard when I still lived with Christopher. He always had international business partners over for business dinners.

"I don't know if Lorenzo would agree, but now that Trelane is meeting with the Council, this is the best timing. We wouldn't want him to see you. Do you have the file?"

"I gave it to your bodyguard."

"Ah, that's why Henri disappeared." Gruber didn't sound concerned, likely a typical exchange for these two. "He must have tucked it in a safe place." The man sounded relieved.

"Hopefully, not in the library."

Gruber giggled, and the sound made my skin crawl. "That would have been interesting with Devon in the room, having no idea what lay in the safe. No. It's in my bedroom. Safe and sound for now."

When no one spoke for several seconds, I lifted my head to see if they'd left, but they were still there. What did they have on Devon?

"Do you have any other assignments for me?"

"Not at this time, but I'll have something next week. Let me take you out through the garage. My new Bugatti just arrived."

"I found a Brough Superiors on my last visit to Tripoli. You'll need to stop by."

Gruber clapped his hands. "I've heard those are very rare. Is the motorbike in good condition?"

The big man shrugged. "It needs a good cleaning, but I think it will look good in my foyer."

Gruber laughed. "You do enjoy showing off your prizes."

The men moved out of the room, and I breathed a sigh of relief. I doubted either would have been pleased to know I'd heard their conversation. Words I wished I hadn't heard. My curiosity screamed to find that file, while another part of me wanted to recover it for Devon. Was someone planning an attack against him? And a tinge of guilt stabbed me when I questioned if maybe Devon wasn't the good guy in whatever those two had been planning.

The dream crashed into me. The feel of Devon's arms as he pulled me close. The strength of his hold. The power in his kiss when I melted against him.

Stop it.

Yes, I was going in search of that folder. But only because you can't just wave a secret file in the face of a thief and not expect it to be stolen. I had job integrity. I smiled and slipped out of the room.

The staircase to the third floor was roped off, and with the number of people milling about, I'd never get upstairs unnoticed. The elevator was out of the question, but there had to be a back staircase for the house staff. And I found it right next to the elevator, completely unguarded. If I had the time, I would have searched for the uniform Gruber made his house staff wear, but I didn't know how long he'd be showing off his new car.

After five minutes of waiting in a storage closet, the hall cleared long enough to remove my heels and race up the stairs. I had no idea where Gruber's bedroom was, but after walking through dozens of mansions in the middle of the night, most master suites were located at the end of the hallway. As luck would have it, the same was true with this mansion. The room was at the opposite end from the elevator, which also made sense. Who wanted to hear the rattle of an elevator first thing in the morning? Assuming he allowed the staff to use it.

When I reached the master suite, I stared at the doorknob. It had a lock. Of course, it did, and I didn't have my tools. But Anna had stuck bobby pins in my hair that could work in a pinch.

It wasn't necessary. The door opened when I tested the doorknob, and I remembered that one of Gruber's men had been up here. He'd been sloppy.

Once inside the suite, I kept the lights off and allowed my eyes to adjust. As soon as I discerned shadows from the dim light leaking through the window blinds, I scanned the room, determining my plan of attack. A massive bed on the left, a seating area in front of a fireplace on the right, a pedestal with a sculpture in the corner, and the dressing room and bathroom on the far end. Dressing tables and armoires filled the rest of the space.

Starting on my left, I checked every cabinet and picture, searching for a hidden safe. I finished with the main room, irritated at not finding anything, and moved to the dressing room. I sulked as I gave the bathroom a quick look. No one kept a safe in the bathroom.

My shoes were killing me again, and I dropped onto the bed and leaned back, considering the room. I was confident I hadn't missed anything, but Gruber said the file was in his bedroom. When I thought about the conversation, he'd said there was a safe in the library, but he didn't specifically mention a second safe in his room. Gruber just said the file was safe and sound.

I stood and retraced my steps, looking at the room from a different perspective. I was heading back toward the fireplace when I walked past a pedestal with a sculpted head. I hadn't realized it was a head when I'd first glanced at it. But now, it seemed strange to have someone's head mounted in a bedroom. No accounting for taste—especially with the rich.

I backed up and studied the sculpted head. As far as I could tell, it was solid bronze. I lowered my gaze to the pedestal, which was easily ten square inches. Plenty of room to stash secrets, and Gruber could keep his eyes on it from his bed. I knelt and started tapping and pushing, hoping a spring door would open.

Time ticked away, encouraging me to move on and forget my curiosity. *Just a little longer.*

I had circled around to the last side when my thumb hit the door. It didn't pop open. Instead, the edge moved under my fingers. That thrill that raced through me on every job made my fingers tingle as I scraped at the door. My instincts paid off. I squinted as I stuck my hand in, hoping that Gruber hadn't left any traps. I wished I had my lockpicks and penlight, but Sorrento had taken them when he captured me. Devon would need to replace them if he wanted me to steal for him.

The first item I grabbed was a stack of bills. No mistaking that feeling—I'd lifted enough of them. The next two items were silk bags, which based on their weight and irregular edges, were stuffed with jewelry. Sorry that I didn't have a larger handbag to take a few items, I refocused on my goal.

A sound made me freeze, and I tilted my head. A door shut somewhere down the hall, and I held my breath, listening for the tread of shoes on carpet heading my way. After several minutes of silence, I huffed out a sigh and continued my search. There were more stacks of bills, and then stuck in the back was a folder. It barely fit, and the edges scraped as I wrestled it out from behind the stacks of cash and bundles of jewelry.

I stepped to the window, using as much of the meager light as I could to see what was inside. Two pages of handwritten notes, but not a letter. The edges of the pages appeared to have been torn out of something. A journal?

The light wasn't bright enough to make out any words, and I cursed my luck.

The doorknob creaked before something bumped against the door.

Shit.

I looked toward the bed, and without further thought, I darted for the dressing room. I slid into the room and dashed behind a plastic wardrobe bag as light filtered in from the bedroom. I worked to control my breathing. Music floated in from the lower floors. Whoever it was had left the bedroom door open. A light went on, and feet scuffled into the bathroom. A few minutes later, the light went out. After what seemed like an hour, but in reality was only a couple of minutes, the bedroom light went out and the door closed.

I leaned my head against the wall as a deep rush of air escaped. Whoever it had been hadn't stayed. They must not have noticed I hadn't closed the door on the pedestal. If they did, I doubt they would have left without contacting someone.

Devon was probably searching for me. I'd lost all track of time. But before leaving, I had to know if the pages were worth taking. I took a chance and flipped on the lights. Surely, no one would see lights from a dressing room in a closed bedroom. Regardless, I probably should have confirmed someone had left and not just gone to bed.

Worry crept over me, knowing I'd spent too much time in my search. My spidey senses made my gut clench, but I took the time to review the pages. I couldn't make sense of the almost child-like writing. The one word I did recognize made up my mind—Trelane. The name alone didn't mean anything, but it was close enough, especially after Gruber's delight over the folder.

Thankful there were only two pages, I folded the paper until it fit in my clutch. I shut off the light and crept into the bedroom, my gaze immediately flicking to the bed. I snorted. Someone had come in and turned down the bed. They probably put fresh towels in the bathroom. How quaint.

I stuffed the empty file folder back in the pedestal and shut the hidden door. After peeking into the hallway and seeing that the coast was clear, I raced down the hall for the servant's stairs. When I reached the second-floor staircase, the sound of Gruber's giggles floated my way. From the railing, I could see him weaving up the stairs, a young man and woman with him, one hanging off each side. I ducked into the first room with an open door and found myself in the gaming room.

A few men glanced my way, some taking a second look, but I ignored them as I strolled to the billiards table. I found a seat next to two men, who lounged in overstuffed leather chairs while drinking something clear. Vodka was my guess, but it could have been gin.

The man closest to me leaned over, his white-blond hair falling over half his face. "Would you like a drink?" His accent sounded Scandinavian.

"Vodka?" I asked. I really hated gin.

"What else?" He grabbed an empty glass from the stack on the table next to him and poured me two fingers. That seemed odd. They had their own bar?

"Now, you bet?" the other man said.

I'd only meant to get out of Gruber's way so he wouldn't see me and remember who I was after he discovered the pages were gone. What had I been thinking? I shrugged—once a thief. The man asking the question seemed to take my shrug as non-committal.

"Which one wins the game?" He pointed a chin to the billiards table.

My gaze turned toward the game in progress. I knew pool but not the rules for billiards, so I studied the players instead. A beefy man, who could have walked straight out of a biker bar, lined up a shot. The tall, wheaten-blonde woman was all class. Her makeup perfectly applied, it looked like she hadn't eaten in days, and her ruby-red lips gave the impression she was excellent at blow-jobs.

I glanced back at my new friend and smiled. "The woman."

I'd just finished my second drink, laughing at outrageous Nordic tales—turned out they were from Oslo—when someone grabbed my arm. I pulled away, but the grip tightened. I glanced up to Devon's fierce gaze, that icy-blue glow striking fear for a split second. Before I could react, the glow warmed to a darker hue, and for an instant, I caught his concern. He must have been searching for me.

One of my new friends rose, but his friend staid his arm and shook his head.

I stood—or maybe I was hauled up—and handed my empty glass to the closest man. "Sorry. I still say the woman will win." I winked at them over my shoulder as I was dragged—no mistaking it this time—away from the room. I figured it couldn't hurt to have friends if they were at the next party.

We'd just reached the first floor when shouts erupted from above. If I had to guess, I'd say it was the third floor, master bedroom. Gruber must have immediately checked his hidey-hole when he got his friends upstairs. I assumed after that there wouldn't be a three-way tonight.

Instead of being dragged, I pushed Devon to go faster. By the time we were out the front door, I was ahead of him, pulling him in tow. I noted his worried expression and the glances from those around us. We were making a scene. Not good.

I stopped at the top of the steps, long enough to put my hand on the back of his neck and pull him down for a kiss. I meant for it to be quick, just to give everyone an idea of why I might be in a hurry. Lustful play rather than a thief getting away. But when I pulled back, his grip tightened around my waist. He skimmed his tongue along my lips before forcing his way through. I didn't stop him, remembering the kiss from the dream, startled by how much it tasted the same. And for a heartbeat, before he kissed me again, I saw recognition in his eyes, as if he knew about the dream. Then he held me at arm's length, and I heard a car pull up.

"What did you do, Cressa?"

Chapter Eighteen

"WHAT WERE YOU THINKING?" Devon glared at Cressa before turning to stare out the window as the limo sped home, the pages crumpled in his hand. Did she have any idea how dangerous a game she played? What would have happened had she been caught? He wouldn't have been able to help, not without more of his people.

"I thought it was timely." Her snappy tone made him surly. "Besides, isn't that why I'm here? To steal stuff for you?"

He closed his eyes to the landscape rushing by. She was right. Why was he so angry? Was it that she dared to steal something without his knowledge or the fact he'd kissed her back? He would have done more if they hadn't been in front of dozens of partygoers. "You steal with careful planning. Not with some foolish idea in the middle of a party."

"What better time with everyone distracted?"

He couldn't argue with her reasoning, and it only fueled his irritation. "You had no backup. And there was no telling how long Gruber would be preoccupied. Neither Sergi nor I could have done anything to help. Consequences for stealing aren't as forgiving in our world."

When she didn't have a witty retort, he glanced over. She stared out the other window, arms wrapped around her waist, looking small. But when they passed under a streetlamp, he caught her tightened jaw and the thinning of her mouthwatering lips. She wasn't disheartened. She was angry. For some reason, her defiance intrigued him and lessened his own anger. "Who were your new friends?"

The question seemed to startle her, and after a moment, she shrugged. "I don't know. We were still in our getting-to-know-you phase before you dragged me out of the room."

He let the last piece go without comment, already tired of that conversation. "They looked familiar."

She snorted. "White-haired, almost twin vampires. You have a lot of those running around?"

He smiled. "More than you can imagine."

She returned a tentative smile, but there was still fire in her gaze. "You live in a strange world."

"More than you can imagine."

Cressa considered his statement and slowly nodded. "All I know is they're from Oslo, have some gruesome tales they think are hilarious, and love their vodka."

"The Larsen brothers?" Sergi commented from the front. "Why are they in town?"

"Was that who they were? I didn't recognize them with their long hair." Devon's fangs had lowered while watching Cressa with the twins, her head thrown back in laughter at whatever the vampires had been saying. That wasn't jealousy. Was it?

"It's been over two decades since they left Norway." Sergi eyed Cressa in the rear-view mirror. "And they told you stories?"

Cressa appeared surprised that Sergi spoke to her. He didn't talk to most people he didn't know well. She shrugged. "More like tales from the crypt, but yeah. It might have been the vodka."

"Alcohol doesn't affect vampires." Devon's comment was rote, distracted by this new information. "It might be good to see why the brothers are in town."

Sergi nodded as he turned the limo into the driveway.

When they entered the house, Cressa headed for the stairs, but Devon caught her arm. "Let's finish our discussion in my office."

She rolled her eyes but didn't say anything as she followed him with Sergi trailing behind.

Devon laid the stolen pages on his desk while Cressa scanned the ceiling. After seeing her at the party, he recognized her reflexive behavior for entering any new room. Probably something she'd picked up after years of thieving. Had she learned the practice because she was a thief or for another reason? If he considered his own habits, they were similar.

He dropped into his chair, more tired than he realized. The impromptu Council meeting at the party, something unheard of in his lifetime, had been Isabella's show of strength in reminding everyone that only facts, not rumors, could be brought forth in Council chambers. Then Cressa risked everything by stealing those papers, and it made him question his plans.

"I'm sorry."

Devon swiveled around to face her, surprised by her admission.

She clutched her purse in her lap, but she didn't drop her gaze, meeting his stare head-on. Not aggressive or complacent—just confident. The only thing giving away her true feelings was the tight grip on her purse. "I shouldn't have taken the pages. I risked your plans, even though no one noticed me." Her chin raised an inch. "I'm good at my job." She didn't hold the boldness for long, probably realizing it was wiser to stay on her conciliatory track. She dropped her chin and slumped in the chair. "I'm not used to waiting for someone else to make decisions for me. And when I heard Gruber talking, well, it seemed worth the risk."

He turned his gaze to the pages he'd straightened and laid on the desk. He pulled them over, tapping a finger on the corner of the first page. It had only taken a second for him to see his family's name in the recognizable handwriting. Though he hadn't read the pages, he knew Cressa had done him a great service. Possibly lifesaving.

"The one thing I've learned this evening is that you require weapons training."

When she opened her mouth, most assuredly to object, he waved her off. "Don't bother. You are now required to master, in the five days remaining, one weapon of your choosing. That is, one weapon from the options I present you." He glanced at Sergi. His good friend wasn't going to like this.

"Your time with Anna will be cut in half, and you'll finish your morning with Sergi. He will be your weapons trainer."

Sergi and Cressa stared at each other before returning their gazes to Devon.

"You need your rest." He flicked a hand at her. "Go to bed, Cressa."

The emotions racing across her face enthralled him and left him curious as to which one she'd leave with. If he'd been a betting man, he wouldn't know which emotion to place his money on— contrite, irritated, arrogant? Demure hadn't been on his radar and didn't fit her, which led him to believe she was probably planning revenge for his flippant statement. He'd be disappointed if she wasn't.

After Cressa left, Sergi poured drinks and handed one to Devon. "Why weapons and why me?"

Devon tapped the aged paper lying on his desk. "I don't know how recovering these plays into our plans, but these pages have proven one thing."

Sergi's brow lifted, but he remained silent.

"Gruber is not our ally."

Sergi grunted. "He always was squirrelly. It was only a matter of time before he showed his greedy nature."

"We need to use more of Cressa's talents. But if we're going to use her for the main event, we need her alive. Her martial arts skills are improving, but against a vampire, she'll need something more."

Devon drained his glass and stood. "As far as why you? I'm surprised you even asked." He stopped long enough to squeeze his friend's shoulder. "I need the very best to keep her alive."

THE DEWY GRASS was cool on my bare feet as I raced through the garden, my peals of laughter floating around me. I ducked under an arch of crimson roses, the scent heady, urging me on.

The rattle of leaves told me he was closing in, and instead of fear in the dark undergrowth, tingles of anticipation shot through me. A slow ache, deep in my core, grew as I rushed ahead, leading us farther into the garden. I recognized the grotto as soon as it came into view, but I'd barely reached the secluded spot before an arm grabbed me by my waist and swung me around.

He wrapped me in his embrace, his head lowering to meet my waiting lips, his eyes glowing silvery blue. The heat of his touch fired small eruptions of joy. It had been days since I'd seen him, worried over him, and when his tongue met mine, the empty days fell away, leaving only Devon and me. The two of us alone in our special place.

He trailed kisses down my neck, his tongue sweet rapture on my skin. How could one man fill me with such content that only a few days without him felt like weeks? His fangs scraped a heated path to my collarbone, and I arched into him, wanting his hands on me, his skin on mine. I opened my eyes, and with my head thrown back, all I saw was the full moon. The velvet sky wrapped around the silver orb as if lovers. I ran my fingers through his hair, pulling him to me, daring him to bite.

For long days wandering the property, I fretted over the not knowing. No one had any word as to his whereabouts. It had been the plan, but I hadn't been the only one suffering in his absence. And now he was here. Safe.

I ran my hands over his muscled shoulders, ripped with tension as he held me close. I breathed in his heady scent and licked the sweet spot at the dip in his collarbone. He shivered, and I felt a nip on my ear. Smiling at his hungry response, I plucked at the buttons of his shirt, needing to feel his skin on mine.

He pushed my nightgown down until he freed a breast, his fangs teasing the nipple before his hot lips suckled and pulled. The erotic sensation scattered my thoughts to nothingness. The buttons no longer within reach, I ran my fingers through the soft waves of his hair. I gripped the locks tighter when his hand reached under my nightgown and found the wetness between my legs.

I opened to him, wanting more, unable to wait. The heat of his lips on my breasts drove me to a fevered pitch.

Cool air brushed my breast before he replaced my nightgown and stepped back, pulling me with him. A single brow rose in his silent invitation, or more likely a dare. His wicked smile revealed the tips of fangs. He knew I'd play.

He led me to the edge of the lake. Across the pond, a large party was in full swing. His entire family milled under a large canopy, the figures dancing and playing under lit torches and colorful lanterns.

Music drifted to us, and Devon slid an arm around my waist while taking my right hand. He swung me around, and we swayed to the slow and sultry rhythm. I felt his hardness pressing into me, but we were content in this moment. We held each other, and no one could hurt us. I laid my head against his chest, and he rested his cheek against my hair. We moved as one. There was still danger outside our refuge, but for now, for this one night, it was only the two of us, breathing in each other's essence. I wanted to remember our time together, when no one else intruded, in case it never came again.

When the song ended, he stepped back, pulling me with him

as he led me down a dirt path to a grassy knoll under an oak tree. A blanket lay on the grass, facing a quieter portion of the lake and lit only by the moon. Before stepping farther, he leaned to reach behind me. I heard a soft snap. He offered me a crimson rose. The petals were a deep, blood red, and without a single blemish. The rose's heady scent filled the space between us, and the glow in his eyes darkened with desire. The longing between my legs returned.

"Let me see all of you, Cressa. It's been so long." He pulled me to the edge of the blanket.

I didn't utter a word and might have nodded. But I didn't stop him when he pulled the nightgown over my head. I stood there, his gaze a gentle caress as my body heated with need.

I reached for the buttons on his shirt to complete my earlier task. When the last button was freed, I ran my hands up his chest, sliding the shirt off his shoulders. At last, there were no barriers between us. I circled his nipples before tasting each one. Then I reached for his neck, pulling him down to me.

His kiss, needy and filled with longing, devoured me as he pulled me down to the blanket. Then he moved away, standing to stare down at me, his manhood straining for release. When he didn't move, I smiled, knowing how to get him to return to me. A warm breeze tickled my skin as I ran a hand over a breast, moving slowly to the spot between my legs.

Boots then pants hit the ground, and he stood over me, fully naked, his shaft thick with need, his gaze lit with love. He fell to his knees, and his day-old stubble rubbed against my inner thigh as he dipped his head to run a tongue over my overly sensitive skin. His fangs grazed the same area as he moved up until he reached...oh my god...that was it. I opened my legs, aching for more, the feel of his tongue on me and then in me. No one else had ever taken me to such heights, to places where time didn't matter and no one existed but him and me.

Then we were entwined, our lips demanding, unable to get enough of the other. Had it been days or years since we'd been together? I held on with an urgency I'd never known. Suddenly, time was against us. The weight of it dragged me down as his arms slipped away, his face fading to shadows.

"Cressa! You're going to be late for your session with Anna."

I lifted my head, which had been face down in my pillow. My brain was fuzzy, but I distinctly smelled roses and an intensely masculine scent—something spicy.

"You'll need your breakfast if you're training with Sergi before lunch."

I face-planted back into the pillow. It had happened again. And when I touched a hand to a sensitive spot on my thigh, I felt the abrasion. As if someone had rubbed their whiskers against it. I remembered the glow of his gaze as he watched me from between my legs. How was he doing this?

Chapter Nineteen

"Cressa, at least let me know you're alive in there."

I shot up, the sheet slipping down over bare breasts. I swiped along the bed, searching for my nightgown. Where was it? I jumped out of bed, almost tripping over the nightie that had fallen to the floor.

"I'm here." My throat was raw and sounded more like a cough. "I'm awake," I tried again. "I'm not hungry. Go away." The last part made me feel bad. Lucas didn't deserve my attitude, but I needed alone time.

I grabbed the nightgown and threw it on before diving back under the covers. What the hell?

The dream.

The thought of it instantly created an intense yearning between my legs. When I closed my eyes, I could see his warm hands over me as he torched my skin with his tongue and took me over the edge with the tips of his fangs. My eyes shot open. I reached between my legs. Yeah, I was wet. From just now, or whatever the hell happened last night?

I went to bed with my nightgown on, still not feeling comfortable sleeping naked in a house full of vampires. Well, maybe not entirely full of vamps, but there were enough of them walking around.

I'd been so tired. And the kiss.

Not those from my dream, but the one in front of Gruber's house. We'd raced out so quickly, and with people milling about and Gruber screaming, I didn't want anyone to remember us running like thieves. I only needed a distraction, and the kiss was the best option I could come up with at the time. The tea party had been filled with sexual innuendos from the minute we'd entered the house. It only made sense to go with the theme for the evening.

I'd meant for the kiss to be chaste. Just a sweet taste of promised expectations, but Devon's lips had tasted so good. His shocked expression, then his arms clamping around my waist, had only encouraged me. Who had slipped tongue first? I couldn't help but grin because I think it might have been me. Then his shock disappeared, and he returned the kiss. And the second kiss was more powerful, more erotic. So much so, the entire car ride home filled me with overwhelming mixed emotions. I thanked the gods we could fight about my rash action. Otherwise, I might have thrown myself at him, ignoring Sergi's frowns from the front seat.

That had to be why I'd had such an erotic dream. I must have ripped off my own gown because there was no other explanation. Now that I had time to consider my current state, why did it feel like I'd actually had sex last night? My legs weren't sticky from that type of exploit, but when I touched my cheek, I distinctly remembered the feel of his scratchy whiskers. I loved the roughness of them against my inner thighs.

Oh my god.

I threw the covers across the bed and raced for the shower, making a quick side trip to the door. It was locked. Devon must have a key. Had he drugged me? I stood under the hot water until I heard pounding at the door. I called out a greeting, not ready to leave the false security of the shower.

"It's Anna. I'm leaving a tray by your door. We need to start in thirty minutes. In the library."

"Okay," I shouted and dropped my head to the cool tiles. At least I wouldn't have to face him yet.

The tray held a bowl of oatmeal, a fruit cup, and a small carafe of coffee. I ate and tried to recall everything that happened after locking my door last night. Nothing special. The only alcohol I'd had was at the tea party, but my senses had been fully engaged for the robbery. I'd had two drinks with the Oslo twins. Had they drugged me? If so, would Devon had known? That seemed unlikely.

Maybe there were other ways a vamp could mesmerize a person, and he'd put some hoodoo spell on me in his office. No. Not with Sergi there. Nothing added up with the sedate lifestyle the vamps in this house appeared to lead. It could be a ruse, though why bother if he just wanted to have sex? Why the game? There were so many other ways to go about it, including drugging me. There just hadn't been an opportunity for him to do that.

At the crux of it all, I had no one to ask about what was happening. I slipped on my workout clothes, groaning when I remembered my new sessions with Sergi.

This was day three. Only four more days and I would walk away from this world. From Devon. And I was okay with that. I ignored the sense of regret and the loss of something important as I ran downstairs to meet Anna.

I STARED at the array of hand weapons displayed on a table of white linen. If the linen was meant to dampen the deadliness of the weapons, it wasn't working. I didn't like carrying weapons, terrified I might kill someone—or myself. A few quick spins and kicks had always gotten me out of scrapes before.

A glance at Sergi confirmed that Devon wouldn't take no for

an answer. I was grateful for the shortened sessions with Anna, who'd changed her lessons from which fork to use at any given time to which ensemble to wear at a particular event. All of it was boring as hell, but I wasn't convinced time with Sergi was a fair trade.

For the last hour, he'd grudgingly discussed in excruciating detail each weapon Devon had considered appropriate for me. There were three different pistols and various sizes of knives, and if those didn't provide a solid opportunity to kill myself, the throwing stars would definitely get the job done. Instead of one or two sharp edges, they sported several.

"I don't like any of these. I'm better off with the moves Devon and Lucas are teaching me." Though my gaze lingered on a bone-handled dagger that had fit well in my hand. I couldn't do all the fancy moves Sergi had demonstrated with the knives, but the weapon was beautiful enough to steal for a private collection.

He grunted, a deep sound that, combined with his brows moving into a straight line, clearly conveyed his dismissal of my opinion. "Vampires are twice as strong as you. And while martial arts will work in distracting and evading many, if not most, situations, there will come a time when you will simply be outmaneuvered. You won't kill a vampire with any of these weapons, but you'll do enough damage to escape."

I nibbled my lip as I considered his words. After watching Devon and Lucas spar, no amount of training would make me vampire fast. And witty remarks wouldn't work like they might with human security patrols.

"Here." He picked up the bone-handled dagger and handed it to me hilt first.

The hilt was cool to the touch, and like before, fit as if made for me. I considered Sergi's wry smile. He was rather charming when he did that, yet it irritated me. "What?"

He shook his head and packed the remaining weapons into a duffel. "Devon said you'd choose that one."

"I didn't select it. You handed it to me."

He grunted. "You've been ogling it since the first time you picked it up."

I opened my mouth to object, then grunted back.

His lips quirked, and his smile widened. "Protect yourself."

I'd dragged my sorry ass off the mats enough times to know these vamps meant business. I immediately stepped back into a fighting stance, my new dagger held out in front of me.

His smile morphed into a leer as he circled me. I turned with him, never giving him my back. Something didn't feel right, and his gaze watched my hand with the dagger. I was holding it wrong. Or maybe he was psyching me out.

He licked his lips. "I think we're going to miss lunch." Then he dove for me.

THE LEAVES RUSTLED with the ocean breeze, and I mentally surveyed my body as I stared up from my prone position on the grass. Every muscle ached, and I took advantage of the day's warmth in hopes of restoring my body after the earlier session with Sergi. I wouldn't have thought learning to wield a dagger could be so exhausting or that I would discover new muscles that even Devon's training hadn't uncovered. They must have been dormant since my birth.

With my body melting into the grass, I was left with nothing but my thoughts. For the first few minutes, I replayed the sparring session, trying to understand what I did wrong and where I could have done more damage, making notes for the next session. It didn't take long for the garden dream to worm its way into my conscious. Try as I might, there wasn't anything I could do about it other than face it.

If I closed my eyes, it brought me closer to him. The heat of the sun as searing as the touch of his hands. He reeled me in as if the dream had never been broken.

I opened my eyes and focused on the stirring leaves, the sound similar to the scrape of cloth on cloth, then skin on skin. His lips roving over my breasts, the feel of his tongue, then fangs. His scent drifted over my wrought senses—so close, so familiar.

"Is this where you hide?"

I sat up quickly, throwing a hand across my chest as if I were naked. My aching muscles made me grimace. When I stared up at Devon's bemused expression, there was a glint of intimacy that made me wish I had a jacket to cover myself as his eyes roamed over me. It wasn't a leer but a glimmer of appreciation, which didn't make me feel any better.

"That's me. Hiding in plain sight." I forced my fingers to release the tight grip on my shirt and attempted a weak smile.

"Or maybe this was as far as you could crawl after a session with Sergi?" His sensuous lips curled into a knowing smile.

"I found new muscles I didn't know I had." I scowled. As expected, my complaint slid off him like rain off a slicker.

"Sergi likes to push, especially if he thinks he has a student who won't give it their all. He tells me you were a sufficient student."

"Sufficient. Thanks."

Devon leaned against the tree, arms folded across his chest. "High praise coming from him. I wouldn't be so hard on yourself."

I shrugged a shoulder. "I'll be better tomorrow."

He shook his head. "You get the day off tomorrow, as well as the rest of today. Let your muscles heal." He paused and glanced toward the ocean. "Lucas can take you to your apartment to pick up anything you might need. Or anywhere else you might want to stop."

I pushed my hair back with both hands as I studied him. "Why?"

He shook his head. "You're not a prisoner here, Cressa. I've told you that. But I also can't have you running all over town until the mission is completed. That doesn't mean you have to hide. Although, I'd rather not have anyone who knows you as Pandora discover you're posing as my Blood Ward."

I thought about that and nodded. "I get it. I wouldn't mind seeing Ginger. Make sure she's okay."

He hesitated. "No one else?"

"No." I said it so fast it wasn't until after it was out of my mouth that I wondered if he thought there was another man. Would it have been better to let him believe there was? Would the dreams stop? I decided the best policy was honesty. Once the lies started, they'd be hard to keep track of. If he touched on a topic I didn't want to talk about, I'd let him know. Easy enough.

Tired of his penetrating stare, I shifted my gaze toward the ocean and then glanced up at the house. Drapes fluttered in the third-floor window. "Who lives in that third-floor room?"

His gaze flew to the house, but his answer was slow and practiced. "No one."

I snorted. "The drapes just moved."

"Even empty rooms collect dust. Letty sends a girl around to all the empty rooms to keep them clean in case I have unexpected guests."

His answer made sense. My mother always had staff cleaning empty rooms as if someone had thrown a party and left invisible filth behind. But I'd distinctly remembered the door handle moving. If it had been a housekeeper, they would have come out. But if I asked about it, he'd know I'd been snooping after he'd clearly told me to stay away from the third floor.

Then another thought came to mind after sneaking around Gruber's house. "Can Lucas drive me by my supplier?"

His lips rose into a half-smile. "You're not using, are you, Cressa?"

I rolled my eyes, thankful he was going to make this easy. "He's the best security man in the business."

He studied me with that watchful look that suggested he knew more than I thought he did. But I might be imagining it, too overcome between the dreams and the thrill of having my lockpicks. I had to admit I wasn't the average woman.

He disengaged from the tree and walked toward me, stopping long enough to stare down at me. His hand brushed over my hair before he brought my chin up to meet his gaze. "Be careful, Cressa, of whatever games you're playing. I guarantee I play better than most." He scraped his thumb over my lips, zapping a flash to my core that heated my cheeks. Then he walked away.

Dangerous games, indeed.

Chapter Twenty

THE STRESS DRAINED AWAY when Devon drove past the gates of Oasis. This was his true home, unknown to all but his vampire family and most loyal friends and staff. The Council and the rest of vampire society assumed his home was the dreary coastal mansion that had been his childhood residence, filled with memories best kept buried. Yet he was still tied to the relic, thought he would be forever until Cressa came into his life. She was the single person who could free him from the place, but only if he uncovered her secrets.

After driving along a winding driveway, he crested a knoll that looked down on the two-hundred-acre estate. A lake, partially hidden behind trees, lay some distance behind the main house. Smaller bungalows were strewn along the wandering paths, providing additional guest quarters for his family. Every room on the estate would be filled to overflowing.

Devon spent months designing the house built of wood, stone, and glass. Its modern design had the feel of a massive two-story bungalow that blended with the natural environment of forest and meadows. A home more in tune with an alpha shifter than a vampire. But that was part of his future plans, something only a handful of his closest allies were aware of—vampires and shifters whose political leanings were his own.

He parked the car in front of the broad veranda with tall wood columns and an open porch that skirted the front and sides of the house, eventually drawing people to the tiered back patio. He tossed the keys to a vampire on his security team and ran up the steps, eager to be home. One of the two hand-carved front doors opened before he reached them, and standing inside the cream-colored foyer was his administrator—a six-foot-tall vampire who ran the house in his absence.

"Simone." Devon reached out, and the two hugged. He gave her a tight squeeze before pulling back to arm's length, his hands resting on her broad, powerful shoulders. "You look wonderful, ma chérie."

Her smile showed perfect white teeth and a bit of fang. Of Somalian heritage, she carried the stature of royalty, the lean, powerful body of a fighter, and the sultry beauty of a runway model. She'd spent the last two decades in Milan, Tokyo, and New York and dressed like it. Her hair was kept short and was currently dyed white, matching her flowing caftan suit.

Devon moved to rest a palm on her cheek. "It's so good to see you. It's been too long."

Simone's eyes shimmered with what Devon knew to be tears, but his favorite vampire merely blinked them away. "Your house welcomes you home, Father."

Devon's lips twitched at the reverence. "Really, Simone. I'd expected something less formal from you."

She turned to walk with him, their arms entwined as they strolled to the main living room off the foyer, the one usually used for greeting guests. Two large sitting areas filled the space, sharing a large, circular fireplace set in the middle of the room and floor-to-ceiling windows that showed off the tiered patio. During the day, automatic blinds lowered from the ceiling. The shades filtered varying levels of light, depending on the sensitivity of the occupants. At night, outdoor lighting displayed the stunning beauty of the backyard all the way to the woods. Today, Simone had left the blinds at fifty percent, enough for most vampires to feel comfortable and adequate light to make Devon happy.

"Wasn't it you who said I needed to hold my emotions in check?" Simone led him to the bar and poured two drinks. They sat near the unlit fireplace, her in the comfortable, dark-leather chair, and Devon on the matching sofa to her right.

"Not all the time. And certainly not with family." He sipped the scotch while studying his administrator and most cherished friend.

She smiled. A feral image that intimidated people but wasn't meant to. Simone couldn't help that her natural smile came across like someone ready to take your head off, but it suited them both for her role. It wasn't her smile you had to worry about, it was when her fangs were fully exposed. By then it was too late to run. She carried incredible patience for idiocy, much more than Devon, but once someone stepped over that line, they deserved whatever action she took. And a break of trust—that didn't get past any leader.

She leaned over, her hand running over his. "The new butler seems to be judging my behavior."

Devon squeezed her hand and frowned. His original butler had been human and died peacefully in his sleep a few months earlier. "I thought Spencer would fit in. He's not normally one to judge." Spencer had been in his employ for several years and had been his valet when he traveled.

Simone frowned. "Really? He's always staring and seems to jump from the shadows."

Devon threw his head back and laughed, enjoying the first unencumbered discussion he'd had in weeks. "I think it's more infatuation." At Simone's scowl, he only laughed harder. "I'm sorry, ma chérie, but why is it you can't see your own beauty?

When I walked in just now, I thought I must be meeting the Queen of Sheba herself."

"She was Ethiopian."

He shook his head, unaffected by her tart response. She'd had a horrible life as a child, and it was worse after she'd been turned. When Devon had found her in the employ of a miserly and spiteful vampire, he convinced the man to allow Simone to join his family. It took years for her to learn that not everyone was cruel. It was decades more before she found her footing. A century and a half later, she still didn't understand the power she held with her beauty alone. And maybe that was okay for now. But she would need to harness all of her assets before she found her true potential as the leader of a House.

Simone sat back and sipped her chilled vodka, her shoulders relaxing as she considered his words. "You're telling me he's following me around and staring because he's enthralled by me?"

He smiled and patted her hand. "I think you need to look in the mirror more frequently, but I'll have a talk with him."

"No." Her quick response brought a raised brow from Devon. "I must learn to handle these things myself." She gave him one of her seductively wicked smiles. "I'll be nice. I need to spend more time with him. Let him get to know me as a person and not the administrator."

"You're a wise woman, Simone, and you will rightly deserve your House." When he saw her eyes turn liquid, he stood, not wanting her to feel weak. "Let's finish our drinks in the study. Sergi should be here soon. Has everyone else arrived?"

"Everyone except Bella and Jacques. They should arrive shortly after midnight." Simone walked him by the bar to top off their glasses before continuing arm in arm down the long marble-floored hallway.

"Problems with their assignment?"

She shrugged. "A delay, but their information is better suited for your ears alone. Dinner is planned for ten in the banquet hall."

The hall could fit two hundred, so there would be plenty of room for his small family of seventy-five.

He nodded. "Lucas won't be able to make it. I have him on another assignment."

"With your new Blood Ward?"

Devon grimaced. "I meant to discuss that with you before now, but I'll catch you up once Sergi arrives."

A young woman, no more than sixteen, all but ran to them. She bowed when she reached them, her eyes looking up through long raven bangs. "Sire, I was told to tell you Sergi was waiting for you in the study."

Devon lifted her chin. "Rise, child." He studied her. She looked familiar. He turned to Simone. "Lydia's girl?"

Simone smiled and gave a slight nod.

She was a Sangre Azul—a blue blood. True vampire. Not turned. They were precious and, over the last century, not as rare. No one knew why the natural procreation rate had improved, and while studies continued, most didn't want to question good fortune. "You're Tamara. I didn't recognize you. You've grown since I last saw you."

"Yes, sire. Maman says it has been a decade since you last visited us." She stood but continued to bow her head.

He lifted her chin again. "First, my name is Devon, not sire. You may call me Father in public and in private if you prefer. Second, no one bows in this House. You are all equal here. Some just have more privileges due to rank and seniority. Never lower your head to anyone in this household, even if being reprimanded for something. And never lower your head to anyone outside our House, including members or leaders of other Houses. If someone is your elder and deserves your respect, never look them in the eye unless directly spoken to, and always respond with reverence. But never lower your head again. Understand?"

She gazed up, her eyes filled with a mix of confusion and delight. "Yes...Father." Then she smiled.

"You have a beautiful smile, Tamara. Now, go get some rest. It will be a long night, and I'm sure you won't want to miss any of it."

"Yes, Father. I'm looking forward to it." She began to bow, remembered she shouldn't, gave him an apologetic grin, then raced off as quickly as she'd arrived.

"Lydia has made great progress with her." Simone took the lead, pulling Devon down the hall as he nodded greetings to others.

"Make sure she gets everything she needs to continue Tamara's education. I'd like to know if the child has revealed any special talents yet. If so, I want to see a quarterly report on the growth rate and potential. And, as always, I'll want your opinion included with each report. We must take good care of our Tamara."

"I'll see to it."

They turned into the study, this one twice as large and brighter than the one on the coast. Today the blinds had been darkened, the lamps and fireplace lit to provide a warm glow to the room. Sergi stretched out on a sofa next to the fireplace with three glasses, a bottle of scotch, and a bucket of ice that chilled the vodka. When he heard their approach, he filled the glasses and pushed them across the low table. He picked up his vodka, drank half, then refilled it before leaning back.

After Simone sat, Devon dropped into the chair between the two vampires and gave Sergi an irritated glance. "I have the feeling you didn't bring me good news."

He gave a non-committal grunt with a shrug of one shoulder. Then he drank a third of the glass.

While Sergi gathered his thoughts, Devon spent ten minutes bringing Simone up to speed on Cressa and how she came to be in his employ. He didn't have to explain the importance of Cressa being the best cat burglar in the region.

"Have you already discussed your plans with Decker?" Simone asked. She was one of the few who knew his entire history with Decker.

"We discussed that it was the right time to make a move, but I haven't shared the entire plan. He knows I have a thief on retainer, but that's all. He doesn't know who the thief is, and he would never consider it might be a woman." Devon turned his attention to Sergi, rotating his glass in his hands as he considered his friend. "Tell me what you have."

"It's still not much, but I was able to speak to a handful of family friends. I claimed to be a reporter for one of the tabloids."

"And you thought that would open doors?" Simone seemed appalled at the idea. Yet, curiosity lurked in her gaze, and Devon knew she would be filing the information away for her own use.

"Easier than it should be. Humans have no problem talking about their friends and associates if they think it's anonymous." Sergi placed a finger on his lips. "All hush hush and all."

Devon resisted drumming his fingers with impatience. He focused on the amber liquid in his glass, wondering what Cressa was doing while he listened to a report regarding his investigation into her background. The pang of guilt surprised then irritated him. She had vital information worth any cost. But as soon as he thought it, he knew it wasn't true, and he sneered. Sergi must have thought it was meant for him, so he hurried on with his report.

"There's no love lost for Christopher Underwood, Cressa's stepfather. Her mother is the perfect hostess, wife, and mother, apparently in that order." Sergi paused when Devon raised a brow. "That was one of the few things everyone agreed on. From there, the opinion of the two daughters differs greatly. April is the biological daughter of Christopher and Willa Underwood. She's five years younger than Cressa and the darling of the family. Most people like her; however, many of them believe her to be manipulative. A trait from her father. Everyone agrees April and Cressa are close, even though Cressa was a troubled child. She settled down when she turned ten, and her grades were above average until she turned sixteen. She had a sealed juvenile record for theft when she was seventeen. Nothing major and never did time. Her stepfather has many important friends, so friction between the two began almost immediately. Seems Underwood was embarrassed by Cressa's unseemly activities. However, when I pushed a couple of her old friends, they claimed she started stealing from her stepfather much earlier. From what I gather, she stole frequently and only got caught a handful of times. It took Underwood some time to uncover her habit."

"So our little thief started early." Devon rubbed his chin, a new appreciation for Cressa shaping a different image. "That certainly explains how she became so good at it."

"There was some other trouble that occurred the day before Cressa graduated, but if anyone has details, they're not talking. She left home the day after graduation. Underwood tells his friends he kicked her out after making a promise years before to let her graduate. Which she did, after regaining her above-average grades."

"A smart thief. Experienced. But does she have the right connections?" Simone asked though she didn't seem all that impressed.

"The respect of her street name implies she does," Devon replied, then turned to Sergi. "Best to confirm."

Sergi nodded. "As far as her biological father, I have no further information. But I have a couple of leads that should provide something."

"And why do we care about that?" Simone asked.

Sergi stared at his drink, which Devon appreciated, but there was no reason to shut Simone out, and she would be hurt otherwise. "She might have more abilities than just burglary." He waited, anticipating Simone would put it together. He hadn't meant to hold anything back from his friends, but the dreams were too intimate and would break an unspoken trust with Cressa. So, he'd only told Sergi and Lucas that she could dream walk and that their meetings were short, which was true enough.

"You think she can help Lyra." It wasn't a question, just a sad sigh that happened to escape Simone's lips. Her gaze was full of pity, and he glanced away.

"I can't tell you much at this point, but you'll know everything soon. I promise." He waved a hand at both of them. "You know I appreciate the patience the two of you have with me. Lucas as well." They nodded, and Devon sighed inwardly, thankful for his friends. At some point, they might not be as understanding. "If there's any possibility that Lyra can be helped, I have no choice but to follow that path."

Chapter Twenty-One

I STARED out the window as Lucas drove from the lush coast manor to the ghetto where my apartment and life existed. The joy I'd felt at going home to see Ginger faded as the neighborhoods grew dingy with trash piled in the gutters, gang bangers trading on the corners, vacant shops with boarded windows, and finally to the four-story apartment building with the familiar graffiti. Away three days and I'd already grown accustomed to life at Devon's estate.

Lucas followed behind as I mounted the steps. I noticed the freshly painted red dick on the left side of the front door with the name Greco written below the sadly curved image. Bulldog patrolled the area, but the neighborhood belonged to Greco. Apparently, someone was attempting to squeeze in, and Bulldog had missed the taggers. Or maybe not, and we wouldn't see any new graffiti for a while.

I cringed when I found the front door keypad smashed again and pushed the door open to the horrific odors inside—piss and vomit mixed with the cloying scent of gardenias from Margo, the landlady. She was a wiry seventy and carried a bat when collecting rent. No one messed with Margo.

When we reached the third floor, I stood in front of my apartment and debated whether to use my key or knock first. Since my stepfather had stopped by before, I decided knocking would be less of a shock. I'd called Ginger as soon as Devon had released me for the day, but she hadn't answered. After the third knock with no answer and sensing Lucas's impatience, I dug the apartment key out of my back pocket. It had been the only personal item on me during the heist, other than my backpack. It seemed Sorrento hadn't cared to confiscate it when he captured me. What a guy.

The apartment was dark inside, and Lucas put a hand on my arm before I took more than two steps. I felt it too. The apartment wasn't as empty as it appeared. He closed the front door then moved in front of me as he scanned the tiny living room and then the kitchen, which was blocked off by two screen dividers. We moved down the short hallway, and I pointed to the closed door on the left, which was my room. After a quick check of the ten-by-ten bedroom and simple closet, he shook his head. When he tried to move in front of me at the second bedroom door, I pushed him away. If Ginger was in there with her headphones on, the last thing she needed was to be surprised by a vamp.

I knocked on the door. "Ginger? It's me, Cressa."

I heard a gurgle, something of a moan, and tore through the door before Lucas could stop me. He was so close behind me that I felt his breath on my neck.

Ginger was in the opened closet, huddled with a blanket and her stuffed bear. What the hell?

I dropped to a knee in front of her. "Ginger." I kept my voice low, horrified by her tears. "What happened?" Then I noticed the bruise forming on her cheek. I turned her face to get a better look in the dim light filtering through her curtained window.

"Who did this?" I felt the old anger brewing. "Did Christopher do this?"

She shook her head then shrugged. Her gaze moved to Lucas and widened.

"This is Lucas. He's a friend. Tell us what happened."

Ginger stared down at her stuffed bear—a leftover childhood toy her father had given her before he died. She blew out a long, exaggerated sigh and wiped her eyes before pushing her hair back. "It was one of Christopher's guys. Said he was looking for you—for something you stole."

"Let's get you up." I grabbed her hands and pulled her up, letting the blanket and bear fall to the ground.

"I don't know why I'm so fucked up on this." She gave a shaky laugh. "It's not the first time we've had a break-in. Someone looking for a fix."

I glanced at Lucas. His emotions were shielded behind a blank expression, and there was no judgment in his gaze.

"I'll check the halls and stairways. Lock the door behind me." He nodded toward Ginger before leaving.

I locked the front door before guiding Ginger into one of two chairs in the kitchen and put a tea kettle on. Lucas returned by the time I handed Ginger a mug of minty tea, one of her favorites.

She took a sip before glancing up. "What did you steal, Cressa?"

I shook my head. "The last thing I took from Christopher was a thousand dollars in cash when I left home. I haven't stepped in his house since. I meet April behind the pool house whenever she contacts me, but it's been three months since I've heard from her." I shook my head. "If he's missing something, he must have assumed I took it." I hated having to contact my stepfather, but this shit had to stop.

I could see Ginger didn't quite believe me, so I grabbed both her arms, sloshing the tea, and stared her straight in the eye. "It wasn't me. I know how dangerous he is, and I would never put you at risk. You know that, right?"

She closed her eyes and set the mug down. "I know. This guy, he scared me. He was big and ugly, like one of those bouncers they have at the Lowdown." The Lowdown was a dive four blocks away where we hung out when we tired of our tiny apartment. It's where Bulldog kept an office.

"I didn't know Christopher used that kind of muscle."

"Is this going to be a problem?" Lucas asked.

When I turned on him, fire blazing from my glare, he raised his hands. "You know your first duty is to the mission, but I also ask to determine if I need to call for security. Devon won't want you worrying about your friend..." He smiled. "Ginger. He'll want your full attention."

I hated it, but Lucas was right. "I'm sure after this second visit, Christopher will see Ginger doesn't know anything. But I'll contact him, try to set everything straight."

"Why are you here?" Ginger gave Lucas a longer perusal, and I could see she was getting her groove back. "You're gorgeous. What did you say your name was?"

"Lucas." He smiled at her before crossing the room to peer out the single window in the living room that looked down on the street. "I wouldn't know what to look for that's out of place."

I stood to make another cup of tea. "They'll be in black SUVs of some type. Christopher always had at least one tailing his limo."

"Hmm. A man who wants to be noticed. Someone who thinks highly of himself."

"Yeah. Sound familiar?" I didn't know why I poked at Devon. Lucas was being kind, but anything to do with Christopher drove me crazy.

Lucas never stopped surveying the street and didn't seem to take the jibe at Devon personally. "Devon has the flashy cars and limos because he can afford them, and it's expected of his status as leader of a House. And as a Council member, he required the security. But he's never cared what anyone thought of him." Lucas seemed to stare at nothing when he muttered, "except the Council." But I didn't think he meant for me to hear that last part.

And when I considered what I'd come to learn about Devon, I had to agree with Lucas. There was a huge difference between

Devon living up to expectation, and Christopher's need for others to ogle, admire, and envy.

"I know it's still early, but I think it's time to party. I'm done playing the victim." Ginger rose and stretched like a lazy cat, which I'm sure was to show off her womanly curves should Lucas be interested.

I noted that he paid close attention to Ginger.

He ignored my glare. As with all the vamps I'd met so far, he wasn't apologetic about staring. He gave Ginger his hand as he walked her back to her room. "Cressa hasn't mentioned it, but she has free time to spend with you today."

"Just the day?" Ginger gave him a sly wink.

He grinned. "And evening. She's due back at eight a.m. tomorrow."

"Is that when you turn into a pumpkin as well?"

"I have no limitations unless I have an assignment."

"Good to know." Then she winked at me before sliding into her bedroom and closing the door.

"I think it's best you stay away from her." I gave Lucas my scariest look, but he just laughed.

"I think Ginger knows how to take care of herself." When I glowered at him, he smiled. "Devon supplied spending money. Perhaps a shopping trip before clubbing?"

"We don't need Devon's money." Hands on hips, I stared him down.

"But we'll take it anyway," Ginger said as she bounced into the room, fully recovered in leggings and pullover. With the wiggle of her eyebrows at Lucas, I could only laugh. She was old enough to make up her own mind. But as soon as I told her Lucas was a vamp, she'd cool her jets.

The next several hours were spent in one of the most posh shopping centers in Santiga Bay. I wasn't sure how Lucas did it, but he didn't bat an eye as we moved in and out of stores, some of them more than once as Ginger decided on what to buy. Lucas finally put a stop to it as the day waned to twilight and purchased three outfits for Ginger and one for me.

The next stop was dinner at a bistro overlooking the ocean. Ginger discovered Lucas was a vamp during one of our dressing room conversations, but the news, while titillating for Ginger, didn't stop her from flirting outrageously with him. If anything, she became more starry-eyed.

Lucas took us back home and crashed in front of the TV while Ginger and I took showers and giggled in the bathroom, preparing for a night of clubbing.

"How did you get mixed up with shifters and vamps?" As soon as she asked, her levity broke down. "It all circles back to me, doesn't it?"

I dropped the eye shadow to pull her around, holding her face in my hands so she was forced to look at me. "Never, never apologize for that. Didn't we say we were in this together?"

Tears formed in her eyes, and I turned on my fierce momma-bear expression and tone. "You're going to mess up your makeup, and I think we've pushed Lucas to the limit on babysitting the women."

She snorted. "Please. That man has stamina. I can tell." And she wiggled her brows. "And I've never done it with a vamp." She kissed my hand before pulling away, blinking and using a tissue to catch the excess liquid before it damaged her mascara.

I sighed at her new obsession with vamps, remembering my dreams of Devon. In the dreams, we never got far enough for me to test the stamina theory. Was it really like that? I inwardly cursed the tingle that coursed through me, centering uncomfortably between my legs.

"Oh my, god! I know exactly where we should go tonight." Ginger bounced on her toes before wiggling her ass.

"I thought you wanted to go to Freddy's."

"Not anymore. Have you been to the Serenade Club?"

"No. Isn't that on the west side?"

"Yep." She lowered her voice and leaned toward me. "Word is that vamps and shifters sometimes go there. At least, some of the regulars seem to know about them. I know someone that works there who could fill us in."

"I think I've had my fill of vamps the last few days." I finished the last touch of mascara and stared at my reflection. What little I'd learned about vamps while staying at Devon's wasn't as much as I'd hoped. No one sat me down and explained all the ins and outs. Anna had been the most forthcoming, but even then, most of the information was limited to etiquette rather than real-life examples. Nothing about the basics, like how often they really drank blood, why they could walk around during the day, or if they could they fly. I snorted.

"Okay. Let's see what we can discover while clubbing with a vamp."

Ginger all but squealed as she raced out to the living room in her three-inch heels and a skirt that barely covered her backside. At least the off-the-shoulder top she threw on covered most of her breasts. I tried to ignore the quick flash that lit up Lucas's eyes. If Ginger noticed them, she didn't miss a beat as she grabbed his arm. "Can we go to the Serenade Club? Do you know that one?"

His lips twitched. "I'm aware of it. There aren't as many vampires there as you'd hope, but if you want gossip, it's probably one of the safer places."

We got a quick pass at the club's door. Having a vamp along meant we didn't have to stand in long lines. Once we entered, Lucas left us on our own.

I was three drinks in before Ginger waved over a woman heading for the back. She glowered until recognition lit her gaze. She plowed through a group of men, ignoring their complaints as they jostled their drinks. It was either her six-foot, lean but muscular frame or her growl that quickly appeased them. She wore a muscle shirt that showed off her tight abs and skin-tight jeans that accentuated her long legs.

She grabbed Ginger and twirled her around. "God bless, woman, where have you been lately?"

Ginger laughed. "Laying low. But I just met my first vamp and had to drag Cressa out to meet you." She turned to me. "Trix is one of the best bartenders around."

Trix grabbed a stool from another table, growled at the customers when they began to object, then plopped down between Ginger and me. "So, you got your netherworld cherry popped, huh?"

"Not as much me as Cressa." Ginger grabbed my hand under the table before leaning in to whisper in a not-so-low voice considering the ear-shattering music. "But I've got my eye on her bodyguard over there at the end of the bar."

Trix turned toward Lucas leaning against the bar, sipping a drink as he kept an eye on the room, his gaze constantly roaming. When he noticed the women staring at him, he lifted his glass with a wry smile. Had he heard Ginger over the crowd and loud music? Trix answered my unspoken question.

"He is fine. But they all tend to have that look about them. Even the ugly ones, and there aren't many of those, seem to have a glow. And I'm sure he's hearing every word about how fine his ass is."

Lucas's quick grin and wink confirmed her statement. I shuddered to wonder how much I'd said while at Devon's estate, not understanding how good their hearing truly was.

Trix turned back to us and lowered her voice as the music got louder. We had to lean over the table to hear her. "I know more about shifters, but I can tell you it's not only vamp hearing you have to watch for."

"You mean their blood sucking?" Ginger asked.

Trix laughed. "Oh, those fangs aren't just for show." She shook her head. "But they're not as blood-thirsty as the stories say. Oh, they need it, but it's only the young ones that need it regularly. I've heard they go as long as five or ten years before the urge lessens.

The older ones can go months, even years without having to feed on blood, but some just enjoy it." She took a sip of Ginger's drink. "They're smart, crafty, and sometimes shifty—all rolled into one. Down here, in this part of town, you mostly get the young ones, and while their makers keep a fairly tight rein, there are rogues who aren't friends to any human. I keep a silver-tipped stake with me in addition to my Glock. And I always have security walk me to my car before heading home. Every once and a while, someone ends up dead around here."

"That's true for any of these neighborhoods," I countered.

"True enough, but their blood loss is from a gun or knife wound. These unfortunates are nearly drained dry." She shrugged. "Shifters aren't any better, but they usually cart their food away."

I grimaced at the thought of The Wolf dragging someone off to a dark corner for feasting.

Trix watched our faces and laughed. "Looks like I just scared the shit out of you. Hey, vamps and shifters have their own code, vamps more so."

I thought of all the hours I'd spent with Anna on the myriad etiquettes for dinners, parties, and balls.

"But..." Trix stood and bumped shoulders with Ginger. "Word is vamps can fuck all night and know how to make a woman's toes curl. They'll make you so wet, you'll never want a human lover again."

When Ginger's mouth dropped open, and she looked toward Lucas, Trix laughed again. She patted Ginger on the shoulder. "Let me get you another round, on the house."

I hadn't wanted to think of Devon and those frickin' dreams. But Trix's words wouldn't go away, nor would the last dream image of a fully naked Devon just before he knelt between my legs.

Those thoughts took the innocent pleasure out of the evening, especially when Ginger kept glancing at Lucas, even when she danced with other men. Maybe she was planning a three-way with him. Nothing surprised me where Ginger was concerned. And as much as I noticed Lucas keeping an eye on everyone in the club, he always had time for Ginger.

I was grateful when last call forced us out into the night. I had a headache from too many rainbow sliders and knew I'd pay for it in the morning. The evils of party-colored vodka shots. It wasn't so much the vodka as the various liqueurs used to make the sliders.

Lucas walked between us, a hand on each of our arms to steady us as we stumbled to his car. He rolled us both into the back seat, and we giggled as Ginger offered suggestive ideas on how to spend the rest of the evening. Lucas merely smiled, but I caught his raised brow in the rearview mirror. This would have been a very different evening had Sergi been my bodyguard. That vamp was no fun at all.

He parked the limo in front of the apartment, and paid one of Bulldog's men to keep an eye on it. He half-carried Ginger up the stairs. It was a ruse on her part, and his patient grin suggested he knew it. I wondered if Ginger would try to drag him to her room. That's all I needed, and I hoped I would pass out before any gymnastics started.

When Lucas unlocked the door and stepped in first, he immediately blocked us from entering. I pushed Ginger aside to look over his shoulder. And froze—not sure whether to be afraid or downright angry. Someone had tossed the place, leaving nothing but destruction in their wake.

Chapter Twenty-Two

I DON'T KNOW what scared me most about living at Devon's estate. Whether my mission would fail and leave my debt in place, or the seductive allure of my dreams. Both paled in comparison to Devon's rage as he paced his office. His gaze flashed an icy blue as he ran hands through his hair.

Lucas and Sergi didn't seem phased by the dark emotions ready to burst like Mount Vesuvius, but they gave Devon plenty of space. They stood on the far side of the office with blank expressions and stony gazes. I wasn't sure if that should reassure me or not. I had begged Lucas not to say anything to Devon, especially after he mentioned Devon not wanting to be disturbed except for emergencies. That ship had sailed. Still upset at Christopher having the apartment tossed, I wasn't sure how any of this was Devon's concern.

While I waited for Devon's quiet fuming to mark my fate, I took the opportunity to check out his office. The only time I'd seen it was after the tea party when I'd stolen the journal pages. I was beginning to think of this room as the principal's office. But the space was day and night different than the rest of the dreary mansion. Where most of the mansion was dark and gloomy, this room was filled with light, or would be once the blinds covering the bay window were opened to the morning which was still a couple of hours away. Even at this ungodly hour, the office shone with bright lights strategically placed to be warm rather than glaring.

It was obvious this room had been recently remodeled within the last two years based on the modern light fixtures, remote-controlled blinds, and other features I'd only seen in the most expensive homes. My mouth watered at the massive espresso machine on the long, marbled bar. The only old items in the room were the antique knickknacks, but I was too tired to give them a second glance.

I'd considered asking Lucas for a cup of whatever the espresso machine could pour while waiting for Devon's arrival, but even the jovial Lucas had shut down as he drove us back to the mansion and parked my butt in the office. When Devon returned with Sergi in tow, I noticed his expensive suit, which fit him like a hand-tailored glove. We must have interrupted an important party or date. The last thought made my gut tighten. Why should I care if Devon had been on a date? I pushed away the unwelcome images from my dreams, preferring to deal with Devon's wrath.

"Is the girl safe?" Devon finally spoke.

"Yes, sir." Lucas stepped forward, perhaps signaling Devon's initial anger had passed. "She's at a hotel a few blocks from their neighborhood."

Devon stopped his pacing, but instead of facing us, he stared at the closed blinds as if he could see through them to the landscape beyond. "Sufficient for tonight, but I want her moved. Someplace across town, perhaps the Stonegate Bungalows. Give her whatever she needs and enough money to get around." He turned to Lucas. "Make sure she understands how critical it is she doesn't return home or anywhere in the neighborhood."

Lucas bowed his head. "I'll see to it at first light."

Devon turned to me. His gaze softened, but I couldn't tell if his anger had melted away or was well-hidden under his look of concern, which only confused me. I thought he was angry with me. "I won't keep you long. You need your rest. Sergi, get Cressa a cup of espresso. She's been eying the machine since I walked in the room."

Sergi didn't hesitate, and within seconds I heard the whirring of the machine shortly followed by the heavenly scent of coffee.

"Make that two." Devon moved to sit in a chair close to me, heaving out a sigh before leaning back. He waited until our espressos were served, then I heard the whirring of the machine again. No doubt Sergi making cups for Lucas and himself. I couldn't take my eyes off Devon as I waited to hear my fate.

"I apologize for my outburst, and I suspect you believe that your troubles are your own." He seemed to be waiting for a response, but his comment surprised me. He excelled at always saying something I wasn't expecting. So, I nodded, unable to stop my chin from rising in defiance, which only made him smile.

"Under normal circumstances, I would agree. But Christopher Underwood has too many connections and resources to ignore."

I almost spilled my coffee when he mentioned my stepfather's name. I flashed a look at Lucas, but he'd moved to stand next to Sergi and the espresso machine, seemingly ignoring the conversation.

"Don't blame Lucas. Whatever your stepfather is looking for, he seems convinced you're involved. As long as he's pursuing you, or anyone you know, it could have an impact on my interests. And I can't have anyone in my world knowing about you, other than what I personally leak to them." He studied me, looking for a crack, anything that would reveal my thoughts.

I doubted he'd find anything but confusion and turmoil. As I sipped the espresso, my entire focus was on trying to stop my hands from shaking. After the second long sip, the strong brew revitalized me enough to consider Christopher's actions from

Devon's point of view. There was no telling how far Christopher would go to find whatever the hell was he looking for.

"How do you know about Christopher?" I couldn't stop the tremor in my voice, and I cleared my throat.

"You must have known I'd run a background check on you." He shrugged when I couldn't hold back my shock. "You're an unknown element integral to an important mission. I had to know if I could, I don't know. I suppose trust is too strong a word, considering how little we know of each other and how few the days." His smile was tender but his gaze remained severe. "I had to know there wasn't anything in your past that could come back around to me."

I opened my mouth, ready to fling the standard rhetoric about how my business was my own. But was it? I was a thief. He didn't know me. Any crew of worth would dig into someone's background, ask around, do whatever was needed to be sure they could trust a new member of the team. Just because we were playing for higher stakes with the elite didn't make that necessity go away. It only made it more crucial, especially in the world of vampires.

I nodded. "I hadn't considered it before, but you're right." I gave him a half-shrug. "I haven't really been looking at any of this from your perspective."

He seemed pleased, which only confused me more, but I settled back in the chair and finished the espresso, setting the cup on a side table. "As I told Lucas, I have no idea what he's looking for." I stared into Devon's eyes, which had changed from their icy blue to something warmer. "This was all a surprise. Ginger, the girl as you called her," I hesitated when he bowed his head either in apology or acknowledgment. I took a shaky breath and continued, "She told me a couple of days ago that Christopher had stopped by looking for me. I didn't know why or how he knew where I lived. Quite frankly, it irritated me. I left his house and that life years ago for reasons that aren't important to this conversation."

When Devon nodded, the tightness around my chest released,

and I could breathe again, thankful to get past that single point. I didn't want anyone to know about my past and why I ran. I found it unsettling that I didn't want Devon, most of all, to ever learn of it. "Christopher is into a lot of shady stuff, and I've kept out of his circle of influence, especially with my line of work."

"I believe you." Devon set down his cup, and his expression softened. I ignored why that simple statement meant so much to me. "I knew his name and a bit about his business before I ever met you. But once I knew you were...part of his past...I did more digging into Underwood. His business ventures don't cross any of mine with the exception of a few minor investments. And those will now be put under the magnifying glass. I'm more concerned with why he thinks you have something of his. Is it just because you're a thief?"

This part was easy to share and, while satisfying Devon's immediate concern, might be enough for him to believe it was the only reason I left home. "Christopher suspects what I do for a living, though I doubt he knows everything. I stole from him while still living under his roof, though it wasn't anything of real value. A few bucks here and there or small items I didn't think he'd notice were missing." I bit my lip. "I might have stolen one or two things that I knew would piss him off."

Devon nodded again with one of his deadly vampire smiles, almost as if he approved of my thieving ways.

I gave him a steely glare. "But I haven't touched one thing of his since I left that house." *Slow down. Don't make it so personal.* "I do stop by a few times a year, but only when I know he's traveling."

"To see your sister."

That surprised me.

"It's part of the background check. Underwood, your mother, Willa, and one sister. I believe her name is April."

"Yes," I sighed. How much more would he find out about me? Like how there was nothing more to me than being a worthless thief. "I think it's possible that April might be involved with what

Christopher is looking for, though it could just as easily be some other thief. If I knew what he was looking for, I'd have a better understanding of what was going on."

"All right. I think you've had a long enough evening. You need your rest. We're only a few days away from the main event, and I need your full focus on the mission. Not on Underwood. Ginger will be safe and quite busy in her new bungalow where you'll be able to see her whenever you want. I'll make a decision later today on what, if anything, we do to curtail Underwood's interest in you."

I rose on shaky legs, but if Devon noticed, he was too much a gentleman to say anything.

Before I left, Devon whispered, "Rest easy, Cressa. You're safe here."

I closed the door behind me. His words brought more comfort than I thought possible.

DEVON WAITED until he heard Cressa's footsteps move down the hall before turning to Sergi. "Her statement seems to track with what you shared earlier this evening."

When Lucas's gaze lit with confusion, Devon asked Sergi to give him the rundown. After listening and taking a moment to consider Cressa's responses, Lucas nodded in agreement.

Sergi shook his head. "She conveniently sidestepped why she left his house in the first place."

"That's none of our business." Lucas shot Devon a glance. "She said it had no impact with whatever Underwood's searching for, and she's not obligated to divulge all of her past." His voice quieted. "It could be more personal than we know."

Something twisted in Devon's chest as it had with Sergi's report. Thieving alone would be enough to leave, or be kicked out, as Underwood had claimed. But something in Cressa's tense reactions to anything involving Underwood told him there was more to the story. Thought of possible domestic abuse made his gut wrench as if he'd drunk acid. How had this woman wormed her way into his soul? Was it only the dreams?

"Maybe." Sergi relented to Lucas's concerns. "But she gave us an opening."

Devon nodded. "We need to know what Underwood is searching for. Find out who his muscle is and see if there's a way in." He felt his fangs grow long when he smiled at Sergi. "Use whatever means you think necessary, but nothing that tracks back to us."

Sergi acknowledged Devon's smile with his own. "Happily."

Devon laughed. "It's been some time since we've found you a decent fight. Our mission is a long one, remember to pace yourself."

"Please." Sergi acted as if his feathers had been ruffled, but the man couldn't hold back the delight in knowing he had full rein to find answers. "What about her true father?"

Devon steepled his fingers and bounced them gently off his stubbled chin. This critical information would be the most difficult to unearth. "I doubt Cressa knows who he is, but it's a possibility." He studied Lucas. His bodyguard had been protective of Cressa, which only made sense with the amount of time he spent with her. Lucas was special in that way. He didn't have the baggage so many vampires had where humans were concerned. And it made him the perfect person in this regard.

"Lucas, see what you can find out. Test the waters, as safely as you can, with both Cressa and her friend, Ginger."

He nodded, almost in relief, and Devon suspected that had more to do with Sergi. The two of them were polar opposites, which made them the perfect team—good cop and bad cop.

"I want a report this evening." He turned back to the blinds. "I don't think Underwood will impact our current mission, but he needs to be removed from the playing field as quickly as possible. That's all."

Devon waited for his men to leave before he leaned back and rested his feet on the wide ledge that ran along the bay window. The expensive sculptures and antiques had been strategically placed to allow for his favorite thinking position. The light tap at the door surprised him, and he wondered if Cressa returned. He smiled at the thought. "Come in."

He glanced over his shoulder, surprised to find Lucas there. He sighed. "What is it?"

"I wanted to ask about the search for Cressa's true father."

"You're right. You should be told what Sergi and Simone now know." When he saw the hurt in Lucas's gaze, he waved for him to pull up a chair. Lucas complied, and he placed his feet on the ledge as Devon touched a button to raise the blinds, revealing the landscape lights glowing in the early morning darkness. Farther in the yard, another light swayed in slow arcs before stopping at the sycamore tree.

"She's up again," Lucas stated for no particular reason. "She's been more active lately."

"I've been having dreams. Cressa is in them. I believe she's creating them, most likely without knowing. At least that's the feeling I get."

"Ah. Now it makes sense."

They sat in companionable silence. Within the closest circles of his family, each vampire had a different preference on how to spend time with him. Sergi preferred a good scotch in front of the fire. Lucas enjoyed the daytime and viewing nature as Devon did. Simone preferred her private meetings accompanied by an intimate dinner with good wine. He grinned. The burdens of running a House and keeping his family happy.

"I don't know if Cressa is a key to helping Lyra, but the turmoil she had as a child in Underwood's home tracks with what I've pieced together over the years. People with her type of talent first become aware of it as small children. But without training, the dreams could seem like nightmares. I have to believe her mother knows the truth, possibly at a subconscious level."

"That's a difficult proposition, especially with Underwood in the way."

"So, let's find out if Cressa ever tried to find her real father. But she can't know our interest. Not yet."

Lucas shifted uncomfortably.

"It's not only because I don't believe she's ready. This is a delicate time, and we must stay focused on the mission. Right now, she believes her dreams are nothing more than that. I have reason to think they're more than reality."

"You believe them to be premonitions?" Lucas couldn't hide his awe.

"Maybe." How else would Cressa know about the garden? Or was she capable of seeing into his mind? That was an interesting thought. "If they are premonitions and word gets out, her life would be in constant danger. And that, I won't allow."

Chapter Twenty-Three

I WOKE LATE the following morning. Not surprising after the long nightclubbing, a house invasion, and an office visit with Devon. Having survived the evening, I'd slept hard with no dreams or cares. But once awake, worries about Christopher cast shadows on the sunshine bathing the room in golden colors. I hurried to dress, hoping it wasn't too late to grab breakfast.

As I scurried down the stairs, I was surprised to hear voices coming from the dining room. I slowed, not sure what to expect, but found the usual suspects, Lucas and Anna, along with Sergi. This was the first time the aloof vampire had shared a meal with us. I wasn't sure why he joined us now, other than he'd also been here until the wee hours of the morning, though I doubted that was a problem for a vamp.

Conversation stopped when I entered.

"Cressa. We thought you'd sleep in longer. We didn't wake you, did we?" Lucas stood and pulled out a chair for me.

"Doubtful. I slept like the dead. I'm as surprised as you that I'm up, but I feel rested." I glanced at Sergi, who stuffed an omelet in his mouth, registering my existence with a slight nod in my direction. At least it wasn't a glare. Progress.

"I must have been dead to the world as well. I didn't hear any of you." Anna sat back, a large mug held in both hands, half of her breakfast uneaten. When she noticed me glance at her plate, she blushed. "I shouldn't have eaten anything; this is my second breakfast. I was up at my normal hour and couldn't wait for everyone else." She pushed her plate away as Cook hustled through the door, placing new platters down.

"Here's more hot food. The other has grown cold." Cook took the time to fix me a plate.

"Where's Letty?" I asked. I'd never seen Cook serve the food. He hated to leave the kitchen.

"Letty has gone shopping." Devon appeared, and my stomach did a little flip at how amazing he looked in a tailored black shirt, black pants, and a silver chain disappearing under his shirt.

I'd never seen him wear jewelry before, except for his House ring. It made me curious as to what lay under that shirt, and I tore my gaze away. I already knew what was under that shirt—intimately. Didn't I? Once again, I questioned my dreams—so real, yet they couldn't be. I wasn't sure what triggered them, other than a display of Devon's intense emotions each time it happened. Maybe vamps could project thoughts. Cook's voice snapped me back.

"If you ate breakfast at the appropriate hour, Letty would have been here to serve you," Cook grumbled.

"And we appreciate your service." Devon snapped open a napkin, and Cook appeared contrite.

"I made you crepes this morning." Cook's demeanor softened as he presented Devon with three small crepes, two filled with eggs and vegetables, the third filled with some type of fruit. Before he could step back, Devon touched his arm.

"Thank you, Cook. You're a blessing."

Cook beamed at the praise then surveyed the table. "I'll bring a new pot of coffee." He picked up the platters of cold food and hustled out.

Sergi chuckled. "You spoil him." He licked his fingers after finishing a slice of toast that had been smothered with raspberry jam. "But it's worth it."

"Why the off-schedule shopping trip? Planning a party?" Lucas dug into the scrambled eggs then added a small mound of sausage on top of the two left over from his first helping.

"Under the circumstances, I thought it best to have more people here, at least until after the mission."

"Excellent. I can run through the security systems this morning before the training session." Sergi scraped more eggs onto his plate then lifted his mug when Cook returned with a new pot.

Cook scowled at Sergi but filled his cup and then mine.

I placed a hand on his arm as Devon had. "I could have done that. Thank you, Cook."

He beamed down at me. "Always a pleasure, Cressa. If you look under this cover," he pushed the small plate with a silver dome forward, "I think you'll find something to your liking." He hovered, waiting for me to look before he left.

I lifted the lid, all eyes on me, and laughed with joy. A fresh blueberry scone lay on a white paper doily. A tiny bowl of what looked like homemade blueberry jam sat next to it. He'd been washing blueberries the day he made my picnic lunch, and I had mentioned in passing how much I loved blueberry scones.

"You remembered." I was truly touched.

"Of course." He glared at Sergi and Lucas. "You deserve the best." He blushed as he picked up Anna's plate and hurried from the room.

"Someone has Cook wrapped around her finger." Lucas grinned at me.

When I glanced toward Devon, I found him studying me, a slight upturn of his lips, the precursor of a smile. He seemed to approve of Cook's gift, and a tingle of pleasure ran through me. I spread jam on the scone and tried to convince myself the tingle was for the freshly baked scone and not the hint of desire I caught in Devon's gaze.

"There will be a change in the schedule today. I'm taking Cressa on a field trip. Sergi, you can spend the day with the security system. And set the secondary perimeter alarms." After Sergi nodded, Devon turned to Anna. "The day is yours, so rest up. The next few days will be busy." Anna had appeared hurt when Devon mentioned taking me someplace, but she brightened when hearing she had a day off.

"Lucas, you'll be coming with us."

Lucas nodded and returned to his breakfast. If he was curious about where we were going, he didn't show it.

Devon's gaze rested on me. "After breakfast, why don't you check in on Ginger and make sure she has everything she needs. I'm sure you'll find her quite settled, but let me or Lucas know if she requires anything else. And wear something casual for today." He grinned, and I sensed mischief. "Consider this your day off."

I raised a brow. "A day off that you've prearranged?"

His grin grew wider. "Sorry for that, but I think you'll find the trip interesting."

Intrigued, I simply nodded and stared down at my plate. His grin made him so irresistible, I wanted to run my hands through his hair and pull him to me, hungry for his taste. I dropped the knife, and it clattered against the plate, thankfully snapping me out of my daydream. Good grief.

When I glanced up, his grin had turned into a full-on smile. I gulped. Thank the gods Lucas would be with us.

DEVON'S STOMACH was in knots. A sensation he hadn't felt since the first time he'd stepped onto a battlefield. And certainly not something he should experience driving to his sanctuary, Oasis. He gave Cressa a side glance, curious as to what her first impression would be. He wasn't sure why it was important for her to like the house he built. Or maybe he did, but this wasn't the time to dwell on it. They had a long path before them. A dangerous game. He pushed all those thoughts aside and focused on this first step, schooling his emotions to present what he hoped was a bland expression.

Cressa leaned back in her seat, and her head lolled to one side as she stared out the window, obviously tired from little sleep. She hadn't asked any questions about their destination and had said little on the drive through a blend of green pastures and forest. Her call to Ginger must have gone well, or he would have heard about it. He wasn't sure how to handle a quiet Cressa. A reflective Cressa.

After several more miles of rolling hills, Devon turned into the driveway. When a rod-iron gate opened automatically, Cressa popped up.

"Where are we?" Cressa perched on the front seat, her head turning about to take it all in. Her brows were scrunched, but she was smiling, and her mixed emotions eased his tension.

Devon slowed as they dropped down the other side of the knoll. "This is Oasis." He hesitated a moment, keeping his eyes on the road. "My home."

Cressa gaped at him. "I thought the mansion was your home."

He gave her a half-shrug. "It's my ancestral home. I inherited it from my parents long ago, but I never felt comfortable there. I wanted something of my own." He glanced over at Cressa, her questioning gaze focused on him. "And the house is too dark for my tastes. It was added to the Historical Society registry before I took possession, and now there's not much I can do with it. It took five years and several compromises to gain approval for updating my office."

"That's why the room was so different from the rest of the house." Cressa's voice took on a reverent whisper as the car pulled in front of the main house. "This looks twice the size of the other house."

"The square footage is about the same, but with two floors rather than three. It also has a basement. I wanted a single residence that could fit my entire family if required. This main house isn't large enough for everyone, so I had the bungalows built, spreading them out to provide privacy."

"It's so sleek and...I don't know. Natural. It's a perfect fit with the setting. You had this built from scratch?"

"Yes. I spent years designing it."

She snorted. "Years doing this, decades doing that. No matter how much I learn about your world, I can't seem to wrap my head around how long vampires live."

"It takes some getting used to."

After handing his keys to the valet, Devon climbed the short steps to the front door with Cressa at his side.

Simone met them at the door. Her demeanor was cool as she kissed both his cheeks then held a hand out to Cressa.

Cressa didn't stare, but it was obvious she was intrigued by Simone. When she slid him a look, he wondered if she thought they were lovers. Would it matter to her?

"Simone runs Oasis and many of its businesses while I'm away," Devon explained.

She nodded. "Like your second in command."

For the first time he could recall, Simone gave Cressa a genuine smile. She'd never given humans more than slight nods of approval when they performed to her satisfaction.

"Yes." Simone's silky voice held a note of approval, and perhaps amusement. "Exactly like that. Welcome to Oasis."

Devon was thankful Sergi and Lucas hadn't heard the exchange, or he'd have to spend the entire day mediating everyone's insecurities about their position in the family. He turned when Lucas drove up and sighed with relief, knowing he'd dodged a bullet.

Once Lucas joined them, Devon led them into the foyer. "We won't get in your way, but I was hoping we might have lunch together. If you have time." Devon had called Simone before the drive, but it had been more of a last-minute thought.

She shot him one of those smiles that gave no hint of what she was truly thinking. "I've already given a menu to the chef. It's a beautiful day, so I thought the terrace would be a good choice. Shall we say two?"

"Perfect."

Simone gave them a nod then sauntered away. Her coral caftan suit floated around her as two other vampires joined her on their stroll down the hall. After a glance at Devon, Lucas followed.

Cressa turned in slow, wide circles as she took in the foyer, the grand staircase to the right, and the room beyond with its floor-to-ceiling windows. "This is amazing. How can you stand living at the mansion with a place like this?"

Devon pressed his lips together. "It's not easy."

She turned to him. "Then why don't you stay here?"

He gave her a tolerant smile. "It's a long story, but the short of it is that I have enemies. No one knows about this place. Its true ownership is buried under miles of subterfuge in county records and land transfers. It's a sanctuary. A safe place for my family to come whenever they need, whether they're on the run or simply require a place to reenergize."

"You can never live here?" She seemed appalled at the idea, and it matched his own feelings so well he had to look away.

"I've been known to stay for a few days, but usually no more than a week. And I always reserve hotels in faraway places for the same time period, making arrangements for people to spend time at the hotel, pretending they're seeing to my needs."

"That seems like a lot of work."

"It is. Someday, hopefully soon, I'll make a move to put an end to my enemy, or at least take the teeth out of his hold. Then I'll be able to make this place my own."

Cressa touched his arm. "I'm sorry. As much as you love this place, it must be difficult to come here for only short periods of time. Thank you for bringing me."

Her touch and words pleased him in a way he couldn't decipher. He cleared his throat. "Let's give you the grand tour, then I'll leave you to your own devices while I take care of some business."

She smiled with excitement. "So, I do get some time to myself?"

He couldn't help but match her enthusiasm. "As long as you stay out of trouble."

She only winked as she took his proffered arm.

Chapter Twenty-Four

I FLIPPED through the pages of the women's magazine, the odd aroma of perfume mixing with the scent of early spring roses from the pots lining the terrace. Ginger would love it here, but based on our earlier call, she was the lucky one. The exclusive, members-only hotel was treating her like royalty. She had to cut our call short so she wouldn't miss her morning facial followed by an hour with the masseuse.

My left shoulder twinged, a leftover ache from my last training session. It seemed I didn't warrant spas or daily massages. But I couldn't begrudge Ginger's pampering. She'd never experienced that type of life and this might be her only opportunity. Fortunately, Ginger understood the world she'd been dropped into was a one-time shot, and she planned on taking full advantage. That was what it was like when you grew up poor, hungry, and battered. You grabbed what pleasures you could find and held on as long as you could.

Footsteps quietly approached, and I turned to see a young man refill my iced tea. He nodded when I smiled my thanks then disappeared with the same stealth. This was the life. When I'd lived at Christopher's, I never received this kind of treatment. That was for the adults—and April. I was always the outsider. Not here. Even in this massive estate filled with vampires, where I only knew Devon and Lucas, I felt more welcome than I ever did growing up in Christopher's house. I blew out a breath, pushing back the pain I felt every time I thought of my mother and how distant she'd become over the years. Ever since my sixth birthday. I couldn't remember most of it, that event that forever split the bond we'd shared after my father left us. Today wasn't the day for a trip down memory lane.

I tossed the magazine on the table and stood, raising my arms for a long stretch. I walked to the edge of the terrace and leaned against the glass railing to view the amazing backyard. It was reminiscent of the English gardens I'd seen in historical movies, full of wandering gravel paths, lush flower beds, and small sitting areas under trees just beginning to leaf out.

Lunch had been a simple affair, but Devon had invited two other vamps—Bella and Jacques—who had apparently returned late from an assignment. While Devon spoke about the job, which was basically tailing people I'd never heard of, Simone distracted me with nonsense about entertaining, dealing with the personal requests of seventy other vamps, and ensuring the liquor cabinets remained filled—the drama of running a household. I couldn't help but think of Anna's boring lessons. I'd drink myself silly if I had to deal with needy vamps for more than a day.

But Simone didn't fool me. While I had no doubt she knew a little something about everything she spoke of, I doubted she personally dealt with any of it. And if she thought I couldn't listen to more than one conversation at a time, she sorely underestimated an accomplished thief. Or someone who grew up an outsider in her own home. I might not know anything about Devon's business, but I could remember names and details. Who knew if they'd come in handy one day?

After lunch, I'd been left on my own as Devon and the others disappeared down the hall. I'd dipped my feet in the infinity pool and read magazines to the sounds of jazz. Now, it was time to explore.

The English garden beckoned, and I surveyed the paths from the second-floor terrace. A smaller dirt path meandered through the flower beds before trailing out through trees toward the lake. For a second, I saw a flash of a different lake, this one shining at night with large tents and dozens of people.

Curious, I raced down the stairs then slowed to a more moderate pace to the lower-floor terrace. The back of the house didn't have the typical solarium with glass walls and elegant French doors. Instead, these glass walls slid back to open an entire wall to the fresh spring day, with exposure to the early afternoon sun that kept the room warm.

I found the dirt path and forced myself to a steady pace, with time to appreciate the colorful blooms and emerging leaves. But I didn't see the flowers. Instead, images from the dreams emerged. After we'd waltzed to the music flowing from the tent, Devon had taken me to a spot under an oak tree. I stopped just before the wooded copse and turned in a circle, surveying the trees and elevation, searching for that knoll. My heart skipped a beat when I noticed a single oak, its stately branches a perfect dome. Could this be the same tree?

My feet moved without thought. The path moved toward the tree then turned toward the direction of the lake. After weaving through trees, the path opened to a small clearing that overlooked the lake. I braced my hand on the nearest tree, my breaths puffing out in short, rapid intervals. I forced several long inhales to slow my heart rate, then closed my eyes. Images of tents and colorful lanterns popped in my head. The song we'd danced to, the one I'd only ever heard in my dreams. This was the lake.

I touched my lips, could taste Devon's on mine, feel the warmth of his breath on my neck, the strength of his arms as he held me close, the whisper of my name. I shook myself. *What the hell was happening?*

I raced past the lake, following the bend in the path as it headed back to the house. After a hundred yards, the path ended at a rod-iron gate, decorated with impressive scrollwork. In the middle of the gate was the three-triangle symbol of the House Trelane. I didn't remember a gate, but I pushed on it, sure it would be locked. It wasn't. It opened quietly, and I stepped through, knowing what I would find. I closed the gate behind me and took the path to the left, stepping under the overhead vine covered with crimson roses and ending at a tree-shrouded grotto.

The same place I had waited in erotic anticipation. Where he'd held me and kissed me as if I was the only woman in the world. His head had been between my legs, making me writhe and moan until I screamed his name. Did that happen in the dream? Or was I projecting, knowing how it would end?

I dropped to my knees and ran my hands through the grass. Should I be able to remember the feel of the grass as my lover laid next to me? I fell back and spread my arms wide, staring into the azure sky—just a shade darker than his eyes, warm and inviting. I didn't know what the hell was happening to me. But rather than being terrified, I wondered if I ever wanted the dreams to stop.

DEVON STARED down at his private garden from the second-floor balcony. No one had access to his master suite except for the house staff and Simone, who only came in when she required access to his private office. The garden had two entrances. The gate that Cressa must have come through and the door that led to the stairs to his suite.

The gate to the garden should have been locked. On their arrival, he'd forgotten to confirm that with Simone. He'd been too worried over what Cressa would think of the place to remember the garden. He hadn't meant for Cressa to find it. Certainly not.

No. He just hadn't expected her to wander that far. He should have known better.

And the view of the garden simply surprised him.

After his meeting with Simone, he'd come to his personal suite to review the mission reports Bella and Jacques had filed. Somehow, he would determine the significance to his plans. The reports were filled with several avenues to explore if he could connect the dots. There had to be something in them he could exploit to his advantage. Lorenzo was excellent at covering his tracks. But everyone made mistakes—eventually. Devon was convinced he'd already made one. The trick was finding it.

Tired of thinking about Lorenzo, he'd thought instead about how to spend the rest of the day and evening with Cressa. One more meeting to go. He'd retrieved a glass of water from the bar and strolled to the balcony to let the fresh air revive him.

When he'd glanced down, he almost dropped the glass. Cressa was stretched out on the lawn in front of the grotto. Her short, sable tresses spread out to form a crown. Her arms were flung wide, pressing her pert breasts upward, her nipples pressed against the fabric.

His cock stirred and grew hard. Images from the dreams rushed past like an old black-and-white movie reel. But this film was full of color and sensory images. He smelled the roses, her spicy citrus scent mixed with the heat of her skin, the texture of her neck beneath his fangs. The evenings had been warm in the dreams, and there was always the lightest sheen on her skin from running. He remembered the glass in his fist seconds before he crushed it.

She had to know this garden was the one in her dreams. Would she ask him about it or continue to ignore the possibilities? And if she feigned ignorance, how would he bridge the gap? He hadn't meant to discuss the dreams with her until after the mission. Damn, but she knew how to stir trouble. He only had one response. She would have to make the next move.

Chapter Twenty-Five

I STRETCHED like a cat waking from a long nap, the sheets warm with their clean linen scent. I couldn't remember when I'd had such a restful sleep. The only thing marring the memory of yesterday's visit to Oasis was the lack of a garden dream. My discovery that the garden of my dreams was real should have frightened me. It had certainly shocked me. Yet, it only confirmed my suspicions that Devon was to blame. He had somehow mesmerized me, though I couldn't remember when. But I wouldn't remember the act, right? I hadn't suspected anything when Margo had mesmerized me. I didn't know if I could approach Devon about this— something so intimate.

I'd experienced detailed dreams before, but never with tactile imagery. The crux of the issue was why he had done it. And why drive me across town and into the country just to have sex? For what purpose? I couldn't wrap my head around it. Maybe it was a waking dream. Or maybe he didn't know he was doing it. Then there was the question of how I had woken in my own bed straight from the dream. They were so real I could feel the touch of his skin, the hard muscles of his arms, and the strength of his legs as he parted mine.

Stop it.

I was going to give myself an orgasm just thinking about it. A cold shower was what I needed. Instead, I pulled on a one-piece swimsuit, threw on a light robe, and jogged downstairs. The atrium's glass walls and ceiling made the room bright, even on gray days. The room carried the lightest scent of chlorine mixed with heavy foliage and blossoms from the dozens of scattered potted plants and small trees.

I tossed the robe on a chair before turning to the pool, only then seeing Simone floating on the far side. When I'd first met her, it was obvious the woman didn't like me. I could blame the cool reception on the fact she was a vamp, but the looks she gave me said it all. At dinner, which seemed more like a small banquet with the number of vamps in Devon's family, he confided that Simone had a bad history with humans. It had only been in the last few decades she'd become more comfortable around them, but she still only felt safe with a few hand-selected employees.

Not requiring any more explanation than that, I went out of my way to avoid her. More for her sake than mine. I reached for my robe, intending to tiptoe back out and take that cold shower.

"Don't leave on my account." Simone didn't bother lifting her head, but her cool, rich voice had no problem reaching me.

"Are you sure? You look like you're having some nice alone time." I shuffled my feet. "And I didn't know you were here. At the mansion, I mean."

After a minute ticked by, Simone swam toward me. She stopped when she could stand, and the waterline framed her glorious breasts, nicely covered in a one-piece. This was probably her cooldown after swimming laps.

"Devon didn't tell you."

I stepped to the edge and dipped a toe in the water before committing to the wide steps leading into the pool. The cool water lapped around my legs, giving me goosebumps as my body acclimated to the temperature change. I waded in until the water reached my stomach then leaned back against the edge of the pool, letting my arms flow back and forth, creating small ripples.

"He didn't mention it on the drive back, but I have to admit, I drank a bit too much at dinner. I think I giggled most of the way home."

Simone grimaced. "That must have been painful for him."

I gave her a grin. "Probably. He did say goodnight rather quickly once we got back."

Simone's lips twitched. "I arrived about an hour after you." She moved around the pool, short strides that didn't take her far as she walked a semi-circle around me. Her suit, the color of burnt sunrise, showed off her muscular physique overlaid on a lean body. "I understand Devon has a mission planned. He asked me to be your bodyguard."

I wasn't sure what to say, but I was certain, based on the humor in her gaze, that my mouth must be hanging open. My temper flared, and I gritted out, "I don't need a babysitter."

She let her smile blind me with its radiance. Damn, if she couldn't stop anyone in their tracks. "Not a babysitter, a body-guard. No one will know my role, and I won't be hounding your every step. But you can be assured I won't be far away." She studied me. "I would be upset, too, if Devon gave me a bodyguard. But I'm vampire, and you are only a human. He's simply being careful to ensure the success of your mission." She paused before giving me a side glance. "I also hear you tend to go rogue."

It shouldn't have surprised me that Devon would tell her about my sticky fingers at the tea party. "I'm a thief. It's what I do."

I paced through the water, the density slowing my roll. But rather than circle the same way as the shark-like Simone, I walked to the other edge and silently dropped down until my head was under water. When I rose again, I flipped my head back before running my hands over my head to push back my short crop of hair. Then I walked back to Simone.

"All right. I see his point. I just wish he would have told me."

"It must have been the giggling." She said it was such a flat tone and straight face I had a hard time deciding whether that had been a joke.

Did this vamp have a dry sense of humor? Best not to go there. While I did everything I could to avoid her at Oasis, I couldn't help but watch her through dinner. She took command, even with Devon in the room.

"Why don't you have your own House?" I wasn't sure how that popped out and was a bit horrified at my rudeness.

The look she gave me could melt ice, or the sidewalk, or maybe boil the water in the pool until my skin melted off. All she did was lean her back against the pool as I had done earlier, her arms resting on the lip.

I decided to follow suit, albeit a few arm lengths away. Not that she couldn't reach me and strangle me to death in the few seconds it took to register I was in mortal danger.

Several minutes went by. She laid her head back to stare at the glass ceiling, the sun just broaching this side of the house. "Devon will give me my own House someday. That's all I've wanted for the last hundred years. And within another twenty or thirty, that goal will be achieved."

"Why doesn't he give it to you now?" Curiosity into this world of the supernatural was like a drug. And if I was going to work with vamps, I needed every scrap of info I could gather.

A chuckle rose out of her long, slim throat. "He knows I'm not ready. I know I'm not ready. But soon." She turned her head, her tawny brown eyes boring a hole into me. "Did you know it is extremely rare for a vampire to rise through the ranks to declare their own House?"

"This is my first week. I don't know anything."

Her laugh was a deep, sultry sound that would make most men's dicks perk up and take notice. "I didn't think I'd like you,

Cressa Langtry." Then, she grew serious. "The Houses have always been owned by the aristocracy. It wasn't a rule per se, just a custom that grew over centuries. About five hundred years ago, an ancient Council member gave his most trusted vampire his own House. Until then, only sons or daughters earned that right. But this particular vampire was the most powerful on the Council, and no one voiced their concerns. The practice never took off because so many of us had been ingrained in the old ways. But every once in a while, still too few and far between, an elder or ancient will give a House to someone of great loyalty or for completing a courageous deed."

She ran her hands over her arms as if warding off a chill. "Today, if the Council had their way, they would have outlawed the practice. It's one of the reasons Devon's enemies work to keep his censure in place. One less vote for equality among all vampires, regardless of birth. Devon has always pushed against the old ways. He believes in the future."

"Why doesn't he keep you close like Sergi and Lucas? I assumed they were his top men if they were always around him." When her frown deepened, I knew I'd said something wrong. "I didn't mean to offend. I'm just trying to understand."

For a moment, Simone didn't respond. Her eyes refocused when she glanced down at me, and she moved dangerously close. "I'm sorry. My mind was elsewhere." She touched my shoulder, so light and quick, she might have been brushing away a fly. "I run Oasis in his absence, as well as several of his businesses. It's part of the training to run my own House."

I smiled. "He must have great confidence in you."

She blinked in surprise before blessing me with that amazing smile. "I just know I'm going to hate myself for liking you."

"Until then..." I pulled myself onto the edge of the pool, stood, and dripped a water path to my robe. "I bet you have some great moves you could teach me in the gym. We'll do an early lunch. You can take me to one of those vampire tea houses."

She frowned. "Anna won't agree to that."

"She's been boring me to death with all the rules. Etiquette this and protocols that. It's time to put everything into practice before the main event. We can call it field training. If she doesn't like it, she doesn't have to come. Besides, I don't remember Devon saying I had to take orders from her."

Simone's smile returned as she toweled off. She draped an arm over my shoulder as we walked out. "Yes. Absolutely going to hate myself."

"BUT WE STILL HAVE TO DISCUSS THE different levels of the aristocracy." Anna trailed behind me as I jogged down the stairs.

I didn't know if putting distance between us would make this easier, but she kept pace with me all the way to the front door. "Look, Anna, it's just for today. I want to put what I've learned to use at least once before the big show. In a real place where I won't expect what's coming. Practicing in the gym and pretending I'm fighting bad guys isn't the same thing as facing a real threat."

"I'll have Thomas get the car," Simone said, and turned, her turquoise caftan floating around her as she made her escape out the front door. Who would have thought the lethal vamp could be scared off by someone as innocuous as Anna? And after a short training session with Simone, I'd rather go up against Devon and Lucas combined before facing her in a dark alley. The woman had mad skills.

Little lines crinkled on Anna's forehead and her eyes squinted, reminding me I had my own battle standing in front of me. She shook her head. "I don't think that's what Devon had in mind. And we can practice a tea service here. Cook can put something together while we go through the Houses and their structures."

I could already envision stabbing my eyes out.

"Here's an idea. Come with us, then you can see me in action."

She hesitated for a second, then placed her hands on her hips, her lips thinning. "No. That just won't work for me."

"Look, I need to spend time with Simone if she's going to be my bodyguard. We need to learn each other's peculiarities. We only have today. I know Devon doesn't want me leaving the house tomorrow."

She wanted to go. I could see it in her eyes. But she had her stubborn on, and nothing was going to change her mind when she got like that.

I shrugged. "We'll be back in a couple of hours. Maybe we'll have time to run through the Houses after my session with Sergi?" Without bothering to wait for an answer, I hurried out the door to meet an impatient Simone, who had to be the one honking the horn.

The vampire tea houses were nothing like their tea parties, where sexual exploits were the name of the game. Vampires took their tea very seriously, as essential to their identity as it was with Asian cultures. But vampire tea houses looked nothing like their Japanese counterparts.

On the drive over, Simone explained how the tea service had changed over the centuries. Not quickly, but subtly absorbing bits and pieces of other cultures and blending it with their own social conventions. Each tea house would be different in decor, but the basic layouts were the same, boasting expansive rooms they called dens. The interiors were dark, blocking out any exterior light to accommodate the vamps' sensitivity. But the house lights provided more than enough illumination to easily appreciate the sleek furnishings. Decorative screens and plants added a dimension of privacy between the intimate tables placed spaciously around the room. A necessity with a vamp's excellent hearing, though the spacing would never block conversations from being overheard. This was not a place to share secrets unless you reserved a private tearoom for such meetings.

Five different teas were served with five light courses of cuisine

I'd never seen before and, hopefully, would never have to eat again. All in all, it was an entertaining adventure, and I grudgingly had to thank Anna for the long mornings. Simone said I'd only made a couple of minor mistakes and insisted they were acceptable, considering I was human.

Simone was warm and chatty, something I hadn't expected. I wondered if she retained her cool exterior around Devon and his House vamps for appearances. But we didn't speak of ourselves or of Devon. And though we had little in common, we both liked antiques. Although, she typically bought hers where I stole mine. I shared insights about my job, and Simone appeared captivated as I explained the different techniques I used to enter homes and bypass security systems. I even divulged one or two trade secrets for safecracking I'd never shared with anyone else.

We didn't realize how long we'd talked and had to literally race to Simone's valet-parked car. She didn't let off the gas until we skidded to a stop in front of the mansion. Words of thanks flew out of my mouth as I rushed up the steps.

I ripped off one set of clothes in exchange for my workout gear, hopping to the door as I shoved on my sneakers. I ran the rest of the way to the gym. When I slammed through the door, I doubled over, panting to catch my breath.

To my surprise, Sergi, Lucas, and Devon were all there, working through a routine.

"Sorry," I wheezed out. "We didn't notice the time. Simone almost flew the car here. I wasn't sure I'd make it back alive."

I stopped talking when I realized Sergi and Lucas had stopped to stare at me.

The only response out of Devon was a quirk of his lips. "Anna was quite upset with the both of you," he said. "You could have at least invited her to take the sting out of it."

I frowned. "I did."

"Ah. I thought she might have made the situation more than it was. That's all right. She'll have you all day tomorrow."

I grimaced and then scowled when I noted his grin before he turned away and waved at Sergi and Lucas to both come at him.

I watched them spar, each taking turns being the single man fighting two vamps. Then the three of them turned, and Devon waved me over. I gulped, knowing I was going to pay for being late and already sorry for stuffing down that last dessert course.

Chapter Twenty-Six

I SMILED and positioned my body so the hot jets of the jacuzzi hit my sore spots. I moved every five minutes to make sure other tender areas received the same treatment. After an hour in the training room, Devon had taken pity on me. I'd spent most of the time hitting the mat, usually being tossed over someone's head.

The three vamps had kept at me, never relenting until Devon whistled us to a stop. One of them would always hold out a hand to pull me effortlessly from the floor. After a five-minute break to wipe the sweat from my face and pits, drink some water, and settle my breathing to a normal rate, we were back at it. By the end, I'd felt defeated and whipped.

"Don't frown. This was an intense session and you've held up better than most humans." Sergi had grimaced, or maybe it was meant to be a smile. He didn't do it often enough to be recognizable.

"Right." I had collapsed on the bench, not sure how I was going to make it up the stairs to my room. I thought about dragging myself to the backyard and dropping into a lounger, or maybe just crawling back to the mat.

"Sergi's right. And he rarely gives compliments, so I'd take the one he gave you seriously." Lucas had handed me a bottle of water. "You've really improved this week. Just don't forget that one of your options is to run."

"Yeah. That's what I should have done the first time Devon waved me to the mat."

That got a chuckle out of them. I had somehow found the energy to leave the room, the three of them already circling each other since they hadn't worked up a sweat. Damn vamps.

I'd determined the stairs were too much for my spaghetti legs but managed to make it to the atrium and jacuzzi. I kept a swimsuit in the changing room. This was not my first time easing sore muscles after a workout. After turning my left hip toward a jet, I considered my next big decision between a dry sauna or a nap when Anna entered the room.

I perked up. "Are you joining me?" This would be a great way to make up for ditching her earlier.

Anna seemed surprised by the suggestion and took a moment to stare at the bubbly tub. "No." She paused, and I thought she might change her mind. "No. I only came to deliver a message."

I waited, but she continued to stare at the hot tub.

"I'm sorry." Anna blurted it out so fast I wasn't sure what she'd said.

Then I realized what she meant. I shook my head. "It was my fault. I just couldn't take another minute of which spoon went where and with what event." I gave her my most earnest expression. "I thought putting everything you taught me into practice would help. And it did."

Anna finally met my gaze.

"Really," I insisted. "Simone seemed to be tolerating me, so I wanted to spend some time with her since she's going to be my bodyguard tomorrow night." I shrugged. "I honestly thought you'd come with us."

Her shoulders drooped. "I should have. I took the whole thing the wrong way, and by the time I realized how foolish I'd been, the two of you had already left."

"Maybe we can go after the mission is over. I know I won't be living here anymore, but I can always meet you."

When Anna gave me an odd stare, I shut up. Devon hadn't mentioned what happened after the main event, but I assumed I'd go back to my old life and forget all about this place. Maybe the simplest answer was that she didn't think of me as a friend. Uncomfortable that I said something wrong, I stepped out of the jacuzzi and grabbed a towel.

"Silly thought." I wasn't sure what else to say when she continued to stare. "Was there something else?"

Anna nodded, but she seemed to be somewhere else as she played with the tips of her hair. She suddenly snapped out of wherever she'd been. "Sorry. Devon wants you ready by eight for dinner. Wear something casual." Then she was out the door.

I STARED AT MY CLOSET, waiting for inspiration to strike. The amount of clothing I'd amassed in less than a week astonished me, and it didn't help my current dilemma. I had no idea what an ancient billionaire vampire meant as casual. Worry simmered to miffed.

What if I didn't feel like going out to dinner? He'd said I had freedom, yet for the last six days I'd done everything he'd asked. My thanks was a single day off, and that was with a bodyguard in tow. It was intolerable.

I was being testy. I had a debt to repay. This wasn't a week at the spa, regardless of the luxuries that surrounded me. Although, as I rubbed my shoulder, the time spent wasn't exactly pain-free. I knew my nerves were raw. Finding the garden from my dreams had startled then consumed me until my flesh burned for his touch. The mission was one day away, and as each hour grew closer, my stomach churned. What had I gotten myself into—walking into a house full of vampires to steal a letter? We'd only gone over the job once. We'd spent hours planning it, but any crew worth its salt would have replayed the entire mission from entry to exit dozens of times. And now I was supposed to find something casual in this closet stuffed with finery. Yeah, I was on edge and not ready for a night out.

What I wanted was the exact opposite. A night to curl up in bed, watch pathetic date movies from the eighties, and gorge on ice cream. The only missing ingredient was Ginger to make snarky comments on the bad dialogue. I should beg off dinner in favor of going to Ginger's bungalow for a sleepover. But that wasn't meant to be. Not until after tomorrow night.

I ran my fingers over the most casual clothes Devon had procured, which still seemed like dressing up to me. My gaze fell on my jeans and pullover sweater. I smiled. He did say casual.

Butterflies whipped around in my stomach. I could swear I heard them pinging off the sides, and I ran a hand over my belly as I wandered through the first floor in search of Devon. I found him in the library, sitting in a high-backed chair, reading a book. He was relaxed, one hand rubbing the fabric of the armrest, one leg resting on a knee. The only thing missing was a fire and a glass of whiskey. Was this how he spent most evenings? I wasn't much of a reader, but I was curious what vampires read.

Before entering, I straightened my shoulders and lifted my chin. I bounced on my toes to release nervous energy, enjoying the feel of my sneakers. A touch of rebel sneaked through my defenses and gave me a source of bravado.

He glanced over when I walked in, half turning in his chair. I waited for his disapproving look, or some witty comment that meant go change, but he turned back to his book and marked his place before standing. His casual attire was a pair of pressed black chinos and a blue shirt that matched the color of his eyes. The sleeves were rolled up to his forearms, and the top of a medallion grazed just above the opened collar. He'd left his late-afternoon stubble, and the tips of his dark-blond hair curled at the edge of his collar. He was the sexiest man I'd ever seen.

"I see you got my message." He gave me an appraising look. His expression gave nothing away, and I couldn't tell if he was amused or irritated by my choice of clothing. His eyes glittered with mischief.

A warmth flowed through me that I ignored in favor of pestering him. I crossed my arms. "Don't you own jeans?"

He swept out an arm, directing me out of the library. "I don't know."

I took the lead as we strode toward the foyer. "How can you not know that?" Then it dawned on me. "Don't you buy your own clothes?"

"Most suits and evening attire. Anything I need that requires meeting with a tailor. But my assistant procures everything else. He has a sense of humor, so it's possible he bought a pair, though I don't remember seeing them."

Sometimes I never knew whether to be exasperated with him or laugh. I settled on being happy he wasn't making me change.

His sleek BMW waited at the bottom of the stairs, but before we left, he handed me a long duster raincoat. It wasn't supposed to rain, but one never knew in the spring. I took it rather than start an argument and let him open the door for me. We were out of the estate, heading toward town before I couldn't wait any longer to ask.

"Where are we going?"

"It's a surprise."

"Not even a hint?"

He kept his eyes on the road, but I saw the slight grin. "I thought it would help to get your mind off tomorrow. And that's the most I'll share."

"I can hardly wait to see what a vamp considers playtime." I didn't mean for the remark to sound flippant, but after seeing some of the ways vamps released tensions at the tea party, I wasn't sure I wanted to know what was coming.

He surprised me by laughing. "I think you've had a very narrow window into our world, and it has left you biased. I expect this evening will toss everything you've learned about us into complete disarray."

"And that's supposed to make me feel better?"

His laughter only got lighter. "Nothing about us should ever make you feel better."

My only response was to cross my arms, stare out my passenger side window, and try to ignore the laughter he couldn't seem capable of holding in.

When he pulled into valet parking at Baxter's, an upscale microbrew, pizza, and gaming establishment, I could only stare.

"You're kidding." I'd never been to one. It was an adults-only gaming pub that Ginger and I could never afford and would never be willing to pay, though I'd always wanted to see what all the hype was about. There were two in the city, and as far as I knew, they were always packed.

"You should know by now that I never kid."

Devon dropped his keys in the valet's hands along with a tip, then took my elbow to steer me up the stairs into what turned out to be a three-floor restaurant. Each floor had a bar, gaming areas, and plenty of tables—all crowded. We'd barely made it three steps through the front door before a hostess met us.

"Mr. Trelane, good to see you again. We have a table for you on the second floor, if that's acceptable." The hostess was a short, dark-haired, buxom beauty who smiled warmly at Devon and then at me. I was surprised this wasn't his first time here, and the thought of him being a regular at this place blew my mind. I knew vamps played games. They'd been all over Gruber's house, but he had kinky rooms too, so I wasn't sure if that was the norm. I'd seen one gaming room at the mansion, but it was always empty. Come to think of it, I also saw one at Oasis, but I hadn't seen anyone using it. Maybe they played at night.

The floorplan was spacious with games on one side, the bar on the other, and the tables arranged in the middle, separated by sectional dividers and plants. We settled into a private nook for two, which gave us a clear view of the gaming area. Devon ordered a beer, and I decided on a hard cider.

"You look uncomfortable." Devon took a long drink from his porter while studying me.

"I feel like I dropped into a different world." I sipped my cider and glanced around. "You're full of surprises, Devon Trelane."

"Is there anything you don't like on your pizza?"

"Anchovies and sausage."

Devon ordered a large pizza and two side salads.

"Doesn't this go against your organic eating rules?"

He shrugged. "This isn't a place we visit every day, maybe once a month or so. I normally reserve the entire third floor, and they're very accommodating with special orders. But I thought you could use a real pizza." He lifted his mug. "You've earned it."

I clinked my glass with his mug. "Not yet."

"You've accomplished a great deal these last six days. More than I could have hoped for." He lifted one of my hands and kissed it. "Now, enough business talk. Tell me what you and Ginger normally do to relax."

It seemed like an odd request, but it was better than him asking about my childhood or Christopher. The time flew as we ate pizza. I shared my close calls as a cat burglar and the crazy antics of the crews I'd worked with. He told me stories about Sergi and Lucas that had me laughing so hard I snorted cider out my nose.

That was when he decided to test my abilities at the games. He was so different in this environment, more relaxed than I'd ever seen him. His quick reflexes as a vamp could be considered cheating, and I advised him of that.

He stared at the floor in front of the dartboard. "I'll take four paces back."

"Five."

He scowled. "Fine."

It didn't matter, and he couldn't stop laughing after watching my first two darts hit the board and fall to the floor. "You can't even play."

His chortles were infectious, and I laughed with him. "Nope. I always figured I'd poke someone's eye out."

"Then why all the fuss about where I stood?"

"I just wanted to see if you'd do it."

He actually patted my ass when he moved us to the air hockey tables. It wouldn't matter how many points he gave me before we started, there was no way I could match him at this game. When we moved on to the pool tables, I finally found a game where his vamp speed wouldn't help. His quick mind would be able to read the bank shots better, but experience turned out to be my advantage. After three games, Devon gave in.

"Be honest. Do you hustle for money in your spare time?"

I winked. "Sometimes there's a long break between jobs."

"So, you played me?"

"Please. Like I haven't been dealing with your meteoric vamp skills the entire night."

He grinned. His laughter had been lighthearted throughout the evening, but this time, his smile traveled to my core, spreading a warm tingle through me. "It appears we're evenly matched then."

Those words played in the back of my mind the entire drive home. Was there more to his words, or was I reaching?

His banter continued as he parked in front of the house and guided me to the library, where he poured two snifters of cognac. We sat side-by-side on the sofa, and the conversation became more serious. He spoke of his vamp family and his plans to expand the bungalows at Oasis to accommodate other species like shifters.

With his acreage, they could shift and run, though the hunting would be scarce.

"Why would you want shifters at your home?"

"Not all the time, but for specific meetings and gatherings." He stared at the small fire he'd started in the hearth, then at the snifter, the firelight dancing with the warm color of the cognac. "One of the areas I differed from several Council members was the need to share policies and rulings over all magical beings. A Council with equal representation from both the vampires and the shifters. Times have changed. As the human population increases and our numbers remain relatively the same, we need to combine efforts."

"At dominating the human race?"

He shook his head. "I do hope that was a joke." When I didn't respond, he blew out a frustrated sigh. "I agree there is a faction in my world that considers humans a lesser species. But most of us just consider them a different species—no less or better than another. I admit, consideration of equality among all the species is a more enlightened approach that some have difficulty subscribing to. But there are many of us, most still guarded about publicly voicing it, that feel our species will be in trouble if we don't find a balance."

I nodded. "Simone made some mention of it, I think. It has something to do with not having your censure removed."

His expression soured. "She shouldn't have told you about that."

"It wasn't just her. There was a lot of gossip at the tea party. And I'm sorry if I divulged a confidence I shouldn't have mentioned."

He shook his head and set his brandy down. "It's obviously not a secret in my world. I didn't see a reason to mention it, and you have enough to think about. I'm still allowed to entertain and mingle with high society and Council members. However, I have no voting privileges on Council matters, and my business interests among the vampires are curtailed."

"I'm not judging. Shit. I'm a rebel and outcast myself."

He seemed to relax, though I sensed there was something riding just below the surface he wanted to broach with me. Was it the dreams?

"As I said, we seem to be evenly matched in many areas." He took my glass and set it on the table next to his. He turned to me, lifting one of my hands, his thumb running small circles over my skin and sending small shivers through me. "I know you're here to pay off a debt, but you've done more than what's been asked. You've stepped up to learn more skills and suffered under Anna's tutelage."

That made me smile. One would think martial arts and weapons training would create the most suffering, but it seemed Devon and I both silently endured the etiquette of his world. "Is that why you don't attend the parties. All the stiff rules?" I'd meant it as a jest, but he appeared sad when he glanced down at our hands, his gentle massage never stopping.

"In part. Our family had been ostracized by many in our gallant society long before the censure." When he sensed my question, he shook his head. "That topic is something for another day. Let's just say, many had reason to shun us from the more formal gatherings, yet they couldn't outwardly stop us from attending larger gatherings open to Council members and the aristocrats. But even with that, yes, I found the old ways stuffy. If someone should take a single perceived step outside of those conventions, they could be off a guest list for months, even years. That in itself could damage a person or family's reputation, as well as their business interests. Just one more reason for me to be considered an outcast since most of my business has always been with shifters and humans."

"Sacrilege?"

"To many, but not all."

"It sounds like you've been building an army of like-minded

Houses. Are you waiting until you have enough to tip the balance?"

He let go of my hand and caressed my cheek. "You are an enigma, Cressa. Intelligent, courageous, reckless, unpredictable."

I quirked my lips. "A bit of a mixed compliment."

His gaze caught mine and wouldn't let go. Or maybe I refused to let go of the intimate moment. "You think so? I think it fits you perfectly."

Then he kissed me. A light brushing of the lips, a tentative test, nothing I'd ever experienced in the dreams, which were seductive and hot. His lips pressed harder. The tip of his tongue traced the outline of my lips as if memorizing their borders, their feel, their taste.

I leaned in, welcoming the parting of my lips as his tongue explored. I tried to be patient, to see where this would go with only his own need moving us, but my body had other thoughts, wanting to meet his growing demands as our tongues met. Somewhere in the back of my mind, I felt his hand travel up my body until he was cupping my head with both hands, his fingers weaving through my short locks as my arms ran over his shoulders.

The kiss lasted forever and not long enough as he pulled away. The warm glow of the vampire raged with something primal. And I wanted more. The need between my legs more intense than I could imagine.

He stood, his hand cupping my chin as he lifted my head to meet the fire in his gaze. His voice was low and husky, such a promise of more. "Get your rest, Cressa. You have a busy day tomorrow." He kissed my forehead and almost dashed out of the room.

I touched a finger to my swollen lips, closing my eyes as I remembered the real deal. Exactly like the dreams. For the hundredth time, how was that possible? I smiled. He might think he can get away from me. But somehow, I knew there would always be the dreams.

Chapter Twenty-Seven

I SLUMPED against the window and watched the morning break slowly along the coast. Remnants of a light mist softened the landscape. The grave markers were hidden within the shadow of the sycamore. The mysterious woman was all but forgotten between the events of the last couple of days.

No dream. I'd expected one after last night. I touched my lips, still able to feel his on mine. The kiss had been passionate, heat burning under the surface. I'd been disappointed when he walked away, certain he'd finish what he'd started. The dreams had always come after Devon expressed high emotions. Why not this time?

I'd been left with nothing but a sleepless night, my thoughts jumping between Devon and the job before me. Anxiety clawed, churning my stomach. Day seven. The main event was less than sixteen hours away. Not that I'd been checking the time every fifteen minutes, waiting for the house to wake. I'd never been this nervous—felt so off—before a job. It must be the vamps. An unknown equation no matter how many times I mentally reviewed the mission.

Devon drifted back to me. The line between the man in my dreams blurred with the leader of a vampire House. I could say it was his tailored suits that couldn't disguise what lay hidden beneath the clothes. The snug fit of his workout attire that revealed toned muscles and hinted at the ridged lines of his stomach. But those images weren't the ones that tugged at me.

It was the quiet moments. Devon relaxed at a meal, teasing Anna over some silly incident. His routine of reading the newspaper in the solarium before dinner, a slight wrinkle along his forehead. Each time he'd stop to talk with Lucas or Sergi with a casualness that spoke of years of camaraderie. Those were the moments I remembered the touch of his skin—hot and scented with long, sultry nights. It would taste of deep desires, sweet regrets, and everlasting satisfaction. And those few times, when he looked at me in a different way, if only for the barest of moments, I had no doubt he was aware of the dreams, yet I had no idea how.

Instead of fearing the dreams, I welcomed them. And I couldn't decide whether it was because, even with a house full of people, I was still lonely, or because I wanted to take my pleasure where I could.

Everything about Devon Trelane rattled me, intoxicated me, terrified me, and pulled me in like I was a helpless kitten. Which was why it perplexed me that the real man hadn't taken our attraction a step further last night, considering how daring and seductive he'd been. Tension had been there—for both of us. And not just sexual tension. Tonight was the big event, and we were both worried, albeit, I'm sure, for different reasons.

I wasn't sure what Devon's motives were. He never confided his thoughts with me—not those that counted. But something simmered on the surface, and I wondered what it meant that I could read his emotions so clearly now. I might not know what he was thinking, but I could determine his mood by the way he walked, his speech patterns, and how he interacted with others. With me. Whatever had him worried, I had no doubt they were much larger stakes than mine.

For me it was simple. Do the job. Get out alive. One wrong

move and I would only have myself and my training to rely on. And Simone—wherever she would be.

I glanced around my bedroom and realized I'd grown accustomed to living here. To being near Devon. The thought of moving back to that dingy apartment in a bad neighborhood twisted my guts. Was it the luxury I'd been living in, the one I'd known all my life growing up, that I missed? I'd been happy a couple of weeks ago. Well, maybe not happy, but satisfied. I had a job that I enjoyed and a great friend in Ginger, who was outrageously fun to spend time with and who kept me on track. Once my debt was paid off, we could save for a better apartment in a safer neighborhood, and I would still have money to stash away.

What would I do when I thought I had enough money? That was the problem. Enough for what? I'd been fighting for survival for so long, I had no idea what my hopes and dreams were. Who was Cressa Langtry?

Damn. That question circled more frequently these days. And rather than face my next steps when I finished this job, all I could think about was why I hadn't had the dream last night.

My growling stomach ripped me from my musings. With little sleep, I'd need nourishment to get me through the evening. After a hearty breakfast, I spent a few hours with Anna reviewing the protocols for a Blood Ward attending this particular event—a formal ball. All of the elite vampires would be there, including the Council members. There would be other humans mixed in the crowd, but the bulk of the guests would be vamps of various ages. For once, I paid attention.

After a light lunch and an hour break, I met Sergi and Lucas for my last round of dagger and martial arts training. I wasn't sure who was more impressed by my new adaptive responses to their attacks, mixing my martial arts training with a dagger—me or the vamps. We were all surprised when Devon joined us.

He prowled the room, closing the gap between us as he circled. He must have been working out in the gym because his skin glistened with sweat, his hair was damp at the temples, and his eyes glimmered with that low pulse that happened whenever he exerted himself. He was agitated, and as the circle tightened, his pacing slowed, his fingers flexing into tight fists that made the muscles in his arms strain.

His gaze pinned me, and I readied myself, knowing how fast he could attack, how brutal he could be. And whatever riled him to his current state, I was thankful Sergi and Lucas were in the room with us. At least, I assumed they would hold him off from actually killing me. One of the few things I'd learned about vampires was that once their true nature got past a certain point, especially when hunting, it was extremely difficult for them to pull back. That was not a point I wanted to find myself in, not with vamps who were supposed to be on my side.

Sergi and Lucas divided, each taking a position to my left and right. I released a brief sigh when they turned to face Devon. I settled into a defensive crouch.

"Leave us." Devon's growl raised the hairs on the back of my neck.

A cold tingle of fear ran down my spine, and I glanced at Sergi and Lucas, questioning gazes already passing between them.

"I won't ask again."

With a great amount of reluctance, Sergi straightened, bowed his head, and walked out without a backward glance. Lucas followed until he reached the door.

"Devon," was all he said, but he waited.

"She'll be fine." Devon bit out the words, which did nothing to comfort me.

Lucas gave me a long look before turning away, the soft click of the door signaling I was alone with a ramped-up vamp.

His attack wasn't as fast as it could be, but he still caught me and flipped me to the ground. When he moved to pin me, I rolled away and was up, swinging out a leg that knocked him off his feet. I only had a few seconds reprieve before he was up and on me. We sparred for fifteen minutes—full speed and without a break. When I landed on the mat for the fifth time, I released my muscles and melted into the floor, refusing to get up.

"You're never going to best a vamp, little thief." He stood over me, legs apart, arms folded.

"One day," was all I could manage.

"Never. And it seems I need to spell it out since you've had an entire week and have yet to grasp the objective of these training sessions."

"Oh?" That piqued my interest, and I managed to rise high enough for my elbows to brace me. "Are you going to share with the class?"

He smiled, or maybe it was a leer. It was tough to tell. The glow in his eyes had receded, but his gaze held a steely edge. The man had ice for blood. Did vamps have blood? After a moment of glaring at each other, his leer shifted. A bit of a smile and something else. Respect? No, that seemed impossible. He held out a hand to me.

Resigned, I accepted the offer and let him pull me to my feet. Once there, he didn't let go of my hand but gripped it tighter and pulled me close. "Your objective wasn't to beat me or Lucas, and certainly not Sergi. Your mission was to last long enough for help to arrive or for you to find a way to escape. And you've proven yourself capable. It's becoming more difficult to take you down."

My temper flared, and from Devon's expression, it didn't surprise him. "Why didn't you tell me that from the beginning?"

He let go of his grip and turned toward the table with the weapons. "Because no one fights for their life unless they have to." He picked up a steel blade and ran his fingers over the edge. "And for a human, fighting to escape is the same thing. Always know you're fighting for your life, Cressa."

"I thought I had been."

He was on me in a flash, and once again, like on that first day of training, I found myself pressed against the wall, feet dangling.

This time the hand around my neck didn't pinch as tightly, but the glow in his eyes was back. Not the scary ice blue, but the soft glow of moonbeams on the surface of a warm lagoon. My body responded with an urgent tightening between my legs.

He leaned in, breathing in my scent, as his other hand rested on my hip, a thumb rubbing soft circles. Did he know he was doing that? His lips were close, and I parted mine, hoping for a kiss. Wanting it. Needing it.

I was positive he was going to kiss me, but something shifted in his gaze. His lips grazed my ear, his voice barely a whisper. "What are you, Cressa Langtry?"

The next thing I knew, I was on the floor, dropped like a spent rag, and Devon was gone.

~

"WHAT ARE YOU, CRESSA LANGTRY?"

Devon's words pounded in my head as I tripped up the stairs to my room. Not *who* am I, but *what* am I? Maybe it had been a slip of the tongue. But he didn't make those types of mistakes. Not in a world of magical creatures.

My body felt stronger than it ever had, and I considered Devon's earlier words. I might not be able to best a vamp, but it had taken longer for them to pin me down. I would be able to elude them as long as I wasn't locked in a room with one. And once I was back to my old life, any street hood I ran into better watch out. I had to smile at that. Devon had been right. The skills I'd learned in the last seven days would serve me well. My gut lurched when I thought about leaving this place, but I tucked the thought away when I found the two women waiting for me.

Anna was already pulling out undergarments and jewelry, while Ingrid, the masseuse, stared at me with a frown. She was a lumberjack of a woman, who seemed out of place in this feminine room. I took a quick shower before I was oiled and massaged until my bones melted. Just barely, I made the short walk to fall face-first into bed. I had two hours for a nap before a steamy bath and the spackling of makeup.

The dream surprised me, but this time there wasn't a garden. We were on a balcony, and I was nestled in Devon's arms as we watched the sunset over the lake. His scent of cinnamon and cloves mixed with wood smoke, and I turned my head to see a fire lit in the enormous hearth on the far side of the bedroom. The glass doors had been slid back, and the room was just warm enough to counter the effect of the light breeze coming in from the lake. I laid my head on his shoulder as if we did this every night, and he held my hand, caressing it with his thumb.

The scene changed.

I was cold. The intense pain ripped a cry from my throat.

"You'll be okay, Cressa. Focus on me. Everything will be all right." Devon's soothing voice called.

I lifted a hand, barely able to raise it. Blood. All over my hand. Dripping.

Every breath was torture. I tried to sit up but didn't have the strength. Any movement tore through me with blazing agony. Tears leaked, streaming a path down my temples. I lay on something that pricked at my back: my insides felt like mush. On a second attempt, I was able to move my head enough to glimpse my gown, catching a quick flash of more blood. My beautiful crimson dress drenched in it.

Devon leaned over me. His face marred with fury—and worry. He pressed a hand to my cheek. "You'll be all right. You'll be fine."

His hands moved over me, and I moaned. A hot flash of searing pain like hundreds of nails pressed into me. I just wanted the torment to pass. He ran his blood-stained hands through his hair, his earlier rage overshadowed by fear.

My body grew cold.

He wiped the tears from my face. "There are no other options, Cressa. This must be done. I'm sorry."

Something was pressed to my lips. I rolled my head, shuddering as something sharp as razors dug deeper into my back.

"Just a taste. Then all will be well."

Unable to do anything else, I licked at the drops on my lips. But instead of the water I expected, the sweetest taste enveloped my senses. Exotic. Sinfully sweet like double-chocolate velvet cake. Honey straight from the comb. But underneath the luscious flavor, I tasted Devon. The memory of his kiss warmed the chill that had sunk into my bones.

More drops fell, and I sucked at them. The erotic flavor raced through me, and I gave in to the overwhelming sensations.

When I opened my eyes again, all I saw was Devon's face. The fear had subsided, replaced by something my brain refused to decipher.

"Hold on, Cressa. This next part will hurt."

My eyes flashed open, and I sat up, scanning the room and finding myself alone.

"What the fuck?" My hands shook, and for a split second, I remembered the pain. The sheer intensity as it drilled through every raw nerve. The fight to take each tormented breath. I touched my lips. This wasn't like my earlier dreams. It started out the same—kind of. I'd never seen Devon's bedroom at Oasis, but I knew with every fiber that was where I'd been.

Then, I'd shifted locations. That had never happened before. Once again, I'd been in a place I didn't recognize. Not much of a surprise, since I'd been on my back with nothing to see but the stark sky and Devon. His face was almost a blur beyond the sensation of someone trying to rip my spine out. Such deep, soul-crushing pain.

I dragged myself back to the bathroom and ran a cold washrag over my face, wiping the sweat from my brows before starting a bath. I tossed in the scented salts Anna had selected and eased my body in as if I still felt the pricks of daggers piercing my flesh. She found me there thirty minutes later. The water had grown cold and goosebumps covered my exposed limbs and breasts. I cared little for my modesty, my entire focus reliving the dream—nightmare—over and over.

She helped me out of the tub, clucking about something. We were back in the bedroom before any of her words found their way to my consciousness.

"I understand being nervous about this evening, but catching a chill isn't the best way to begin." Anna turned me toward the bed. "Now, wait for me to find a robe."

She disappeared into the walk-in closet as my gaze wandered around the room. My eyes snapped back to the dresser.

A single crimson rose in a crystal bud vase stood out among the disarray of jewelry and undergarments. It hadn't been there before. I was sure of it.

"Anna?" I called out. It took a moment before she rushed out with the robe.

"I'm sorry. I grabbed the robe then noticed your dress had arrived and got distracted." She held the robe open for me to step into it, and I gathered it tightly around me.

"Devon has such wonderful taste. The emerald dress would have been fine, but this dress—well, I think you'll be a knockout."

"Did you send the rose up?"

"What?" She scanned the room and did the same double-take I'd done earlier. "That wasn't there before." She walked over and bent to smell it. "What a lovely aroma. So many of the newer varieties don't have a scent, and it's so disappointing. What good is a rose that doesn't provide a heavenly smell?"

"Who do you think sent it?"

"Devon, I imagine. He has hundreds of roses in the garden at his estate." Anna froze, then seemed flustered. "Let me go see if the hairdresser arrived. She'll be doing your makeup as well."

She nearly raced out of the room, and I realized she probably hadn't known Devon had taken me to Oasis. That I'd seen not only his English garden but his private garden as well. That I'd lain prone in front of the grotto for Christ's sake. But I didn't have to spend time in his gardens to know where I'd seen a crimson rose before.

The rose had been in my first dream. Its thorn had pricked and left a mark that stung after I'd woken. And when I recalled the other dreams, there had been roses in each one. Crimson roses.

A flash from my last dream forced my steps to the closet, drawn as if some alien power controlled my body. Each step created more dread, not wanting to know but unable to stop.

Anna had left the closet light on, and I stopped at the doorway. My heart pounded in my chest, and a rushing sound filled my ears. I noticed nothing else, my vision pinned to one spot at the back of the closet. The dress hung so it faced me. The color of the dress matched the deep red of the rose.

And it was the dress from the dream. The one drenched in my own blood.

DEVON GASPED as he woke from the dream, trembling from the abrupt change of scenery. Of darkness and blood. He shook himself before quickly scanning the room. Alone. He blinked into the late afternoon light, not remembering falling asleep. The last thing he remembered was leaving Cressa in the training room. And he felt shame creep over him.

He'd done it again. A call from a shaky Decker had dredged up old images and times better forgotten. After all this time, Decker still had the ability to bring out Devon's dark side as if the Magic Poppy had seeped its roots into his inner core, never leaving him truly free.

And instead of leaving well enough alone, he'd felt a deep desire to see Cressa. That she alone could balance him. Shake him free. He couldn't remember what changed and sparked his irritation past all good sense. His desire for her had overwhelmed him to the point of idiocy. She had the single ability to push him to blood madness. He'd been far from that, but if anyone could push him all the way there, it would be Cressa. His thief.

The images of the dream returned, and unable to face them, he jumped out of bed and stalked to the shower. He stood under the chilling spray until he could think straight. Unable to take the cold any longer, he switched to hot water and washed his hands over and over. He stared down at them. The blood wouldn't come out. One moment, he'd held Cressa in his arms as they watched the sunset from the bedroom balcony at Oasis. They hadn't made love in the dream, but they must have before the dream started. He knew that lazy feeling, the serene warmth of the afterglow of their lovemaking—the nuzzling of her ear, her hand resting on his thigh.

Then, the insanity. Cressa on the ground, soaked with blood, her body broken. His anger, fear, despair. Knowing what he had to do, but terrified to do it. They'd never discussed it. Why would they?

He hadn't been able to move. The dozens of options, and the pros and cons of each, floated through his head. All he'd been able to do was watch her writhe in agony, her eyes glassy and unfocused. Somehow, her gaze pinned to his—imploring, scared, angry. Worst of all was the dress. The dress he'd bought especially for tonight. The crimson gown that had been drenched in Cressa's blood.

Chapter Twenty-Eight

DEVON GRUMBLED as he opened and closed drawers. *Damn it all*. Where could he have put it? It wasn't like him to misplace things. He checked the safe again. Not there. He grabbed his phone, checked the time, cursed, then hit a button.

"Yes, sir." Sergi's voice was crisp, his tone relaxed.

"Where's the letter?" Devon's tone was anything but relaxed, and he reined it in, taking a deep breath until his hand stopped shaking.

"I put it in the cash box after finding it in Lyra's room again. I thought I told you."

Christ. He had. Maybe they should cancel this. Try something different. Everything seemed to be out of control.

"Sorry. I forgot." Where was his head? He should never have kissed Cressa. Shouldn't have interrupted her training session. Then the dream. He hung up. There wasn't anything he could tell Sergi that wouldn't sound like he was falling apart.

A knock at the door startled him. She wasn't ready so soon, was she? "Come."

Simone strode through the door, her body wrapped tightly in a purple so dark it looked black. She could wear a bag and still turn heads. But this particular bodysuit showed every part of her lean, muscular frame and was shrouded with a matching caftan that didn't flow like her signature ones. But it was close enough for no one to think anything of it. Simone was a stickler for wearing the same style of clothes, the only difference the myriad colors and patterns. She would be noticeable but blend in. And if necessary, she could shed the caftan and become almost invisible in a crowded room.

"You seem on edge." She poured a scotch and handed it to him. "Relax."

Devon unlocked the cash box and found the letter on top. He ran a hand over it in a vain attempt to remove the wrinkles and torn pieces, then moved it to the corner of the desk. He accepted the drink and emptied it in one swallow, the bite of it a balm as it burned its way down.

"Something feels off." He sat down, too wired to lean back.

"It will be fine. Everything is in place, and we've planned for all possible contingencies." She wrinkled her nose. "Is she not ready?"

He relaxed as the scotch did its job. He liked talking about Cressa. Even when it was an aggravation. "She's ready." Flashes of the last dream poked at him, and he shook his head. "I think it's me."

Simone's deep chuckle brought him around. "You've been preparing for this moment for decades. And now that it's here, there are bound to be questions. Once we start this, there's no turning back." She studied him until he wanted to squirm. "Would you prefer to let it go?"

"Never." The word was out of his mouth before he had time to think. But what did it matter? He would never be able to let it go. None of them would. It held them back like chains around a junk-yard dog.

Simone poured him another scotch and left it on his desk. She brushed her fingers over the letter. "Then get your head in the game. The only one that could truly lose tonight is Cressa."

Her chilling words filled his office like the bad omen it was as she closed the door behind her. He stared at the scotch, then swallowed it one gulp. The burn did nothing to squelch the cold dread that lay like a twenty-pound stone in his stomach.

Another knock made him frown at the door before he yelled, "What?"

A moment passed before the door opened. Cressa peeked her head around the corner. "Anna said to meet you here."

He ran his hands over his face. "Yes, sorry, come in."

She was stunning. Even in the stark lights of the office, her skin glowed warmly. Her short, cropped hair had been tamed and brushed back from her face, showing off the diamond stud earrings and emphasizing her long neck. The crimson dress was cut low, not enough to bother her mission, but enough to show off the simple diamond pendant that hung at the edges of her breasts.

The dress flowed around her as she turned toward the bar. Her long legs teased through the slits that ran up the gown and halfway to her thighs, allowing the eye to travel to her firm backside. A lump formed in his throat, and all he could do was watch as she knocked back two fingers of the same amber liquid he had.

"So, what exactly is the object I'm stealing for you this evening?"

He didn't hear her words, still mesmerized by the beauty in front of him. This was his first realization that he knew every inch of that body wrapped in crimson. *Holy hells.* How had he not remembered that every time she'd walked into a room? Because he'd pushed it away, knowing he wouldn't have the strength to only stop at a kiss. As he'd done last night. Shouldn't have done. He'd had a devil of a time locking down the beast within. The one that wanted to carry her to bed and take what had only been offered in dreams.

The dream. The crimson dress drenched in blood. Now the beast wanted to lock her in her room until morning. They were all damned.

~

THE LANDSCAPE RUSHED by as Sergi drove us to the ball in Devon's luxury sedan. I stared down at my shoes, classic pumps with short heels in the same blood-red color as my dress. Shoes I could run or fight in. Devon had thought of everything. "All this effort for a letter?"

"Words have power." Devon never lifted his gaze from his phone, either scrolling through email or social media.

When I'd first walked into his office, his eyes caressed me. I held some power over him, as he did with me. It had everything to do with the dreams. Although we'd only shared a single kiss the night before, electricity surged in the room, and the scotch hadn't dampened it. My gaze roamed over his tux, which only confirmed his hard physique. I couldn't help but lick my lips, and the next thing I knew, he rushed me out to the front steps to wait for Sergi.

The cool air tempered the heat that had sprung up between us. There was no doubt he remembered the kiss. Had he seen me lying in a pool of my own blood? I shook my head to bring me back to the present.

"How will I know which letter I'm looking for? I won't have time to read through a stack of documents." When Devon had mentioned during the planning session that the object was no larger than an index card, I assumed some type of disk. I guess after stealing part of a journal, I'd thought this would be a larger heist. Maybe it was to him.

He tapped a couple of buttons before sliding the phone into his inside breast pocket. When he turned to me, I immediately read his mood—all business—and squashed my emotions to match his expression. "The letter was written on light-blue stationery."

"Like a love note or something?"

He hesitated. "Or something." His gaze, at first considering, couldn't seem to stop the slow increase of a glow. That warm, liquid azure that melted my insides. "It won't be a problem will it?"

I couldn't seem to pull my gaze away and balled my hands into fists to prevent from reaching out. I wished I was in the limo behind us where Lucas and Simone followed. Anything to put distance between the heat building in this confined space. I grabbed the decanter of scotch and poured a drink for him, then a large splash of vodka for myself. I forced my hand to stop shaking but must not have masked my emotions.

He covered my hand with his own as he took the chilled bottle of vodka from me. "This should go smoothly. There will be many vampires, but you know all the security systems and the floorplan. You said yourself this was one of your easier jobs."

I snorted, releasing the pressure. The poor man thought I was nervous about the job and not that he was less than five feet from me. All I wanted to do was rip his tie, vest, and shirt away—too many layers of clothing—just so I could feel the warmth and strength of his bare chest. Breathe in his masculine scent. I lifted my glass in a salute and downed the vodka, relishing the jolt to my system.

"No problem." I set the glass on the bar then turned to watch the scenery.

We traveled to the north side of town, where extensive estates with impressive mansions swept by. Sergi turned into the drive of one of those mansions and pulled up to the front door where two limos waited in front of us.

By the time our turn came to exit the vehicles, nerves itched below my skin. I couldn't get my legs to move, grateful Sergi hadn't opened my door yet. My eyes landed on Simone, who'd already exited. Her gaze met mine and the jitters fell away. I stepped from the vehicle with a confidence that settled over me like a warm comforter.

Simone gave me a swift head-to-toe review and smiled. "Devon won't let you out of his sight this evening."

And there went those calm nerves. "That will make my little side trip a bit more cumbersome."

Her laughter filled the warm night air, making heads turn. The tension drained away. If she kept people's focus on her rather than me, I might survive the evening.

～

DEVON LED ME IN, his arm wrapped around mine, with Lucas and Simone trailing behind. Sergi followed with a group of singles. His job was to scope out the upper floors, deliver the intel, then remain on the fringes, ready to pull the limo around when it was time to leave. The other driver, Bella, who brought Lucas and Simone, would remain outside, ensuring the vehicles didn't get blocked in. There was nothing worse than having your escape route compromised.

The entrance line took ten minutes, and our group remained silent with the exception of Devon sharing an occasional word with Lucas and Simone. I remained invisible at his side. When we made it to the doors of the ballroom, we were announced to an enormous crowd, who couldn't seem to care less. I silently thanked Anna for the hours of drudgery preparing me for such an event, though it didn't stop the butterflies from returning.

I trotted out my bored expression as if Devon dragged me to one of these every week. If I thought Devon overdressed me, I could stop worrying. Elegance and diamonds dripped from every corner. It was like stepping into a room full of royalty, and I supposed, from the vampire perspective, we were. Aristocracy, Council members, and anyone who was anyone mingled in the richly decorated room.

After the heralding of our names, Lucas and Simone disappeared into the crowd. I stayed close to Devon, chin up, my gaze lowering if anyone spent too much time staring. According to Anna, the ball was not a place for ogling Blood Wards. Decorum was maintained, and Blood Wards were kept under the watchful eyes of their handlers.

For two dreary hours, Devon worked the crowd, greeting obvious friends who weren't at the tea party. They were all surprised to see him at the ball, even more so with a Blood Ward, yet they seemed supportive and genuinely happy to see him. There were several who snubbed him while managing lukewarm greetings, and others who didn't hide behind false flatteries. I marked all of those in the enemy column. While it rankled that I carried no status, being a mere human and all, most ignored me other than a polite greeting and a raised brow of interest. It played into our hands. I had no doubt Devon had expected that. If I was nothing more than interesting wallpaper, like a few other Blood Wards we met, no one would pay me any mind if I were to get lost in the crowd.

We mingled, covering every inch of the first floor, which was widely open to guests. Then we ventured to the second floor, where a sizable open area boasted leather chairs and sofas for private conversations or to rest tired feet—if that ever happened to vamps. I used the opportunity to monitor the security system and bodyguards that patrolled the outer fringes. Everything was exactly as we'd predicted and planned for.

Except for all the touching.

Devon's hands were on me constantly. On my arm, my elbow, and sometimes holding my hand. Whenever a male with lustful eyes wandered by, he placed a protective hand on my ass. I knew why he was doing it, could see other men with their vampiric protective nature keeping their women close. It wouldn't have bothered me so much if I didn't feel a warm tingle course through me each time his hand touched me. And sometimes, I didn't see a reason for his caress, or the need to wrap an arm around my waist and pull me close as he laughed at someone's joke. It felt so natural, so intimate, so provocative. The strangest occurrence was when a vamp, who I later learned was a high-ranking Council member, strolled toward us. Devon pulled me into an alcove and planted a kiss on me, creating sparks that could have singed hair. I don't know how I noted the vamp's disgusted leer as he passed by when waves of desire shook body parts that were best kept dormant.

"Why did you do that? That man stared daggers at the back of your head." My breath rushed out, and I touched my lips, certain Devon had seared them off.

"That was Jacova. High aristocracy and one of the longest-sitting Council members. He considers shifters worse than humans."

"I'm glad there wasn't time for introductions. What was the point of the kiss?"

He gave me his first honest smile of the evening, beyond the ones he gave his friends. "I didn't want to talk to him." Then he whirled me back into the crowd before I could find the right retort. Though I couldn't hold back my grin as I touched my lips again.

We hadn't strayed far when someone called out from behind us. "Devon, where have you been hiding yourself?"

Devon went rigid.

I recognized the smarmy voice and ran a hand down Devon's arm, giving it a gentle squeeze. He relaxed and turned around, sliding an arm around my waist. "Lorenzo."

The asshole was handsome in his dark-silver tux that matched the silver in his hair. I remembered him from the tea party, and his insinuations about adding me to his harem hadn't been forgotten. No one could understand my struggle to not sneer or give him a kick to his solar plexus. Instead, I lowered my gaze like a good little puppet.

"Two surprises in less than a week. First the tea party and now a ball. Although, I suppose it's not against any rules." The man had that not-so-endearing quality of being able to sound like your best friend while belittling you at the same time.

Devon stared into the vamp's haughty gaze. "No. It's not against any rules, as you are so fond of reminding me."

I took a moment to check Lorenzo's date, or possibly wife, but the woman kept her eyes downcast. Lorenzo held onto her elbow with a tight grip. Maybe a Blood Ward of his own.

"As long as you remember your place."

When Devon's muscles tensed, I laid a hand on his arm, drawing the asshole's attention. Probably not the best move, and I groaned when his piercing stare pinned me to a wall. I forced myself to lower my gaze, though I was still considering something more memorable—like a knee to the balls.

"Ah, and your Blood Ward." Lorenzo paused while giving me a more thorough study.

I couldn't help but stare back—he was pissing me off. But I eventually lowered my gaze when Devon pinched my side.

"She could use more taming." His eyes shone with a malice that was strangely offset by his smile. "I'd be happy to trade her for Adele here. It appears yours needs someone with a more forceful hand. Though she'd eventually fit in my stable."

Devon's second pinch made me grimace, and I did my best to turn it into a half-hearted smile. I really needed the vamp to stop leering at me while images of being caged in a basement with nothing but a king-sized bed and handcuffs flashed. Not that I wouldn't try kink, but not with this creep.

"I'll do my best to muddle through." Devon's muscles tightened. "If you'll excuse us, I wouldn't want to tarnish your reputation by taking so much of your time."

Although the words were meant to show respect to an elder, it was obvious by Devon's tone he was dismissing the other man. I only knew it hit the target by the response of his Blood Ward, who gave Lorenzo a quick, worried glance.

Lorenzo's lips thinned, and he gave Devon a tight nod before pushing his way past us, saving some grace.

"Why is he always picking you out of the crowd?" I whispered as Devon moved us quickly to the second floor.

"He knows I've started something, and he wants me to know he's watching, as if the warning to the Council wasn't enough."

"Does this mean we're aborting?" I kept my voice low, whispering into his ear.

He shook his head. "I'll keep an eye on him."

I glanced around and found Simone leaning against a marble column, a drink in hand. Some man chatted away as if she was paying attention. I finally found something to smile about.

"Stay away from him."

I snorted. "Yeah, that won't be a problem. Although, Anna must have forgotten the lesson on stables in her curriculum."

"Let it go."

Right. That wasn't going to happen, but I agreed tonight wasn't the time.

He leaned down and kissed my cheek. "Showtime."

Chapter Twenty-Nine

DEVON and I positioned ourselves on the second floor near the balcony so we could monitor most of the ballroom.

"There are two men on the third floor." Sergi stepped next to me and passed each of us a glass of champagne. "One man at each of the two staircases, as we predicted." He nodded at a passing vamp before continuing, "There's no one at the servants' stairs. Also as we predicted. I also confirmed our earlier information about the closet."

Devon smiled. "Raul has always been sloppy about security."

"For as much as he wants to outdo Gruber, it seems they're equally lazy." Sergi's sneer didn't require interpretation.

After reviewing the security system for the mansion, I had to agree. Everything was subpar. But I took the cue and slipped away from the men, drinking just enough of the champagne to prevent sloshing. I meandered through a smaller crowd that dwindled as I worked my way toward the servants' stairs. My nerves jingled—a pleasant feeling of comfort and expectation. I always got that electric kick when I began a job. My body relaxed, and my instincts came alive.

I noted the placement of cameras in the lounging area and

worked my way around them, either keeping to the shadows or walking behind someone. When Sergi had mentioned the closet earlier, he'd meant the security office. He'd been able to confirm our earlier intel that only one vamp manned the security cameras. Even with vampire dexterity and excellent vision, it would be almost impossible to watch every room on a regular schedule with so many guests. While the news gave me a breather, it was no reason to get sloppy. The cameras would be recording, and I didn't want to be caught on any of them once the theft was discovered. Even if they couldn't determine when the object was taken, they'd review the replays until they found what they needed.

The layout for the third floor showed staircases on each end. From there, the hall turned after a few doors, leaving a long corridor with six doors before turning again to meet the other staircase. The door to the servants' stairs was halfway between the two turns. There would be one camera at each corner, but surprisingly not along the long portion of hallway where the servants' stairs, Raul's bedroom, and his personal office were located. Security assumed the cameras would pick up anyone coming from either of the main staircases. Even in the vampire world, or maybe because of it, no one ever considered the servants. All the better for me.

But first, I had to get past the cameras on the second floor. A group of women stood on the far side of the extensive landing. I walked toward them, planning to skirt around them and keep my head down so the camera wouldn't catch my face. But as I passed the first vamp, the taller of the three grabbed my arm.

"Are you lost, sweetie?" Her bright-orange hair was pulled back far enough to get the frizzy ends out of her face. Her makeup was impeccable, and somehow, she'd squeezed her generous breasts into the small bodice of a Regency-style gown. She pulled it off.

I shrugged, not wanting to make an impression, but not sure how to avoid it.

"I recognize you." This came from the short brunette, who

swallowed a half-full glass of champagne then nodded toward my glass. I looked down, shrugged again, and handed the champagne to her. She tipped the glass back then licked the inside dry before setting both empties on a table behind her. "You're with Devon."

Great way to not make a scene.

"I thought so." This was the third woman. She was older in appearance than the other two, but her sable-colored hair didn't have a hint of gray. For a vampire, it was impossible to tell true age by looks alone. "I could almost hear Lorenzo's growl from up here."

The tall woman snickered. "Someone should stake that man."

The other two grinned before the older one glared at me. "Not a word, human."

I crossed my chest. "I doubt Devon would miss him."

They all laughed at that.

The older woman looked me over. "My name is Rachel. This tall one we call Red, and that's Naomi." Rachel nodded to the shorter woman. "I saw you speaking with Simone earlier."

"Yes. She's in Devon's family."

"That's right," Rachel confirmed. "Do you know about Houses?"

Uh-oh. "A little. There's a great deal I still don't know." Should I play this totally dumb? But if I was Devon's Blood Ward, I should be receiving training and would have opportunities to hear things, even if they were rumors. "I know that most of the Houses have been around a long time. And I think it's rare that new ones are created."

Red elbowed Rachel. "She's a smart one. That's the only reason Simone would say two words to her."

"And she's Devon's Blood Ward." Naomi bounced on her toes, and I wondered if she was jonesing for more champagne. Alcohol didn't intoxicate vampires, but maybe it was addictive. Something I'd have to ask Anna.

Rachel tapped a finger against her chin. "True. Tell me, I'm sorry, what was your name?"

"Cressa."

"Hmm. Okay, Cressa. What would you think about a woman, not one born in the aristocracy, being given a House of her own?"

"You mean that hasn't been done before?" I widened my gaze in mock horror.

The three glanced at each other. "Not ever."

I frowned, drawing my brows together in puzzlement. "I guess I've yet to take the class on misogyny—the world order of vampires. Though it shouldn't surprise me, considering the age of the elders. I have noticed most are male, and it's not unusual to be set in one's ways. But if a woman can get a House now, then some progress has been made." I laughed. "Not like we don't have a similar problem in the human world." I shrugged. "Men can be pigs." It was killing me to fake my way through this. These discussions were more in Ginger's wheelhouse.

Red howled, and it echoed around the landing, forcing jaunty comments from a larger group of men. The second floor seemed to be less formal, and it was obviously a place to let your hair down.

Naomi grinned, and I noticed a light glow in her eyes. Not blue like how Devon's got, but a yellow that turned her brown eyes to amber. "We need to take this one to the tea house."

Rachel gave me a thoughtful glance. "Let's walk you back downstairs, so Devon doesn't miss you too much."

"Let's take the back way and avoid the crowd." Naomi took the lead.

I couldn't believe my luck when she headed toward the servants' stairs and not the main staircase. I tucked in tight behind Red, whose height would easily mask me from the camera. Once we approached the right turn to the staircase, about four doors from the servants' stairs, I stopped.

"Hell's bells. I lost my bracelet. It's always coming off." I looked up, a little panicked. "Devon will kill me."

Naomi waved her hand. "He can come off pretty mean, but he's a gentleman." She rolled her eyes back, thinking hard. "Scratch that. I was thinking of someone else." She giggled, then waved again. "Go back and look for it. Just don't stay alone on the second floor for too long. And maybe we'll see you at the tea house."

The three sauntered off, and Rachel yelled back, "Don't call us, we'll call you."

They laughed as they turned the corner while I raced to the servant's stairs. I gave a quick glance around and dove in, shutting the door behind me.

I calmed my breathing and listened. Silence. I found the light switch and turned it on before running up the stairs on tiptoes, though my pumps were quiet as slippers.

When I reached the top stair, I put my head to the door, wishing I had the hearing of a vamp. Nothing. But there could be a vamp right outside the door, and I wouldn't know it. Sucking in a deep breath, visualizing my target location, I slipped the door open and checked the hall to my left. Nothing. Now the larger risk. I opened the door wider, grateful the hinges didn't squeak. I poked my head around, ready to dash down the stairs if needed. No one was there.

After a deep breath, I stepped out and closed the door behind me. The servants' stairs weren't quite in the middle of the hall, and the door to the master suite was several yards away. The private office beyond that. The plan was to make for the private door rather than go through the master suite, and if the house had been empty, I might have followed that suggestion. But something niggled, and when I got one of those feelings, it was best to follow my instincts.

The door to the master suite was unlocked. I quickly checked for sensors, not expecting any, but better to be safe. Not finding any, I slipped inside. The security plan didn't show alarm panels in the suite, but I checked the obvious places—next to the door and in the closet. I grabbed a silk robe lying on a chair and tucked it over my arm, then checked the door leading to the private office. No alarms.

I put an ear to the door and, hearing nothing, made the last nerve-wracking move to open a door that could have someone on the other side. The hinges squeaked. Barely a sound, but to a vamp it would scream "come check it out." I slipped in, careful to not snag my dress on the doorjamb.

I picked a penlight from my clutch and turned it on. The office was filled with heavy, ornate bookshelves, a couch, and an over-stuffed leather chair that reduced the available floor space, leaving enough room for three people to be comfortable. The room must be a man cave rather than a true office, and after glancing around, I determined it was more of a personal library.

The safe was supposed to be in the desk. I sat down and stared at it before trying each drawer. Nothing. Just to the right of the desk, built into the bookcase, was a combination dry bar and wine fridge. It was a strange place for a bar, but if he used this more like a library, it made sense.

Under the dry bar, there was a locked door the size of a mini-fridge. It begged the question of why someone would lock a fridge with all the expensive liquor out on the counter. And there was more than enough room in the wine fridge for food or other liquor bottles.

I took the time to check the room for other possibilities before my gaze turned back to the mini-fridge. I lifted the right slit of my gown to reach my garter. It was a false garter used to hold little tools of my trade. I knelt next to the fridge door, opened the leather pouch, and pulled out a lock pick. Holding my penlight in my mouth, I went to work, and ten seconds later, the door popped open.

I smiled. Not a fridge.

Chapter Thirty

THE SAFE WAS EXACTLY what we'd expected—modern with a digital lock. Devon had considered having Sergi locate the combination. These vamps had better connections than my old pal, Harlow. But I suspected their way of retrieving information was something I didn't want to know anything about. I'd told them not to bother. Most digital safes had backup key locks. This brand was no different. And there wasn't a key lock I couldn't open in seconds, just like the fake-fridge door.

This door swung open as quickly as the first. The small safe was stuffed with various-sized envelopes, documents, and three stacks of cash. I flipped through the bundles of envelopes, finding the blue letter halfway down. I noted that each of the envelopes were either blank or labeled with handwritten names—none the same and none with the name Raul. Was he a blackmailer or an intermediary? The middleman that either passed the package on or kept it safe—all for a fee. There was nothing written on the blue envelope and it wasn't sealed.

I shoved everything back in the safe, leaving it as I'd found it, and shut both doors. It would only take a few seconds to read what was in the envelope. I was so tempted. But time ticked away, and instead, I tucked the envelope in a safe place then stowed my penlight and lock picks. I was standing up when I heard a door-knob turn. Someone was coming from the bedroom.

I glanced at the door to the hall. There was no way I'd make it before the person came in. And two seconds later, the door opened with a soft shuffle of feet.

What to do?

My gaze locked onto the bottles of liquor. I smiled. And then I swayed.

The footsteps stopped. I glanced back. The darkness revealed a tall figure, slight of build, but it hid any details. It was a man, not a woman or Simone.

"What are you doing here?" The tone wasn't aggressive, but an honest question. He was surprised to find me here but didn't consider me a threat. Poor vamp.

I turned, stumbled a bit, then giggled. "Raul?"

He left the door open, allowing a hint of ambient light to stream in from the bedroom. But it kept his face in shadow.

"No." The man took a step closer.

I giggled again. "I couldn't decide what to drink."

"I think you've had enough, human. Why are you here?" He ran a hand through his hair then turned toward the bedroom before refocusing on me.

"I'm waiting for Raul." I leaned on a bookcase but planted my feet for a strike.

"Well, it's not unheard of, but Raul usually prefers dick for dessert."

Great. Of all the luck.

"But if I had the time, I'd help you out."

I had no doubt he'd try. Where the hell was Simone?

"I think I'll wait for Raul. Or maybe just sit for a while." The man had moved closer.

If I tried to leave there was a good chance he'd follow me. No one could see me leaving this floor. I could almost reach out and touch him, but there wasn't enough light to get a good look at his face. So, he wouldn't have a clear image of mine.

When he took another step, I shook my head. He needed a lesson on appreciating one's personal space.

He was too close for a kick. I rubbed my stomach and made a show of looking around the room. "I'm not feeling well."

The man backed up two paces. I kicked out and hit him square in the chest. He flew back, and I followed him with another kick, this time connecting with his jaw. He was down but was getting up. I needed more time for an exit. I punched him in the face, then kicked him in the balls. He groaned and clutched his jewels. He wouldn't be following me now.

I grabbed the robe I'd taken from the closet and cracked open the door to the hall. No one yet. I ran for the servants' stairs, not knowing who was in the bedroom. If it was Simone, she'd be on her own. My job was to get the letter and get out.

When I reached the bottom step, I pulled the robe over me, blocking my face and as much of the dress as I could. Once past the camera, I tossed the robe behind a potted fern and walked briskly toward the open landing. The number of vamps had increased, but they ignored me, too busy with their own conversations and other people coming and going.

I slowed to a normal pace and controlled my breathing, but I felt the sweat on my temples and under my armpits. I couldn't hear a thing beyond the rushing in my ears. I had to calm down, but it wouldn't take long for the vamp to catch up with me unless Simone had taken care of him.

When I started down the stairs, I searched for Devon. Even in the milling crowd, he stood out next to a marble column on the far side of the ballroom. He was speaking with a man and woman, focused on their every word, though I knew he was aware of everything around him. His head lifted and our gazes met. My breathing calmed as I took in his features, the strength of his resolve. But my nerves wouldn't settle until we were in the limo and a mile down the road.

I was taking another step when someone yelled. Heads lifted toward the second floor. I turned with the rest of them as someone screamed again.

"Stop them."

Hell's bells. It had to be the vamp—or maybe security. I continued down, picking up my pace as others were doing. A body smacked into mine, sending me and the vamp next to me sprawling down the few remaining stairs to a narrow landing. I untangled myself from the heap and stood back, getting my bearings. No one was running anymore. A fight had broken out. An elbow caught me in the side with all the power of a hyped-up vamp, pushing me against an ornate, stained-glass window. I spread my arms and caught myself, the coolness of the glass against my back sending shivers through me.

My path down the remaining stairs was blocked from other vamps turning back, their gazes looking up. Not at me. They must have thought the vamp chasing me was up to something. I ducked, barely missing another elbow heading my way. A large man blocked my exit. I kicked the back of his knees and he dropped. Before I could step over him, someone knocked into me, and without thinking, I used one of Sergi's moves with a quick jab to the face, followed by an elbow to the head. The man went down, but I hadn't seen the man behind him, who was in the middle of throwing his own punch. It landed in my gut. The hit was so unexpected and was delivered with the full force of a raging vamp that I went flying—right through the stained-glass window.

DEVON FORCED a smile as he listened to a couple from Italy, who'd arrived two days earlier for a business meeting before hearing about the ball. After a few seconds, Devon became bored with the man's preening. Everyone here thought they were the most important person in the room.

Across the ballroom, he noticed Lorenzo speaking with another council member as they crossed the floor and disappeared into one of the many sitting rooms. He happened to glance up to find Cressa watching him.

She was radiant, if a bit nervous. Only Devon would know why she was truly nervous, and it had nothing to do with being his Blood Ward in a mansion filled with vamps. The yell forced his attention to the right. Someone was running toward the stairs.

It all happened so fast, the scene too familiar, that he froze. She was too far away with a crowd between them. Men barreled their way down the stairs, and guests were being shoved aside. Cressa went down in a tumble but found her way clear. Then she lurched toward the stained-glass window, and Devon's breath caught for an instant before Cressa regained her balance. She made two decisive moves to clear her path before a vicious blow to her mid-section sent her crashing through the window.

He moved instantly, racing toward the front door. Sergi joined him as he ran across the porch. He never slowed as he took the corner to the side of the mansion. He spared a moment to see where the broken window was, and his heart lurched when he saw the pile of old boards and dry-wall. Raul must have just completed remodeling before the ball and hadn't removed the construction debris.

Cressa lay on top, her head turned away from him, one leg bent at an odd angle, her arms flung wide. He only slowed to make sure he didn't create more damage climbing over the broken boards to Cressa's battered body.

"Get the car," he yelled, knowing Sergi was still close. Devon still sensed Sergi's presence. He must have texted for the limo.

Devon made his way over the debris before kneeling next to Cressa. He brushed strands of hair from her face. Blood from the broken glass dotted her pale visage, thankfully missing her eyes. He slid his fingers down her neck, found a faint pulse, and closed his eyes in relief. Shaking off his relief, he scanned her body, taking in the crimson dress drenched in darker red, and shivered as if a cold wind had blown over him.

The vision from the dream had come true. Would it have ended differently if he'd made her change into the emerald dress?

He brushed his knuckles over her cheek. "Cressa, can you hear me?"

When she moved her head toward him, her lashes fluttered. He gently lifted her head, moving with infinite grace to sit so he could cradle her head in his arms.

Cressa moaned as he ran a hand over her limbs and then her body. She screamed when he touched her sides and lower back. Her stomach was hard, and he assumed there were internal injuries. He glanced up at Sergi.

"She won't make it to a hospital."

Sergi cursed. "This is dangerous."

Devon bent his head. What was it about this creature that entangled him? At first, he thought it was her skill as a thief, and then it was his suspicions of her true nature. But it was more than that. The kiss in the library the previous evening had convinced him of that. She led to damnation. He shook his head, running a hand through her increasingly bloody hair. A flap of skin had been torn from her scalp, either from the glass or a nail from the boards she lay on.

"I have no choice."

He bent lower, twisting his body from onlookers behind him who were peering through the broken glass from the landing. "Cressa, I'm going to ask you to do something you won't want to do. But its critical you do as I ask."

She moaned in response. Her eyes were still closed, but they moved beneath her tender lids. He rolled up one of his sleeves and used a fang to slice open his wrist.

Blood dripped onto Cressa's lips. The drops slowed as the wound on his wrist quickly healed.

"Drink, Cressa. It's the only way to heal. The hospital is too far away."

It wasn't enough blood. Devon opened a second slash, this time placing his wrist to Cressa's mouth. "Cressa, you have to drink. You won't survive without it. You need to heal."

As the blood pooled on her lips, she reflexively stuck out a tongue and captured the liquid. A moment later, she licked again, then scraped her teeth over her lip, sucking in all she could. The taste must have been to her liking, as he suspected it would. He sliced his wrist a third time as the precious, life-saving blood was eagerly lapped up. She cleaned her lips dry in a semi-conscious state. She'd hate herself, and most likely him, once she recovered. Hate him if she must. She'd be alive.

Devon heard the car pull onto the grass as Cressa began to wake. He held her close, an eye on her damaged leg, waiting for the right moment to move it into place as his blood healed her.

"This next part will hurt."

"My thigh."

Cressa's whispered words broke his concentration on her broken limb.

"What?"

"Check my thigh." The words were drawn out, but her increased energy showed as she squirmed under the healing blood.

Glancing around and up to the crowd that had mostly dispersed, Devon slid her dress to the side until he found the pouch connected to the garter. He opened it and found the letter. His heart clutched. She'd found it and wanted to complete her mission rather than worry over her near-death experience. Maybe she didn't understand how close to death she'd come.

Maybe she'd seen something past her last vision. Something he wasn't part of. His chest clenched at the thought.

"You are an excellent thief." He kept his tone light.

"Told you." She opened her eyes and looked around, attempting to sit up before Devon restrained her. "I had a plan."

He grimaced. "Let's not do that again."

She glanced up to the broken window and then down at her bloody dress. "The dress is ruined."

"It's not important."

"But it was the only one I liked."

He smiled, catching her head as it fell back. Her face contorted as her body convulsed. The healing had begun. She screamed, and his eyes shot to her leg, which began to move. He laid her back so he could place a hand above and below her damaged knee. With her next breath, he shifted the leg into the correct position as another scream ripped from her. He had to get her out of there.

As if he'd mentally asked for it, Sergi handed him a blanket.

Chapter Thirty-One

I STARED out the window at the gravesite below. Unable to sleep, I'd gotten up in the middle of the night and opened the window. The mystery woman had returned. With the long, wispy robe, it was obvious the figure was a woman. She must be freezing with the chill of the ocean air, yet she stood quietly, arms hanging by her side as she stared down at the headstones.

Several minutes later, she walked away from the house, which made me question whether this person was the one I believed to be camped out on the third floor. A riddle that would never be solved, since I'd be going home soon. I returned to bed, tossing over the events since the ball, wondering if a dream would come.

A few hours later, I stared at the ceiling, dream-free and restless. It had only been a day since the ball, and I was lucky to be walking, but something felt off, my body not quite my own.

After my fall from the second-story window, I'd woken in a bedroom at Oasis. After searching the first floor and not finding Devon, I made my way to the dining room. I'd just finished a healthy breakfast, amazed at how hungry I'd been, when I spotted Simone in the hall. It required all the heated anger I could muster before Simone relented in telling me anything. The only thing she would divulge was that I needed a safe place to recuperate while Devon was out with Sergi and Lucas. If I wanted any more information, it would have to wait for Devon.

It was useless to argue with Simone, and after delivering her two-second response, she left me standing in the empty hall. I'd remembered little after crashing through the stained-glass window —the pain, Devon's voice. I'd woken mid-morning feeling better than I had in ages. With energy to spare, I'd crawled the walls until Lucas picked me up and returned us to the coastal mansion. He refused to answer questions and asked that I be patient for another day.

I'd eaten dinner alone in my room after a two-hour workout in the gym. I was somewhat spent from the physical activity, but I was wired again this morning and sighed when I noticed the silver tray on the dresser. Someone, most likely Anna, had brought me breakfast.

After devouring the croissant and fruit, I sipped coffee, mulling over my current status. I wasn't sure why I hadn't been allowed to go home, but I imagined Devon wanted to confirm we weren't suspected of the theft, assuming Raul had discovered it. I replayed the evening and what had gone wrong. Everything had gone like clockwork until I got to the stairs. I was minutes from being in the clear, but I had jumped the gun, thinking the yelling had been about me. But with the timing, what else could it have been? Everything went hazy after the fall. Bits and pieces had returned since then, leaving the evening a patchwork of images.

I remembered the coolness of the air on my skin and the prickle of sharp needles piercing my flesh. I glanced down at my arms. Not a scratch. In fact, the small childhood scar on my right wrist wasn't gone, but it had faded. I was sure of it.

The pain had been intense. All I could do was stare into the sky. Hard, pointy bits shoved against my back. I shivered and tasted my own blood. That wasn't a good sign. If I ignored the pain and turned my head slightly to the side, I could see the people staring down at me.

I should be dead. I heard the confirmation from the myriad of voices. Could see it through my fuzzy vision.

Then Devon was there. His fingers brushed back my hair as he whispered to me. He dropped something into my mouth. My eyes widened with the shock of it. I touched my lips. Blood. Had he given me his blood?

All I remembered was the rich taste—sweet as honey, thick as melted caramel, and filled with promises of erotic pleasures.

Devon had saved my life.

I wasn't sure how I felt about that. Another image flashed. He'd found the letter from my hidden pouch. Why had he bothered saving me if he had what he wanted?

Before I could hazard a guess, a hurried pounding broke my reverie.

"Cressa. Devon has called a meeting in his office. Five minutes." Lucas didn't wait for a response, not bothering to be discreet as he raced down the hall.

Everyone from that evening waited for me in Devon's office, including Bella, the driver of the limo, who perched near the door. A man I'd never seen before slouched by the bar, but there was an alertness in his gaze that contradicted his posture. Simone sat next to the stranger and ignored my entrance. She'd been avoiding me since that evening.

I turned to Devon, and a bolt of electricity hit me. I caught the erotic warmth of his blue gaze before it evaporated like a hallucination. Had it been an illusion? With an even expression, he extended an arm toward the couch where Sergi and Lucas sat. Though there was plenty of room with the two vamps hovering at each end, it felt claustrophobic when I sat between them, perching on the edge like Bella in case someone screamed fire.

"Cressa, thank you for coming. This is Decker." Devon nodded to the man by the bar. "He's an old friend who will be working with us."

Decker nodded once before returning his attention to Devon. It didn't matter. I wouldn't be here much longer.

"Lucas," Devon continued. "Tell us what happened up to the point Cressa was pushed out of the window."

He said it so casually, as if it were something that happened every day. But the shiver that ran through me each time I remembered the glass shattering had eased. The memory wasn't as personal as that first morning after the event. I'd replayed the scene so often, it was like watching a video of someone else. The image of someone lying on the stack of construction material, staring up at the sky, no longer came with pain. I wondered if I had the vampire blood to thank for that.

"From what I've pieced together, two men were either in Raul's bedroom when Cressa entered or followed her in before Simone arrived. We think they were after the same letter, but we can't be sure."

"They didn't follow her, or I would have seen them. And if they had, I would have distracted them from entering the room until after Cressa left, but I didn't have the chance." Simone sounded defensive, and I realized she might feel partially responsible for what happened to me. That would explain her coolness. She was a proud woman who hated mistakes, and she'd had her hands full with whoever had been in the bedroom.

"I didn't see anyone in the bedroom, but my focus had been searching for alarms." I paused. "I don't remember the window being open, but the drapes had been pulled back. It was the only ambient light." My voice was so low it was fortunate everyone was a vampire. Though I wondered about Decker, who didn't seem like a vamp.

Devon held my gaze and nodded for me to continue.

"The safe wasn't in the desk, and it took me a moment to find it. It was inside what appeared to be the bar's mini-fridge."

"That would have been the last place I would have looked." Sergi sounded both disgruntled and respectful at the same time. If it had been a different place and time, I might have teased him about it.

"It couldn't have been more than a couple minutes later. I was ready to leave when I heard the bedroom door open. I pretended I was drunk. It was a vamp, and he fell for my ruse until I kicked him in the chest. I kept at him until he was dazed enough for me to make an escape. I heard scuffling in the bedroom and assumed Simone was dealing with a second vamp. I didn't stop to check it out."

"Nor should you have," Devon said.

"Cressa was correct. There were two of them." Simone glanced at me, a slight nod that said we were okay. "I hadn't considered the window, but it's possible they'd entered that way. I don't see another possibility, especially if the vampire was surprised to find Cressa in the office. I took out the second vampire and had just run into the office when the first vampire ran from the room. I would have caught him, but a group of morons tried to block me." Simone ground out the last sentence.

"Their mistake," Lucas replied.

"And a couple of them have a broken arm to show for it." Simone sat back, arms crossed over her chest. She wore a pleased expression that suited her regal appearance in a bright-yellow caftan.

"Once he got to the stairs," Lucas continued the replay, "the man was panicked, probably realizing his mistake. By then, everything had turned to bedlam. I think the fight started out of sheer boredom. He managed to slip through the fight before Cressa's flight through the window. I was able to follow him. Anyone who'd been outside was pushing their way in. The man didn't wait for his car, if he had one. He ran six blocks before stopping to make a call. I got the license plate of the car that picked him up. It traced back to Lorenzo."

Decker whistled low. "He must have suspected we'd make a move and tried to intercept."

"Maybe," Devon replied. "Or something else is going on. After Lucas told me the vampires belonged to Lorenzo, I had Sergi track him. Lorenzo left Shadow Island early this morning. He had a meeting at Haverston Gun Club. We arrived in time to see him leave with his lunch companion." Devon's eyes drilled into mine. "Christopher Underwood."

CRESSA PALED at the mention of her stepfather. For a moment, Devon thought he caught a spark of anger, but it disappeared in a heartbeat, leaving a nervous, jittering leg. She had perched on the couch like a bird ready to take flight, her arms wrapped around her stomach. He hadn't meant to blurt out Underwood's name, but it had to be done at a time when she was at her weakest.

Devon didn't require proof that Cressa wasn't working for her stepfather, but the others needed to see for themselves. A flicker in Simone's gaze and a nod from Sergi told him they believed now. He didn't bother looking at Lucas for confirmation. He'd been in Cressa's camp the first day she'd arrived. But that didn't mean Devon believed in coincidences. Or why Underwood was so frantic to find Cressa that he would demolish her apartment and have someone rough up Ginger. No. That was an answer he still needed.

"Thank you, Cressa. If you could wait in your room until I conclude business here." Devon almost blanched at his words and hated to see the confused expression cross her face, though the pleasant blush was the first color he'd seen in her face since that dreadful evening. But he knew he deserved the flash of anger that crossed her features again before she left the room. He would end up paying for that.

Once the door closed quietly behind her, Simone shook her head. "That could have been said better."

Decker choked out a laugh. "I don't believe my ears. Simone concerned for a human." She turned on him so fast, he fell back, his hands up in mock surrender.

"Enough." Devon's words snaked around the room, stopping conversation and turning everyone's attention back to him. "I'll deal with Cressa. Let's finish this business so you can all take some time off. We need our space." No one argued with that. "We don't know the extent of Underwood's involvement with Lorenzo." Devon turned his gaze to Sergi. "Is it possible Lorenzo has legitimate human businesses in his portfolio?"

Sergi snickered. "Not that I've been able to find. But I've only begun my research into Underwood's affairs."

"I can do some digging in the Hollows." Decker scratched his ear before pulling at his collar. "I've never seen him in the club, but that doesn't mean he hasn't visited the other ones. Maybe he doesn't know Lorenzo's a vampire." He shrugged and rolled a beer bottle in his hands. "Maybe he prefers the more high-class establishments, but from what I've read in Sergi's report, I wouldn't be surprised to find him slumming."

Devon glanced at Sergi, who shrugged before downing the rest of his vodka. "All right. Let's see how far into our world Underwood has fallen."

"And if he hasn't, perhaps he needs a push." Simone smiled at Decker, their squabble already forgotten.

"Let's see what he's been up to first, then we'll see what options we have." Devon didn't want to be responsible for getting Underwood involved. Not unless it was of his own choosing. It was risky having someone of Underwood's influence playing in the magical world. And no one, not even Underwood, deserved to have his life ruined for petty revenge. Devon might change his mind once he found out why Underwood was looking for Cressa.

"The last item involves Cressa. Have you found anything more about her biological father?" Devon rubbed his eyes, already knowing what Sergi was going to say.

"No. And I haven't had time to follow up my leads since the ball."

"If they haven't panned out, see what you can find on Willa Langtry before Cressa's birth. I know it was a long time ago, but maybe someone remembers her and who she might have been seeing."

Sergi nodded. "I have a list of her residences going back that far. If there's something there, I'll find it."

"Do you need me to help?" Lucas asked.

Devon shook his head. "No. I need you to find out why Underwood is looking for Cressa. You've built a trust with her and Ginger. Keep at it. See if you can find out something about April, Cressa's stepsister."

Lucas nodded.

"You all know what's at stake. Take two days, then we'll meet at Oasis and plan our next steps."

After everyone left, Devon closed his eyes. They had all worked hard since the ball, trying to figure out what happened, what had gone so horribly wrong. He'd avoided Cressa, wanting to give her time to work through the events of the evening on her own. Seeing her tonight was the first time since the morning after the ball. He'd stopped in long enough to ensure she was all right, and two others from his family had been there to see to her needs. There hadn't been time to speak with her. To be alone with her.

She wasn't going to be happy with him. And maybe that was for the best. There was too much in front of them to dally with personal feelings. And there hadn't been any more dreams. Was that the influence of his blood or something else? He thought he was past his addiction to her. Until he saw her walk through the door this evening.

He left the office and had just started to climb the stairs when Lucas jogged down them. Devon didn't like the look on the young vampire's face.

"Anna says Cressa packed her suitcase earlier today."

Devon sighed. "I expected as much. Don't worry, I'll set it right."

"She's going to be mad."

"Yes. But it will focus her. And that only works to our advantage." He shook his head before Lucas could respond. "She'll be fine. Check on Ginger. See when she'll be returning."

Devon waited until Lucas had moved down the hall before he continued his path to Cressa.

I PACED MY BEDROOM, suitcase packed and nothing else to do. I couldn't relax. I was irritated with Devon for his casual dismissal, sending me to my room like a child after dropping the bomb that Christopher had met with Lorenzo. A vamp. Did Christopher know?

I'd texted Ginger only to discover Devon had given her a rental car. She'd driven to Seattle to visit her family. Her mother was so excited to see her, she begged Ginger to stay a week. She was safe from Christopher, and I had a week to figure out what he thought I'd stolen. Whatever he had going with the vamp had to be related to his other shady businesses. Five years away from his house, and they'd both ended up working for a vamp. What were the odds?

But my job was finished, and it was time to go home—my debt paid. I'd have a week to shrink back to my dull little life before Ginger returned. I had enough money stashed to fix the apartment. But the thought of contacting Harlow about a job made my gut wrench. Maybe it was time to get a higher-class crew.

Thirty minutes passed, and I was still wound up. When the knock came, I pounced at the door, wrenching it open. Devon wore the same navy-blue, tailored shirt he'd worn in his office, and the color brought out the darker hues of his eyes. My pulse, already hammering, sounded like drums in my head with every heartbeat.

He smirked. "Can I come in?" He took a seat by the fireplace while I remained on my feet, already returning to my pacing.

"Please, sit down. You're distracting."

"I can't seem to relax." My body wasn't the only thing ramped up. I was happy to be leaving, wasn't I? Somehow, this wasn't how I'd pictured our last moments together. At odds with each other. It was probably my imagination. "It was torture sitting in your office."

When he didn't respond, I stopped and turned to face him. This was the first time I'd ever seen him uncertain. "What happened to me? How did I walk away from that fall?"

He stared into the barren fireplace before giving me a weak smile. "I gave you blood. It was only a small dose."

I'd expected that answer, and I licked my lips in memory of that sweet taste. "What will it do to me?"

"Heal you. Nothing more."

I wasn't sure I believed him, but he held his expression in check, giving nothing away. I strode to the window, bouncing on the balls of my feet and ignoring him.

"Will you sit down?"

"I can't. I'm hyped up. I'm surprised I've slept at all." I swung around and went back to pacing. "It's the blood, isn't it?"

He stood to face me. At first, the move appeared predatory, but he leaned against the edge of the fireplace, arms crossed. He wasn't going to sit if I wouldn't. But there was more to it, and I realized he was deciding on the best answer. "It has differing effects on humans. With the severity of your injuries, your system would use the properties of my blood to heal you." He lifted a shoulder, his smile chagrined. "I might have given you a touch more than necessary, but I wasn't sure of the extent of your internal injuries, only that you were bleeding out. Once your body healed, my blood would have energized your system, something like a supercharged battery. It should wear off by morning." He studied me. His brows pinched together, forming tiny lines on his forehead. I'd seen that look before. There was something more, but he wasn't going to say it. His expression became guarded, as if he was irritated with me.

He didn't get to be more upset than me.

"I'm not going to apologize for saving your life."

He had me there. And if he was hiding something, no amount of whining or coaxing would make him spill it.

"Will Lucas take me back to my apartment, or should I call a cab?"

He glanced at my suitcase. "You're not leaving."

His voice was so low I was sure I misunderstood. "I was supposed to do a job for you, and in return, my debt would be cleared."

He shook his head. "After the trial period. Which you completed two nights ago."

I blanched. "You can't change the terms in the middle of the contract."

He snorted. "And what do you know of vampire and shifter contracts?"

I couldn't reply to that.

He strode toward me until he'd backed me to the window. "I noticed your wandering eyes that evening The Wolf dropped you at my door. You were more interested in the knickknacks than the discussion about your future. But the contract clearly stated I had a seven-day trial period to determine if your skill met my needs." He sighed and picked up a lock of my hair.

I turned my back to him. Our clothes brushed, the sound erotic to my ears, and I flushed from the heat he radiated. My gaze landed on the gravestones, but I didn't really see them. They blurred as I recalled that first night, remembering it as he had.

"You're right. I wasn't paying attention." I huffed out a breath and went with the truth. "I was confused and angry at being traded from one person to the next like someone's hand-me-down." I shook my head, bringing everything into focus. "And I admit, I was a bit terrified."

"Another testament to your ability to handle adversity. All I saw was a bored young woman, who might have been assessing my valuables while making a list."

I couldn't help but smile. He didn't know how right he was.

He stepped back, and the cool air he left behind felt wrong. I already missed his warmth, and I touched my lips as the remembered taste of his heated skin teased my senses.

"It's impossible to clear a debt of your size with one simple job. Not after expecting more from the Alpha Overlord. Your near-death experience notwithstanding."

The Alpha Overlord. I hadn't heard that phrase before, but there had been rumors that the lead alpha, the wolf that led them all, lived somewhere in the States. Now, it made sense why he was simply called The Wolf. He was top dog, and I rode in his limo, chatting as if he was just another shifter worried about his own small territory, not the frickin' world. Hell's bells. When I fell into something, I always seemed to start at the top.

He studied me, his gaze filled with emotions I couldn't begin to dissect. "I still need your skills."

There it was.

Now, it made sense—why he'd saved my life. My job wasn't finished. I wanted to push him away, race down the stairs and through the door. The hell with the suitcase. I'd leave as I came, with nothing but the clothes on my back. Besides, I had to get back to my old life. I needed to know what Christopher was up to and whether April was involved.

Then he was closer. I didn't know whether he'd taken a step, or I had.

He stroked my cheek, and I couldn't move if I tried. Where was that pent-up energy when I needed it? He took another step until I had to crane my neck to look at him. His familiar scent washed over me. The one that curled my toes and made my nether regions tingle. The heat rolled off him, and it drew me in.

"We're not finished, the two of us." His lips drew closer until they brushed mine. He hovered, and it required every bit of waning strength to not pull him down until his lips devoured mine.

After a long minute, he brushed his lips against my hair before stepping back. Maybe I imagined it, but either way, the magic broke. He stepped back to the fireplace—all business. More time ticked by until I began to fidget, but he continued to stare at the cold hearth. He finally looked at me. "This is my new offer. Your debt will be cleared after the mission, whether we achieve my goal or not. Your efforts toward that end will be sufficient. If we are successful, I'll add a bonus—half of what you owe me in cash."

Earn back half my debt? That was a lot of money. Ginger and I could afford a better neighborhood. Hell, we could go anywhere we wanted and live comfortably.

"There are conditions."

Of course, there were, but I waited to hear him out.

"You'll do as I ask—no questions, no extra side jobs. You'll do nothing without asking first, and you'll stay here with your existing freedoms."

"With a bodyguard, I suppose."

"Yes. You'll require guidance until you learn more of our world."

"All right." If Lucas was my assigned babysitter, I could find a way around the rules.

"And you'll avoid Underwood."

"I don't need help with Christopher."

"I can't have him interfering with my business."

I understood his reasoning, as misguided as it was, but there was no way Christopher could have anything to do with Devon's business. I buried the niggling seed of doubt that struggled for sunshine. I bit my lip, unable to find a logical reason to turn down his deal, as if I had a choice. But it was a good deal. I ignored the hole opening in my chest and asked the next obvious question.

"Then we'll be done?"

"Yes, Cressa, then we'll be done."

His expression didn't match his solemn tone. I didn't believe a word he said. "Spend some time in the gym, take a swim, and get some sleep. Let your body finish healing."

I waited until he was almost to the door before I asked, "What is the mission? You never said."

He paused as if he was unsure what to tell me or not wanting to. "To remove my censure on the Council."

Then he was gone.

I stumbled to the window, holding on to the frame as I glanced out to sea—its turbulence matching my spirit. My gaze traveled to the two gravestones. Clear his censure. I couldn't fathom what that would entail, but a cold shiver coursed through me. It must involve Lorenzo. How long would this job take? Owing Devon might end worse than being indebted to The Wolf.

I touched my lips, sorry he hadn't kissed me, remembering damn well how it would taste. Under all the misgivings about Devon's offer, I feared something else could be my undoing. My dreams. My hunger for them. My impatience when they didn't materialize. The unimaginable passion that inflamed me when they did.

I gripped the window frame as a flash of pain pierced my temple. My vision blurred as a memory flashed. The dream. I'd been with Devon in his bedroom at Oasis. Then the location had changed, and I was staring at the night sky, my body riddled with pain. The dream had come true. How had I not remembered that? The better question was how Devon could have seen my fall before it happened.

I shook my head.

One thing was certain. I needed an exit strategy. I contemplated my next move, though it was pretty obvious. If I was going to survive, I would need to learn everything I could about vampires. It appeared I was in this for the long game.

Then a second memory rocked me. Devon's whispered words the day of the mission, and while they'd been mysterious at the time, now they flipped my world upside down.

"What are you, Cressa Langtry?"

Thank You For Reading!

BUT DON'T GO! Keep reading for a glimpse of where Devon and Cressa dreams take them in *Visions in Blood*.

Visions in Blood

Chapter 1

THE MAT RACED TOWARD ME, or rather, I hurdled toward it but curled into a ball in time to miss planting my face. I sprang to my feet as I came out of the roll and turned to face my adversary, my arms in a defensive posture, waiting for her next move.

Simone prowled the edges of the mat, and if she'd been a shifter, she would have been a panther. Her full-length leotard accentuated her shapely, long, lean legs and toned upper arms. Regal and deadly. She never took her eyes from me, and I refused to lower mine. I caught her grim smile. A predator sizing up its prey. Prey who didn't know it was done for. I was never overly bright.

When her fangs lowered to caress her bottom lip, I sprang. But not in her direction. I wasn't crazy.

I hit the climbing wall a quarter of the way up and clambered to the top like a spider evading a shoe, crossing as I ascended, heading for the rope. As soon as I grabbed it, I pushed off, allowing my body to undulate and pick up momentum. As I swung toward the multi-circled rings painted on the floor, I took a second to glance back to Simone, who waited to see where I'd land.

Grinning, I prepared to release the rope as I approached my mark and almost screamed when I let go. I landed six inches from Sergi, who hadn't been there a second ago. As I hit the floor, he swept my feet from under me and made a stabbing motion at my neck, signifying he could have ripped my throat out.

"That's cheating." I rubbed my knee, which had hit at an odd angle and would probably require an ice pack.

"You never take your eyes off your mark. This isn't an amusement park." Sergi shook his head and marched to the only bench in the ballroom-sized gym. He picked up a towel that he threw over his shoulder. "I taught you better than that. Devon taught you better than that."

"You spent too much time grinning like a young bride after her first plucking." Simone's stoic expression was always hard to read. I could usually tell when she was joking, but I wasn't so sure this time.

"Her first plucking? I think you're showing your age." I crawled on my hands and knees before getting my legs under me, not confident they'd hold my weight before giving in. Sergi's knockdown had been harder than necessary.

"My age isn't the issue. Your focus is. A typical failing of youth." She picked up a bright red caftan and threw it on. "We'll review the meditation techniques for the next couple of days, then try this exercise again."

I groaned but offered no further complaints. I'd just end up with more days of meditation. Something I was already well-versed with after years of working with an earlier mentor. As usual, my education wasn't up to snuff for Simone's standards.

"You have time for a light lunch before your session with Anna?"

I added an eye-roll to the groan. "Why did her sessions get moved to right after lunch? You know that's a human's worst time for getting anything done."

"Exactly. Which is why you must practice remaining alert through all your training sessions. Many assignments will require hours of waiting. You can't become distracted."

"I'm a thief. I'm somewhat familiar with that part of the job role."

"Yet, Anna reports you retain little of what she teaches you."

"Maybe she should teach me mission-critical information

instead of how many forks go with a particular place setting or whether a dress would look better with a belt."

"Blood Wards are expected to know these things."

"But I'm only pretending to be a Blood Ward. I need to know enough for light conversations, not some exam."

"You never know when someone will be watching. Questioning."

This argument wouldn't get me out of Anna's lectures, but I couldn't stop whining. There had to be a balance somewhere. "I didn't realize Blood Wards were trained so extensively. How long is the internship before a Blood Ward is ready to be turned?"

"Three years."

I stopped. "You meant months, right?"

Simone turned and gave me one of her intimidating glares that would have terrified me a week ago, but between training sessions and periods of friendly chats, I only got worried when I saw the tips of her fangs.

"I always say what I mean." Her tone held an edge that, even without fangs, I took seriously.

"Of course. I didn't mean to doubt you. But if it takes years to train a Blood Ward, why is Anna cramming like I'm taking SATs next week."

Her glare didn't waver. "I don't know what that means, but I see your point. Perhaps you should ask her yourself."

Then she increased her pace, and I took that as my signal that our conversation was over. After the mission at the ball to steal a letter, everyone had been given a couple of days off. And they had all returned with improved attitudes—which lasted a day. The tension had increased exponentially since then. That was four days ago. Devon was rarely seen, and I could only guess that whatever he was up to impacted his vamps—his family.

Lucas, the more easygoing of Devon's inner circle, was away on assignment. Simone spent half her time at the mansion. The rest of her time was spent at Oasis, Devon's hidden residence, where she managed the estate and several of his businesses. Besides not being fond of humans, her fluctuating mood stemmed from being away from her domain.

Sergi, Devon's chief of security and intelligence, by nature of his job, was serious, deadly, and not much of a talker. Out of everybody, he was probably the least affected by the growing tension. Then there was Anna. We'd gotten along well initially, but she took her role as an instructor too seriously, and the many times I invited her to shopping trips or quiet time in the pool, she always had an excuse.

If I analyzed my emotions, I'd become more cranky than usual. Ginger was as the end of her week-long vacation with her mother in Seattle, and I worried about her going back to our apartment. My stepfather, Christopher, still searched for whatever he thought I stole. He'd been so positive I'd taken something of value from him that he'd harassed Ginger and ransacked our apartment.

The bottom line—I was lonely. Devon hadn't shared what came next in the mission to remove his censure from the Vampire Council, and the result was days of the same boring routine. The erotic dreams we'd shared had stopped. The last one had been the day of the ball. It had started like the others, intimate moments with Devon until it turned into a nightmare—the premonition of my fall through a second-story window. A fall that should have killed me.

I shook my head and closed the bedroom door, stripping as I headed for the shower, dropping clothes on the floor along the way. When I traipsed down to the dining room, I was surprised to find Simone waiting for me.

"I thought you were on your way to Oasis." I sat across from her, our salads already served.

Simone, dressed in a purple bodysuit and caftan, had dyed her hair lavender. She looked amazing, and I fingered the edges of my locks, giving consideration to becoming a redhead.

"I'll head back this afternoon. Sergi wants to review upgraded security measures."

I glanced at the place settings, but only two had been prepared. "He's not joining us?" No one had time for shared meals anymore.

"He had a meeting. Besides, we haven't had time to talk." She dribbled balsamic dressing over her greens and gave me a quick glance. "I imagine this week has been a struggle for you."

"I'm not used to just sitting around waiting for the next job."

"You seem the type to have them planned ahead of time."

I played with the salad, pushed it aside, and tasted the soup. Butternut squash with something spicy added. "Not really. It's too stressful. And it's not easy to get other crews to plan that far ahead, not unless it's a particularly complex job. But I don't wait for someone to ask me to join. Not that it doesn't happen. Harlow called me in often, but I don't always take the job. I search for my own and then determine which crew would be the best fit."

"A woman who takes charge. I should have known." She sat back and grinned. "It's not the spare time on your hands that annoys you. You don't like being out of the loop."

I buttered a roll then dunked it in the soup before taking a bite, refusing to look at her. She knew she scored a hit. There was no reason to show her how upset it made me. I itched to do something more productive, anything to avoid routine. I hated routine.

"Finish up. We have time for the target range before your afternoon class with Anna." Her grin seemed at odds with her raised eyebrows, her caftan pushed back, fists planted firmly on her narrow hips. She should be on a catwalk somewhere, dozens of flashes going off as she strode in front of the fashion elitists. It didn't seem right she could wipe the floor with me.

I scowled in response, pushed my bowl away, and faced her, incapable of doing anything other than mimic her pose with hands on hips and chin lifted in acceptance of her challenge. "Are you suggesting I might have some aggression to resolve?"

She released the tips of her fangs. "Sergi procured a supply of silver bullets, but I'm not convinced you're worthy of them. I hear your aim is as appalling as your martial arts moves."

"Those are fighting words."

"As if you'll fare any better with that tactic."

Not able to disagree, I turned and headed for the shooting range located in the basement. Simone, as in everything she did, was far beyond my skill level, and after taking a beating in accuracy and distance, I skulked back upstairs.

I made my way to a small room on the first floor that Anna had turned into a quasi-classroom.

Up to now, her training had been in the dining room to properly display the multiple place settings for various vamp events or in my room to review fashion etiquette with the clothes and accessories Devon had purchased for me. After surviving those mind-numbing lessons, she was finally going to share the secrets of vamps. But when I opened the door and found a table filled with textbooks the size of boulders, I began to back up—right into Anna, who struggled with two more books that had to weigh twenty pounds each.

"There you are." Anna pushed me into the room and kicked the door shut with her foot. "Letty will be here soon with the coffee service. I know how difficult it is to delve through books right after lunch. I'm sorry I wasn't able to join you earlier, but I had a devil of a time locating these." She dropped the books on the desk with a resounding thud. "It's really annoying when people don't return books to the spot they found them."

She ran a loving hand over them before turning to a gigantic whiteboard mounted on the wall. "If you take a seat, we can get started on the origins of the vampire houses. We'll have two hours every day, but even with that, it will take some time to get through the material." She continued writing on the board, making columns and writing names in her tiny scrawl.

I stared at the table and the stack of pens, notepads, and folders. Enough supplies for a class of ten people. I cringed. Should I have brought an apple for the teacher? It was one thing to go through etiquette and fashion to blend in with the aristocrats, but I'd left classroom studies in high school and had no desire to return to it. If she was expecting me to write copious notes to fill all those empty pages, I needed to say something now, but the diminutive want-to-be vamp was more intimidating than she should be.

I glanced at the title of the book she'd placed on the table next to the notepads. It was written in Latin. I wasn't without some education and had graduated school with a perfect GPA, but college hadn't been for me. I opened the book to the first of what had to be over a thousand pages, thankful they weren't numbered, which somehow would have made it worse. The title from the cover was repeated on the first page, but underneath the fluid script were the old English words—Houses of the Vampire. As I flipped through the pages, sweat broke out on my forehead. The type was tinier than Anna's writing.

"We're not going through this entire book, right?" I crossed my fingers in case it helped.

"Of course. The houses can be confusing, so it helps to start from the beginning."

"This could take months."

Her tinkling laughter sparked involuntary shivers down my spine. I should probably consider myself grateful there wasn't a chalkboard in the room, though her laugh was growing similar to her nails running across one.

Think, Cressa. This has to be stopped now before I was lulled into a coma.

"You know I'm not actually a Blood Ward, right?"

She stopped writing what appeared to be last names across the top of the board. She didn't turn around and only paused for a few seconds. "Of course. We can always speed this up by working three hours a day, but Devon will need to approve that. I know he has additional sessions planned for the afternoon."

I flipped through the pages. The first few chapters discussed vampires from three thousand years ago. Good grief. "I'm here to train for a specific mission. I'm not sure how understanding the houses from three thousand years ago will help prepare me for that."

"Are you questioning my ability to know what to teach you?" She'd turned toward me, and I recognized the stubborn set of her jaw.

This required careful treading, and I continued to flip through the tome as I considered a response. I didn't want to ruffle her feathers. We'd already had a rough start, and this could spiral out of control quickly. She was a sensitive person who, for a human, hadn't spent much time among us.

I flipped back to the front of the book and ran a finger down a listing of chapters, hoping for inspiration. After scrolling through the first page, it was apparent the book was laid out by the names of houses, but not alphabetically. Perhaps when they were first created? That made sense. My heart rate increased as I searched for the obvious. I found it on the third page. A chapter that covered four houses: Aramburu, Renaud, Trelane, and Venizi.

I dropped into a chair. Devon and Lorenzo's houses had been created at the same time. Had they been enemies from the beginning or amiable, and the rift began later? If I understood what had made them enemies, maybe I could predict their encounters, weave around them, and, best case, find more evidence that Devon needed to restore his seat on the Council. With that knowledge, I might stumble upon other valuable information when he sent me on an assignment. He couldn't be mad at that.

"I wouldn't think to question your knowledge on vampires." Although I had done just that the previous week. Maybe I could redirect her enthusiasm to match my own. "It's just that I don't think Devon expects this mission to last months."

Her mouth opened, then closed, and her shoulders straightened. "What are you suggesting?"

I turned the pages until I found the chapter where the names of the four houses were emblazoned across the top. This crazy idea could bring us one step closer to ending the censure or create my own mortal enemy. Lorenzo wouldn't be happy with me digging into his past. I brushed at the hairs rising on the back of my neck and tapped a finger on the page. "I thought we could start here."

She gave me a suspicious look but stepped to the table to see what held my interest. I could see the wheels turning with her faraway stare as the beginning of a smile formed. She leaned over and whispered, "This is one of the more exciting chapters in the book." She glanced at the door as if worried someone might be eavesdropping. "This was a turning point for the Council and the vampire houses and set the stage for several wars." Her fingers tapped a staccato rhythm on the desk as she nodded, seeming to rethink her training plan. "I'll still need to give you a quick rundown on how the Council was originally created so you understand the importance of this particular time period."

She erased what she'd initially written on the whiteboard and drew a seven-sided figure, rapidly adding names along each side. "Oh yes, I think this will work. It will take about an hour or two to review, then we'll jump into the actions that changed the entire direction of the Council." She clapped her hands together before giving me a look I couldn't interpret. "This will give you a clear picture of what started the House Wars."

My excitement seemed to be gasoline on her enthusiasm. The start of the House Wars was precisely what I needed to know. Something told me that whatever happened during the wars was at the crux of the hatred between Lorenzo and Devon. And that was definitely something I needed to know.

I grabbed a couple notepads and pens, hardly believing this might end up being my favorite part of the day. But something niggled, like tiny pinpricks on skin. Would Devon get upset with the direction my studies were taking? I pushed the thought aside. "Let's get started."

Thank You For Reading!

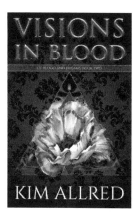

CRESSA DISCOVERS a family heirloom that will bring her one step closer to her true nature as her shared dreams with Devon erupt in new directions. And a new lead could reveal the origins of the conflict between Devon and Lorenzo. Don't miss out on the next release of *Visions in Blood*, **Of Blood & Dreams** - Book 2.

IF YOU LIKE Time Travel Romance...this series will take you on an exciting adventure! (Available only on Amazon)

A Stone in Time, Mórdha Stone Chronicles series

AJ Moore stands on a precipice. Her ambitions stalled after an unexpected loss.

A two hundred year old sailing vessel appears through the fog. This could be the story she's been waiting for. The story to help save her flagging career.

But Finn Murphy, the enigmatic captain, is arrogant, annoying, and tight-lipped. But she's not one to give up easily.

Finn Murphy has only one thing on his mind. Find an ancient stone necklace before someone else does. But he wasn't expecting to be hounded by a reporter. The more she comes around, the more he wants her to stay.

But the stakes are too high, the mission too important...until he discovers the necklace.

Join AJ on an adventure where honor and friendship can beat the odds—and love transcends time.

"Time travel with unique twists and many layers..."

IF YOU PREFER your romance on the steamy side, come visit the romances that ignite in the Masquerade Club.

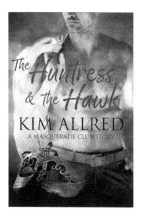

The Huntress and the Hawk,
a prequel to Masquerade Club series

Maude Renaud, owner of Masquerade Club, offers an outlandishly wicked business arrangement to partners of the hottest sex-club in Manhattan—an ironclad deal assuring national acclaim.

However, the deal depends on a personal assessment of Masquerade by one of the partners. Beyond irritated, she grants Gaven Sinclair everything the club has to offer. And his timing couldn't be worse. Preparations for Maude's infamous Valentine's Day Ball are in full swing.

But her perfect partnership may be in jeopardy. Maude never mixes her business with her pleasure. And what she wants from Gaven Sinclair is anything but a partnership.

KEEP up with Kim's latest releases.

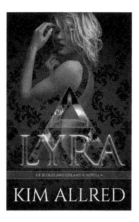

You can also follow her on Facebook, Instagram, Amazon, Goodreads, or Bookbub.

About the Author

Kim Allred lives in an old timber town in the Pacific Northwest where she raises alpacas, llamas and an undetermined number of free-range chickens. Just like AJ and Stella, she loves sharing stories while sipping a glass of fine wine or slurping a strong cup of brew.

Her spirit of adventure has taken her on many journeys including a ten-day dogsledding trip in northern Alaska and sleeping under the stars on the savannas of eastern Africa.

Kim is currently working on the final books for the Mórdha Stone Chronicles series and the paranormal romance series - *Seduction in Blood*.

facebook.com/kim.allred.52831

instagram.com/kimallredauthor

amazon.com/-/e/B07CQY2J8Y

bookbub.com/authors/kim-allred

Made in the USA
Middletown, DE
23 January 2023

22909251R00168